Mrs. Patchet Martin

Coo-ee

Tales of Australian Life by Australian Ladies

Mrs. Patchet Martin

Coo-ee
Tales of Australian Life by Australian Ladies

ISBN/EAN: 9783337082031

Printed in Europe, USA, Canada, Australia, Japan

Cover: Foto ©Andreas Hilbeck / pixelio.de

More available books at **www.hansebooks.com**

COO-EE

TALES OF AUSTRALIAN LIFE
BY AUSTRALIAN LADIES

EDITED BY

Mrs. PATCHETT MARTIN

LONDON
GRIFFITH FARRAN & CO.
NEWBERY HOUSE, 39 CHARING CROSS ROAD

TO THE READER.

—o—

IT is certainly 'a far cry' from the Antipodes to England and back again. Yet in the name of my Australian sisters who have contributed to this little volume, I venture to express a hope that our 'Coo-ee' may succeed in making itself heard on either shore, and that its echoes may linger pleasantly around the Bush Station and by the English fireside. To our kind friends and readers I would therefore only say— 'Coo-ee! Take up the cry and pass it on—Coo-ee! —and again—Coo-ee!'

THE EDITOR.

CONTENTS.

———o———

AN OLD-TIME EPISODE IN TASMANIA.

AN OLD-TIME EPISODE IN TASMANIA.

——— o ———

THE gig was waiting upon the narrow gravel drive in front of the fuchsia - wreathed porch of Cowa Cottage. Perched upon the seat, holding the whip in two small, plump, ungloved hands, sat Trucaninny, Mr. Paton's youngest daughter, whose straw-coloured, sun-steeped hair, and clear, sky-reflecting eyes, seemed to protest against the name of a black gin that some 'clay-brained cleric' had bestowed upon her irresponsible little person at the baptismal font some eight or nine years ago. The scene of this outrage was Old St. David's Cathedral, Hobart,—or, as it was then called, Hobart *Town*,—chief city of the Arcadian island of Tasmania; and just at this moment, eight o'clock on a November morning, the said cathedral tower, round and ungainly, coated with a surface of dingy white plaster, reflected back the purest, brightest light in the world. From Trucaninny's perch—she had taken the driver's seat—she could see, not only the cathedral,

but a considerable portion of the town, which took the
form of a capital S as it followed the windings of the
coast. Beyond the wharves, against which a few
whalers and fishing-boats were lying idle, the middle
distance was represented by the broad waters of the
Derwent, radiantly blue, and glittering with silver
sparkles ; while the far-off background showed a long
stretch of yellow sand, and the hazy, undulating out-
line of low-lying purple hills. Behind her the aspect
was different. Tiers of hills rose one above the other
in grand confusion, until they culminated in the tower-
ing height of Mount Wellington, keeping guard in
majestic silence over the lonely little city that encircled its base. This portion of the view, however,
was hidden from Trucaninny's gaze by the weather-
board cottage in front of which the gig was standing,
—though I doubt whether in any case she would have
turned her head to look at it ; the faculty of enjoying
a beautiful landscape being an acquisition of later
years than she had attained since the perpetration
of the afore-mentioned outrage of her christening.
Conversely, as Herbert Spencer says, the young man
who was holding the horse's head until such time as
the owner of the gig should emerge from the fuchsia-
wreathed porch, fastened his eyes upon the beautiful
scene before him with more than an artist's appecia-
tion in their gaze. He was dressed in the rough
clothes of a working gardener, and so much of his
head as could be seen beneath the old felt wide-awake
that covered it, bore ominous evidence of having been

recently shaved. I use the word ominous advisedly, for a shaven head in connection with a working suit had nothing priestly in its suggestion, and could bear, indeed, only one interpretation in the wicked old times in Tasmania. The young man keeping watch over the gig had clearly come into that fair scene for his country's good ; and the explanation of the absence of a prison suit was doubtless due to the fact he was out on a ticket-of-leave. What the landscape had to say to him under these circumstances was not precisely clear. Perhaps all his soul was going out towards the white-sailed wool-ship tacking down the Bay on the first stage of a journey of most uncertain length ; or possibly the wondrous beauty of the scene, contrasted with the unspeakable horror of the one he had left, brought the vague impression that it was merely some exquisite vision. That a place so appalling as his old prison should exist in the heart of all this peace and loveliness, seemed too strange an anomaly. Either that was a nightmare and this was real, or this was a fantastic dream and that was the revolting truth ; but then which was which, and how had he, Richard Cole, late No. 213, come to be mixed up with either ?

As though to give a practical answer to his melancholy question, the sharp tingle of a whip's lash made itself felt at this instant across his cheek. In aiming the cumbersome driving-whip at the persistent flies exploring the mare's back, Trucaninny had brought it down in a direction she had not intended it to take. For a moment she stood aghast. Richard's face was white with passion. He turned fiercely round; his flaming eyes seemed literally to send out sparks of anger. 'Oh, please, I didn't mean it,' cried the child penitently. 'I wanted to hit the flies. I did indeed. I hope I didn't hurt you?'

The *amende honorable* brought about an immediate reaction. The change in the young man's face was wonderful to behold. As he smiled back full reassurance at the offender, it might be seen that his eyes could express the extremes of contrary feeling at the very shortest notice. For all answer, he raised his old felt wide-awake in a half-mocking though entirely courtly fashion, like some nineteenth century Don César de Bazan, and made a graceful bow.

'Are *you* talking to the man, Truca?' cried a querulous voice at this moment from the porch, with a stress on the you that made the little girl lower her head, shame-faced. What do you mean by disobeying orders, miss?'

The lady who swept out upon the verandah at the close of this tirade was in entire accord with her voice. 'British matron' would have been the complete description of Miss Paton, if fate had not willed that she should be only a British spinster. The inflexibility that comes of finality of opinion regarding what is proper and what is the reverse,—a rule of conduct that is of universal application for the true British matron, —expressed itself in every line of her face and in every fold of her gown. That she was relentlessly respectable and unyielding might be read at the first glance;

that she had been handsome, in the same hard way, a great many years before Truca was maltreated at the baptismal font, might also have been guessed at from present indications. But that she should be the 'own sister' of the good-looking, military-moustached, debonair man (I use the word debonair here in the French sense) who now followed her out of the porch, was less easy to divine. The character of the features as well as of the expression spoke of two widely differing temperaments. Indeed, save for a curious dent between the eyebrows, and a something in the nostrils that seemed to say he was not to be trifled with, Mr. Paton might have sat for the portrait of one of those jolly good fellows who reiterate so tunefully that they 'won't go home till morning,' and who are as good as their word afterwards.

Yet 'jolly good fellow' as he showed himself in card-rooms and among so-called boon companions, he could reveal himself in a very different light to the convicts who fell under his rule. Forming part of a system for the crushing down of the unhappy prisoners, in accordance with the principle of 'Woe be to him through whom the offence cometh,' he could return with a light heart to his breakfast or his dinner, after seeing some score of his fellow-men abjectly writhing under the lash, or pinioned in a ghastly row upon the hideous gallows. 'Use,' says Shakespeare, 'can almost change the stamp of Nature.' In Mr. Paton's case it had warped as well as changed it. Like the people who live in the atmosphere of

Courts, and come to regard all outsiders as another and inferior race, he had come to look upon humanity as divisible into two classes—namely, those who were convicts, and those who were not. For the latter, he had still some ready drops of the milk of human kindness at his disposal. For the former, he had no more feeling than we have for snakes or sharks, as the typical and popular embodiments of evil.

Miss Paton had speedily adopted her brother's views in this respect. Summoned from England to keep house for him at the death of Trucaninny's mother, she showed an aptitude for introducing prison discipline into her domestic rule. From constant association with the severe *régime* that she was accustomed to see exercised upon the convicts, she had ended by regarding disobedience to orders, whether in children or in servants, as the unpardonable sin. One of her laws, as of the Medes and Persians, was that the young people in the Paton household should never exchange a word with the convict servants in their father's employ. It was hard to observe the letter of the law in the case of the indoor servants, above all for Truca, who was by nature a garrulous little girl. Being a truthful little girl as well, she was often obliged to confess to having had a talk with the latest importation from the gaol,—an avowal which signified, as she well knew, the immediate forfeiture of all her week's pocket-money.

On the present occasion her apologies to the gardener were the latest infringement of the rule.

She looked timidly towards her aunt as the latter
advanced austerely in the direction of the gig, but,
to her relief, Miss Paton hardly seemed to notice
her.

'I suppose you will bring the creature back with
you, Wilfrid?' she said, half-questioningly, half-
authoritatively, as her brother mounted into the gig
and took the reins from Truca's chubby hands. 'Last
time we had a drunkard *and* a thief. The time before,
a thief, and—and a—really I don't know which was
worse. It is frightful to be reduced to such a choice
of evils, but I would almost suggest your looking
among the—you know—the—*in-fan-ti-cide* cases this
time.'

She mouthed the word in separate syllables at her
brother, fearful of pronouncing it openly before Truca
and the convict gardener.

Mr. Paton nodded. It was not the first time he had
been sent upon the delicate mission of choosing a
maid for his sister from the female prison, politely
called the Factory, at the foot of Mount Wellington.
For some reason it would be difficult to explain, his
selections were generally rather more successful than
hers. Besides which, it was a satisfaction to have
some one upon whom to throw the responsibility of
the inevitable catastrophe that terminated the career
of every successive ticket-of-leave in turn.

The morning, as we have seen, was beautiful. The
gig bowled smoothly over the macadamized length
of Macquarrie Street. Truca was allowed to drive ;

and so deftly did her little fingers guide the mare,
that her father lighted his cigar, and allowed himself
to ruminate upon a thousand things that it would
have been better perhaps to leave alone. In certain
moods he was apt to deplore the fate that had landed
—or stranded—him in this God-forsaken corner of the
world. Talk of prisoners, indeed! What was he
himself but a prisoner, since the day when he had
madly passed sentence of transportation on himself
and his family, because the pay of a Government clerk
in England did not increase in the same ratio as the
income-tax. As a matter of fact, he did not wear a
canary-coloured livery, and his prison was as near an
approach, people said, to an earthly Paradise as could
well be conceived. With its encircling chains of
mountains, folded one around the other, it was like a
mighty rose, tossed from the Creator's hand into the
desolate Southern Ocean. Here to his right towered
purple Mount Wellington, with rugged cliffs gleaming
forth from a purple background. To his left the
wide Derwent shone and sparkled in blue robe and
silver spangles, like the Bay of Naples, he had been
told. Well, he had never seen the Bay of Naples,
but there were times when he would have given all
the beauty here, and as much more to spare, for a
strip of London pavement in front of his old club.
Mr. Paton's world, indeed, was out of joint. Perhaps
twelve years of unthinking acquiescence in the flogging
and hanging of convicts had distorted his mental focus.
As for the joys of home-life, he told himself that those

which had fallen to his share brought him but cold
comfort. His sister was a Puritan, and she was
making his children hypocrites, with the exception,
perhaps, of Truca. Another disagreeable subject of
reflection was the one that his groom Richard was
about to leave him. In a month's time, Richard, like
his royal namesake, would be himself again. For the
past five years he had been only No. 213, expiating
in that capacity a righteous blow aimed at a cowardly
ruffian who had sworn to marry his sister—by fair
means or by foul. The blow had been only too well
aimed. Richard was convicted of manslaughter, and
sentenced to seven years' transportation beyond the
seas. His sister, who had sought to screen him, was
tried and condemned for perjury. Of the latter,
nothing was known. Of the former, Mr. Paton only
knew that he would be extremely loth to part with so
good a servant. Silent as the Slave of the Lamp,
exact as any machine, performing the least of his
duties with the same intelligent scrupulousness, his
very presence in the household was a safeguard and
a reassurance. It was like his luck, Mr. Paton reflected
in his present pessimistic mood, to have chanced upon
such a fellow, just as by his d——d good conduct he
had managed to obtain a curtailment of his sentence.
If Richard had been justly dealt with, he would have
had two good years left to devote to the service of his
employer. As to keeping him after he was a free
man, that was not to be hoped for. Besides which,
Mr. Paton was not sure that he should feel at all at

his ease in dealing with a free man. The slave-making
instinct, which is always inherent in the human race,
whatever civilisation may have done to repress it, had
become his sole rule of conduct in his relations with
those who served him.

There was one means perhaps of keeping the young
man in bondage, but it was a means that even Mr.
Paton himself hesitated to employ. By an almost
superhuman adherence to impossible rules, Richard
had escaped hitherto the humiliation of the lash ; but
if a flogging could be laid to his charge, his time of
probation would be of necessity prolonged, and he
might continue to groom the mare and tend the
garden for an indefinite space of time, with the ever
intelligent thoroughness that distinguished him. A
slip of paper in a sealed envelope, which the victim
would carry himself to the nearest justice of the peace,
would effect the desired object. The etiquette of the
proceeding did not require that any explanation
should be given.

Richard would be fastened to the triangles, and
any subsequent revolt on his part could only involve
him more deeply than before. Mr. Paton had no
wish to hurt him ; but he was after all an invaluable
servant, and perhaps he would be intelligent enough
to understand that the disagreeable formality to which
he was subjected was in reality only a striking mark
of his master's esteem for him.

Truca's father had arrived thus far in his meditations when the gig pulled up before the Factory gate.

It was a large bare building, with white unshaded walls, but the landscape which framed it gave it a magnificent setting. The little girl was allowed to accompany her father indoors, while a man in a grey prison suit, under the immediate surveillance of an armed warder, stood at the mare's head.

Mr. Paton's mission was a delicate one. To gently scan his brother man, and still gentler sister woman, did not apply to his treatment of convicts. He brought his sternest official expression to bear upon the aspirants who defiled past him at the matron's bidding, in their disfiguring prison livery. One or two, who thought they detected a likely looking man behind the Government official, threw him equivocal glances as they went by. Of these he took no notice. His choice seemed to lie in the end between a sullen-looking elderly woman, whom the superintendent qualified as a 'sour jade,' and a half-imbecile girl, when his attention was suddenly attracted to a new arrival, who stood out in such marked contrast with the rest, that she looked like a dove in the midst of a flock of vultures.

'Who is that?' he asked the matron in a peremptory aside.

'That, sir,'—the woman's lips assumed a tight expression as she spoke,—' she's No. 27—Amelia Clare —she came out with the last batch.'

'Call her up, will you?' was the short rejoinder, and the matron reluctantly obeyed.

In his early days Truca's father had been a great

lover of Italian opera. There was hardly an air of
Bellini's or Donizetti's that he did not know by heart.
As No. 27 came slowly towards him, something in her
manner of walking, coupled with the half-abstracted,
half-fixed expression in her beautiful grey eyes, reminded him of Amina in the *Sonnambula.*   So strong,
indeed, was the impression, that he would hardly have
been surprised to see No. 27 take off her unbecoming
prison cap and jacket, and disclose two round white
arms to match her face, or to hear her sing '*Ah! non
giunge*' in soft dreamy tones.   He could have hummed
or whistled a tuneful second himself at a moment's
notice, for the matter of that.   However, save in the
market scene in *Martha,* there is no precedent for
warbling a duet with the young person you are about
to engage as a domestic servant.   Mr. Paton remembered this in time, and confined himself to what
the French call *le stricte nécessaire.*   He inquired
of Amelia whether she could do fine sewing, and
whether she could clear-starch.   His sister had impressed these questions upon him, and he was pleased
with himself for remembering them.

Amelia, or Amina (she was really very like Amina),
did not reply at once.   She had to bring her mind
back from the far-away sphere to which it had
wandered, or, in other words, to pull herself together
first.   When the reply did come, it was uttered in just
the low, melodious tones one might have expected.
She expressed her willingness to attempt whatever was
required of her, but seemed very diffident as regarded

her power of execution. 'I have forgotten so many things,' she concluded, with a profound sigh.

'*Sir*, you impertinent minx,' corrected the matron.

Amelia did not seem to hear, and her new employer hastened to interpose.

'We will give you a trial,' he said, in a curiously modified tone, 'and I hope you won't give me any occasion to regret it.'

The necessary formalities were hurried through. Mr. Paton disregarded the deferential disclaimers of the matron, but experienced, nevertheless, something of a shock when he saw Amelia divested of her prison garb. She had a thorough-bred air that discomfited him. Worse still, she was undeniably pretty. The scissors that had clipped her fair locks had left a number of short rings that clung like tendrils round her shapely little head. She wore a black stuff jacket of extreme simplicity and faultless cut, and a little black bonnet that might have been worn by a Nursing Sister or a '*grande dame*' with equal appropriateness. Thus attired, her appearance was so effective, that Mr. Paton asked himself whether he was not doing an unpardonably rash thing in driving No. 27 down Macquarrie Street in his gig, and introducing her into his household afterwards.

It was not Truca, for she had 'driven and lived' that morning, whose *mauvais quart-d'heure* was now to come. It was her father's turn to fall under its influence, as he sat, stern and rigid, on the driver's seat, with his little girl nestling up to him as close as she was able, and that strange, fair, mysterious presence on the other side, towards which he had the annoyance of seeing all the heads of the passers-by turn as he drove on towards home.

Arrived at Cowa Cottage, the young gardener ran forward to open the gate ; and here an unexpected incident occurred.   As Richard's eyes rested upon the new arrival, he uttered an exclamation that caused her to look round.   Their eyes met, a flash of instant recognition was visible in both.   Then, like the night that follows a sudden discharge of electricity, the gloom that was habitual to both faces settled down upon them once more.   Richard shut the gate with his accustomed machine-like precision.   Amelia looked at the intangible something in the clouds that had power to fix her gaze upon itself.   Yet the emotion she had betrayed was not lost upon her employer. Who could say ?   As No. 213 and No. 27, these two might have crossed each other's paths before.   That the convicts had wonderful and incomprehensible means of communicating with each other, was well known to Mr. Paton.   That young men and young women have an equal facility for understanding each other, was also a fact he did not ignore.   But which of these two explanations might account for the signs of mutual recognition and sympathy he had just witnessed ?   Curiously enough, he felt, as he pondered over the mystery later in the day, that he should prefer the former solution.   An offensive and defensive alliance was well known to exist among the convicts,

and he told himself that he could meet and deal with
the difficulties arising from such a cause as he had
met and dealt with them before. That was a matter
which came within his province, but the taking into
account of any sentimental kind of rubbish did *not*
come within his province. For some unaccountable
reason, the thought of having Richard flogged presented itself anew at this juncture to his mind. He
put it away, as he had done before, angered with
himself for having harboured it. But it returned
at intervals during the succeeding week, and was
never stronger than one afternoon, when his little girl
ran out to him as he sat smoking in the verandah,
with an illustrated volume of *Grimm's Tales* in her
hands.

'Oh, papa, look! I've found some one just like
Amelia in my book of Grimm. It's the picture of
Snow-White. Only look, papa! Isn't it the very
living image of Amelia?'

'Nonsense!' said her father; but he looked at
the page nevertheless. Truca was right. The snow-
maiden in the woodcut had the very eyes and mouth
of Amelia Clare—frozen through some mysterious
influence into beautiful, unyielding rigidity. Mr.
Paton wished sometimes he had never brought the
girl into his house. Not that there was any kind of
fault to be found with her. Even his sister, who
might have passed for 'She-who-must-be-obeyed,'
if Rider Haggard's books had existed at that time,
could not complain of want of docile obedience to

orders on the part of the new maid. Nevertheless, her presence was oppressive to the master of the house. Two lines of Byron's haunted him constantly in connection with her—

'So coldly sweet, so deadly fair,
We start—for life is wanting there.'

If Richard worked like an automaton, then she worked like a spirit ; and when she moved noiselessly about the room where he happened to be sitting, he could not help following her uneasily with his eyes.

The days wore on, succeeding each other and resembling each other, as the French proverb has it, with desperate monotony. Christmas, replete with roses and strawberries, had come and gone. Mr. Paton was alternately swayed by two demons, one of which whispered in his ear, 'Richard Cole is in love with No. 27. The time for him to regain his freedom is at hand. The first use he will make of it will be to leave you, and the next to marry Amelia Clare. You will thus be deprived of everything at one blow. You will lose the best man-servant you have ever known, and your sister, the best maid. And more than this, you will lose an interest in life that gives it a stimulating flavour it has not had for many a long year. Whatever may be the impulse that prompts you to wonder what that ice-bound face and form hide, it is an impulse that makes your heart beat and your blood course warmly through your veins. When this fair, uncanny presence is removed from your home, your life will become stagnant as it was before.' To this demon Mr. Paton would reply energetically, 'I won't give the fellow the chance of marrying No 27. As soon as he has his freedom, I will give him the sack, and forbid him the premises. As for Amelia, she is my prisoner, and I would send her back to gaol to-morrow if I thought there were any nonsense up between her and him.'

At this point demon No. 2 would intervene: 'There is a better way of arranging matters. You have it in your power to degrade the fellow in his own eyes and in those of the girl he is after. There is more covert insolence in that impenetrable exterior of his than you have yet found out. Only give him proper provocation, and you will have ample justification for bringing him down. A good flogging would put everything upon its proper footing,—you would keep your servant, and you would put a stop to the nonsense that is very probably going on. But don't lose too much time ; for if you wait until the last moment, you will betray your hand. The fellow is useful to him, they will say of Richard, but it is rather rough upon him to be made aware of it in such a way as that.'

One evening in January, Mr. Paton was supposed to be at his club. In reality he was seated upon a bench in a bushy part of the garden, known as the shrubbery—in parley with the demons. The night had come down upon him almost without his being aware of it—a night heavy with heat and blackness, and noisy with the cracking and whirring of the

locusts entombed in the dry soil. All at once he
heard a slight rustling in the branches behind him.
There was a light pressure of hands on his shoulders,
and a face that felt like velvet to the touch was laid
against his cheeks. Two firm, warm feminine lips
pressed themselves upon his, and a voice that he
recognised as Amelia's said in caressing tones,
' Dearest Dick, have I kept you waiting ? '

Had it been proposed to our hero some time ago
that he should change places with No. 213, he would
have declared that he would rather die first. But at
this instant the convict's identity seemed so preferable
to his own, that he hardly ventured to breathe lest he
should betray the fact that he was only his own forlorn
self. His silence disconcerted the intruder.

' Why don't you answer, Dick ? ' she asked impatiently.

' Answer ? What am I to say ? ' responded her
master. ' I am not in the secret.'

Amelia did not give him time to say more. With
a cry of terror she turned and fled, disappearing as
swiftly and mysteriously as she had come. The words
' Dearest Dick ' continued to ring in Mr. Paton's ears
long after she had gone ; and the more persistently
the refrain was repeated, the more he felt tempted to
give Richard a taste of his quality. He had tried to
provoke him to some act of overt insolence in vain.
He had worried and harried and insulted him all
he could. The convict's constancy had never once
deserted him. That his employer should have no

pretext whereby he might have him degraded and imprisoned, he had acted upon the scriptural precept of turning his left cheek when he was smitten on the right. There were times when his master felt something of a persecutor's impotent rage against him. But now at least he felt he had entire justification for making an example of him. He would teach the fellow to play Romeo and Juliet with a fellow-convict behind his back. So thoroughly did the demon indoctrinate Mr. Paton with these ideas, that he felt next morning as though he were doing the most righteous action in the world, when he called Richard to him after breakfast, and said in a tone which he tried to render as careless as of custom, 'Here, you! just take this note over to Mr. Merton with my compliments, and *wait for the answer.*'

There was nothing in this command to cause the person who received it to grow suddenly livid. Richard had received such an order at least a score of times before, and had carried messages to and fro between his master and the justice of the peace with no more emotion than the occasion was worth. But on this particular morning, as he took the fatal note into his hands, he turned deadly pale. Instead of retreating with it in his customary automatic fashion, he fixed his eyes upon his employer's face, and something in their expression actually constrained Mr. Paton to lower his own.

'May I speak a word with you, sir?' he said, in low, uncertain tones.

It was the first time such a thing had happened, and it seemed to Richard's master that the best way of meeting it would be to 'damn' the man and send him about his business.

But Richard did not go. He stood for an instant with his head thrown back, and the desperate look of an animal at bay in his eyes. At this critical moment a woman's form suddenly interposed itself between Mr. Paton and his victim. Amelia was there, looking like Amina after she had awoken from her trance. She came close to her master,—she had never addressed him before, — and raised her liquid eyes to his.

'You will not be hard on—my brother, sir, for the mistake I made last night?'

'Who said I was going to be hard on him?' retorted Mr. Paton, too much taken aback to find any more dignified form of rejoinder. 'And if he is your brother, why do you wait until it is dark to indulge in your family effusions?'

The question was accompanied by a through and through look, before which Amelia did not quail.

'Have I your permission to speak to him in the day-time, sir?' she said submissively.

'I will institute an inquiry,' interrupted her master. 'Here, go about your business,' he added, turning to Richard; 'fetch out the mare, and hand me back that note. I'll ride over with it myself.'

Three weeks later Richard Cole was a free man, and within four months from the date upon which Mr.

Paton had driven Amelia Clare down Macquarrie Street in his gig, she came to take respectful leave of him, dressed in the identical close-fitting jacket and demure little bonnet he remembered. Thenceforth she was nobody's bondswoman. He had a small heap of coin in readiness to hand over to her, with the payment of which, and a few gratuitous words of counsel on his part, the leave-taking would have been definitely and decorously accomplished. To tell her that he was more loth than ever to part with her, did not enter into the official programme. She was her own mistress now, as much or more so than the Queen of England herself, and it was hardly to be wondered at if the first use she made of her freedom was to shake the dust of Cowa Cottage off her feet. Still, if she had only known—if she had only known. It seemed too hard to let her go with the certainty that she never did or could know. Was it not for her sake that he had been swayed by all the conflicting impulses that had made him a changed man of late? For her that he had so narrowly escaped being a criminal awhile ago, and for her that he was appearing in the novel *rôle* of a reformer of the convict system now? He never doubted that she would have understood him if she *had* known. But to explain was out of the question. He must avow either all or nothing, and the all meant more than he dared to admit even to himself.

This was the reason why Amelia Clare departed sphinx-like as she had come. A fortnight after she had gone, as Mr. Paton was gloomily smoking by his library fire in the early dark of a wintry August evening, a letter bearing the N. S. Wales postmark was handed to him. The handwriting, very small and fine, had something familiar in its aspect. He broke open the seal,—letters were still habitually sealed in those days,—and read as follows :—

'SIR,—I am prompted to make you a confession— why, I cannot say, for I shall probably never cross your path again. I was married last week to Richard Cole, who was not my brother, as I led you to suppose, but my affianced husband, in whose behalf I would willingly suffer again to be unjustly condemned and transported. I have the warrant of Scripture for having assumed, like Sarah, the *rôle* of sister in prefer- ence to that of wife ; besides which, it is hard to divest myself of an instinctive belief that the deceit was useful to Richard on one occasion. I trust you will pardon me.—Yours respectfully,

'AMELIA COLE.'

The kindly phase Mr. Paton had passed through with regard to his convict victims came to an abrupt termination. The reaction was terrible. His name is inscribed among those 'who foremost shall be damn'd to Fame' in Tasmania.

MRS. DRUMMOND OF QUONDONG.

MRS. DRUMMOND OF QUONDONG.

—o—

T is a year to-day since I first saw this place,
—since I first saw *her*, I may as well say, for
she is pretty well the centre about which
all my thoughts have turned during this time; and
yet I was not prepared to like her—rather the reverse,
for the Creeks did not, and communicated their un-
favourable view to me. Certainly I was agreeably
disappointed when we met, but I don't think, when I
try really to look back, that I was much struck by
her in any way. I know I did not think her pretty,
only graceful and refined, and far more pleasant in
manner than I had anticipated. I could not help
noticing that she was a different stamp of woman to
Mrs. Creek; and I know the Grettan people were
surprised, and I think a trifle displeased, that I said
so little of my visit to Quondong. The fact is, I
felt rather puzzled what to say. Knowing that the
Drummonds were not liked, I could hardly praise
them; and after the kind reception given me, I would

C

not do the other thing. I went there again soon after. Hope had been told off to bring back the cattle about which I had gone over on my first visit, but he asked me to take his place, as he hated going to Quondong.

I wondered as I rode along if I should find things pleasant this time, and began to be half sorry I had undertaken a duty that was not mine; for certainly many people said disagreeable things about the Drummonds, and possibly my previous reception was only good by accident,—there was nothing in me that I should get more courtesy than others. When I rode up to the house I found Mr. Drummond on the verandah, and I can't say his greeting was particularly cordial. He never offered to shake hands, or to get up; nor, though on seeing him I had jumped off my horse, did he ask me to sit down. He hardly said 'how do you do' before he began business.

'Come for the cattle? But I can't give them to you to-day. Jones is laid up, and none of the other men seem to know where to find them.'

'Will he be able to go out to-morrow?'

'Well, I hardly know, but I suppose you can come over again?'

'Of course I can come again, but I particularly want to get the bullocks to our place by to-morrow night. Molloy is taking down a mob for the butcher, and we want to add them to the mob; and if I get them early in the day, I could run them over to the station in time.'

'H'm,' he said, after a pause, 'you had better see

for yourself. If you ride to Jones' hut, you can find out ; and if it is worth while staying, he can put you up.'

I was savage as I unhitched my horse and rode away, and if I could have done as I wished, would . have ridden back there and then ; but work had to be done, and personal annoyance would hardly have been taken as an excuse if I returned without the cattle, and I could not trust the black boy with me to drive them by himself. The stockman had had what he termed 'a touch of the sun,'—assisted, I suspected, by a good share of bad rum,—but was better, and would be able, he thought, to turn out the first thing in the morning. Neither were other matters quite so bad as I expected. Jones was a married man, and his wife looked after an adjoining hut that was set apart for chance travellers, so my quarters were not so uncomfortable ; and though the being sent off in that way rather rankled, still I was not sure I had any right to complain. So, after making an inward vow never to go again in another's place, I tried to make the best of it, and pass the afternoon as well as I could. Fortunately, after I had had something to eat, and had made my final arrangements with the stockman, I found a readable book, and the day being now pretty well advanced, I did not feel that I had so much to grumble about.

I was so absorbed in the book, *Adam Bede*, that I never heard steps approaching till a voice said, 'Mrs. Jones, I have brought you'—the speaker, who had just entered the door, stopped. I put down my book and jumped up, for it was Mrs. Drummond. I don't think she recognised me at first; evidently she had not thought any visitor was there, and was taken aback for the moment when she found the room occupied; but I knew her at once, and this sudden apparition of a pretty woman set my heart beating a little faster than usual. She did look awfully well in her light grey habit, something blue round her throat, and a knot of ribbon of the same colour under her shady hat; not as you see a riding costume *de rigueur*, but very suitable for the occasion, and it seemed to me also very becoming. I did not say anything, waiting for her to speak; besides, her un-looked-for appearance and the recollection of her husband's lack of courtesy rather confused me. She recognised me, however, almost immediately, and holding out her hand as she came forward, said,—

'What are you doing here, Mr. Verner? why did you not go at once to the house?'

I did not care to say I had been there, so answered as easily as I could, 'Are not these the strangers' quarters?'

'Yes; but no one we know stays here. Of course Mr. Drummond expects you to be with us.' I did not know what to say, but I know what I did—blushed like a girl.

You are very good,' I murmured, after a moment's uncomfortable pause; 'but as I start so early, it might be inconvenient for you.'

I fancy she guessed the real state of matters, or else blushing is contagious, for a pretty pink tinge came into her cheeks, while a look of annoyance passed over her face. She did not say anything more on this subject, but began to talk of her ride, saying she had seen a flower on the border of a scrub that had exactly the perfume of vanilla, but it was too high up for her to get it, or even to see it well. Nothing could be pleasanter than her manner, and though she did not stay above five or ten minutes, she left me with all my ruffled plumage smoothed down.

I had another visitor before long: Mr. Drummond walked in, in about an hour. 'My wife has been scolding me for letting you come here,' he said; 'so put on your hat and come back with me, or I shall have black looks all the evening.'

I daresay it would have been more dignified to have refused, but I forgot what was due to my pride, and did what I was told. I don't think he meant to be rude in the first instance. He simply did not care for my society,—why should he put himself out for a young nobody learning colonial experience?—so he sent me to the strangers' quarters; and he came for me because Mrs. Drummond made a point of having me at the house, and it was easier to do that than to thwart her. He is a man the sole motive of whose conduct is self. He regards it as a matter of course that life should be ruled by that principle, and acts up to it with a serene, unaffected simplicity that fairly astounds one.

When I say that I had not a vestige of regret for
taking Hope's place,—felt, indeed, quite a glow of self-
approval for having done a friend a good turn,—you
may be pretty sure I did not find the evening disagreeable.   Mrs. Drummond sang and played particularly well; perhaps her voice was not really so fine
as Mrs. Creek's, but it had far more expression, and
there was a tone in it that went straight to the heart.
Her singing had the same sort of charm as her appearance and manner.   It would be hard to put into
words what that charm was, though there could be
no difficulty about feeling it.   As I have said before,
she was not pretty, at least she did not strike you as
being so at first; the only actual beauties she owned
were her teeth, small, even, and white, and her ex-
quisitely fair skin.   Her other features were small
and regular, but nothing remarkable; her mouth,
indeed, was rather large, but the lips, fresh as a
child's, were flexible and expressive to a rare degree,
and when they smiled they lighted up her whole face.
Mind, she was by no means prodigal of these smiles.
The prevailing expression of her face had something
of sadness in it, mingled with a certain air of *hauteur*,
and it was this, and a somewhat reserved manner, that
I fancy often repelled people; but when she chose to
be pleasant, as I suppose she did this evening, nothing
could be more natural than she was, simple, kind, and
cordial, and so playful, so light - hearted, that it was
hard to imagine she could be unpopular.

But I am bound to confess she was not always like

this: sometimes her face was like a mask, with a set look on it that never varied, while her manner was chilling to a degree; then that hard expression would melt away, and a sudden softness come into her face. To see that change was as if the soul had come back to those limpid hazel eyes and that tender mouth. Her voice, too, had a hundred different inflections: occasionally it was almost harsh, while at another time there was a caress in its very tone. It was able to express those finer shades of feeling that words are often powerless to convey, and it had a natural pathos that appealed strangely to your sympathy. Of course no one is always bright or always dull. Most are attractive when lively, a few interesting when depressed; but in her it was not the mere change of spirits that charmed. She had very little of what is called vivacity, and her melancholy was less pensive than moody; but whatever her mood might be, her power of attraction never seemed to lessen.

She was a problem that one was always being forced to try and solve. Sometimes her whole nature seemed to open itself to you. It was the real living soul that spoke to you in those soft accents, that looked at you from those pure eyes and ever-varying countenance; then the veil fell, and it was a perfect woman of the world that met your eager glances with calm indifference; or she might chill you with a cold reception, and then by some subtle inflection of her voice call up a thrill of delight that was an ample atonement. Once favourably impressed by her, and

I cannot imagine anything that could diminish her hold upon you. Her outward appearance charmed the eye, as her beauties seemed coyly to unfold themselves as if to you in particular; and her inner nature was one that compelled you to study it, while it could safely bear the closest investigation. You were puzzled, you were repelled at times by a crust of worldliness, by an assumed heartlessness, but never did you find an ignoble thought, a mean motive hidden there; rather was it a lurking enthusiasm, some shy, sweet goodness that lay concealed in those carefully guarded recesses; and she was so pure-minded that the basest man could not have dared to look at, or think of her, with a polluting thought.

Naturally it was not on this visit, or on many succeeding ones, that I formed my estimate of her. I am only trying to put into words—and what feeble, unsatisfactory ones I only can tell—the impression she produced on me during the short time I had the privilege—and the wretchedness — of knowing her. It would be useless for me to deny the feelings with which she inspired me. It was some time before I recognised them myself. I never willingly betrayed them to her, for she was not the woman I took her to be if I could have dared so to do. She may have guessed them, for I was too young to be so master of myself as never to show what I felt. But whether she did, whether in the remotest degree she shared them,—had, as it were, some tender pity for me,— I never knew; she had so strong a will, such an

almost stern conscientiousness, that even if she had
loved me,—and I did not think her an angel, only
the noblest of women,—she would have died rather
than owned her weakness.

But to return to this particular evening. It was
not Mrs. Drummond only, but her husband too, who
was agreeable. He could be a pleasant companion
when he liked, and I suppose I did not find him the
less so because he talked to me about myself. I felt
rather disgusted afterwards when I recalled how I
had prated away on that subject, which, if interesting
to myself, could hardly be so to others. I was not
particularly charmed either to have made a comparative stranger acquainted with all my affairs and
plans, but I never thought of this till too late.
However, I consoled myself in thinking that it would
teach me more discretion the next time, not to say
anything about better taste, and also that certainly
I had not forced my concerns upon him ; and as
both had so kindly pressed me to come and see them
again soon, I could not have been such an insufferable bore as I feared.

I often took advantage of this invite when I could
get an idle afternoon, generally on a Saturday, when
I would not return till the following evening, putting
up for the night at Quondong. I certainly enjoyed
these visits very much ; after the noise of the children,
the somewhat rough-and-ready ways of Grettan, the
lack of neatness and order in things domestic there,
the nicety that reigned at Quondong was very plea-

sant. It may not be of any great consequence, but it certainly is more agreeable to sit down to a table where everything agrees with the snow-white cloth on which they are placed, where the dishes do not look as if they had got on haphazard, or the knives and forks sprawl about anyhow. Mrs. Drummond, too, in her fresh morning dress, a dark rosebud setting off the exquisite fairness of her throat, her slender hands moving amongst the dainty china cups and silver tea equipage, was a pretty object to regard.

After breakfast I used to go with her to feed her chickens; then, if it was not too late, we took a turn round the garden, or I helped her to water her plants in the back-house. We soon got on sufficiently easy terms to be under no restraint, no necessity to make talk; if we had anything to say we said it, if not we read, or simply remained silent. Time never seemed to lag, to me at any rate, and I ventured to flatter myself that Mrs. Drummond found even my society a relief to the very dull life she led.

Dinner was always early on Sundays, to let the maid-servants have a ride in the afternoon, so generally Mr. and Mrs. Drummond would walk with me on my return to Grettan as far as the crossing place, I leading my horse; and when I mounted they would wait till I rode away. How well I can recall her as she used to stand, resting her hand on her husband's arm, and turning her face to give me a parting smile, as, when I reached the top of the opposite bank of the river, I looked back before riding on.

The road to the ford was through a scrub which
on one side was untouched, and ran in an unbroken
wall of verdure, the other had been cut down, but
had partly grown up again; while the climbers,
taking advantage of the unusual light and air, had
flourished mightily, and covered the young growth
with their long vines, almost hiding their supports,
and hanging in festoons from shrub to shrub, or
creeping along the ground and concealing the fallen
logs with their mantle of green leaves; farther on was
the open flat where the station buildings were, that,
luckily for the picturesque, one could only partially
see; beyond them was a sloping hillside, treeless,
but covered with long broad-bladed grass, which the
rays of the setting sun tinged with the richest shades
of golden brown and red. The dwelling-house, which
was about a quarter of a mile away, was not visible
from this point, which was perhaps as well, for it was
hardly a pretty object, and only partially redeemed
by the many fine shrubs that grew around it.

Perhaps it was as well that I could not make these
pleasant visits as often as I could have wished, or I might
have worn out my welcome; but not only had I rarely
the leisure, but I fancied the Creeks rather resented my
being a favourite with the Drummonds, and regarded
my visits to them in some sort a going over to the
enemy; so I had on several accounts to put a whole-
some restraint on my inclinations. I have no doubt
it only made me prize my visits more; certainly I
was not sorry when business sent me one day un-

expectedly to Quondong. I made a little plan in my own mind as I rode along, that I would stay the night, and ride back in the very early hours, for I knew there would be a bright moonlight. Mrs. Drummond would sing me my favourite songs, and I could talk over with her some news I had received by the last English mail, and show her the photos it had also brought me; but 'the best laid schemes of mice and men aft gang agley.'

I must tell you that two young lady visitors had just arrived at Grettan,—an unusual event,—and their expected arrival had been discussed the last time I met the Drummonds. I cannot say their advent had disturbed me much, and I had almost forgotten all about it when I entered the drawing-room at Quondong, where for a marvel on a week-day I found Mr. Drummond. Business did not take long to settle, and then some allusion was made to the new arrivals. Had they come when I left? Yes, I had caught a glimpse of female forms as I passed the verandah on my way to the stables, and Mrs. Creek had called me in and introduced me.

What were they like? Were they quite young and pretty? Did they seem nice girls? Surely I could tell them something about them?

Mrs. Drummond was unusually eager in her questions, for she was the most incurious of women as a rule. As to Mr. Drummond, he always put one through a course of inquiries, so his remarks did not surprise me.

'I only stayed half a minute. I know one is nothing to look at; the other, I think, is pretty,' I said.

'That must be Miss Brown. I saw her last year, and thought her extremely handsome. Don't you remember, Robert, we met her at the Finches?' said Mrs. Drummond.

'Yes,' he answered; 'didn't she talk about *kiows?* But I would not mind that, if I were you, Verner; as her father says, "she carries ten thousand bullocks on her back," and she's worth looking after.'

'Thanks,' I answered; 'but I don't think I shall trouble Brown pater to round up his daughter's fortune.'

'At any rate these visitors will make bush life less insufferable,' put in Mrs. Drummond, and then held her peace; and as she turned her head away she could not see the reproachful glance that I involuntarily gave her when she spoke of finding life—her own, no doubt—insufferable.

Not a word was said, as usual, about my remaining. I presume that Mr. Drummond took it for granted that as these people were at Grettan I should wish to go back; at any rate he said,—

'I suppose it is no use asking you to stay?'

I did not answer for a moment. I wanted her to ask me, for it was a fresh pleasure when she repeated the invitation with that kindly smile in her eyes, but she said never a word; so, after a pause, I replied stupidly enough, 'I suppose not.'

She was at the piano when I came in, and she

remained there all the short time I stopped. When I made that last speech, she began a brilliant run, but blundering, broke off abruptly, and turning to me, said, looking full at me, ' Is it not provoking when one's fingers will go wrong over a passage ; but I forget, not playing, you will not understand.'

I had no particular reason to make any answer, so held my tongue.

I never knew it so difficult to get on at Quondong as that day. Mr. Drummond was as usual, that is, he never put himself out to entertain,—indeed, he went away and had a smoke on the verandah, as he frequently did. But she was unlike herself, seemed preoccupied, and to have no welcome for me. It was plain both thought I had only come over on business, and would be eager to get back to those wretched girls, and with a sinking heart I felt that all my anticipations of a pleasant afternoon were as the ' baseless fabric of a dream,'—my much considered plans quite uncalled for.

I took my leave in a little while, and went back with very different feelings to those I had indulged in as I rode over. The horse, too, seemed determined to add to my annoyance : he always had a trick of boring to one side, and this afternoon he did it till I was downright savage with the brute. I know I made him gallop nearly the whole way home, as he insisted on going like a crab whenever I slacked my pace to a walk ; the consequence of which little bit of temper on my part was, that I had to spend about

an hour rubbing him down and getting him cool
before I could turn him out.

I did find these visitors pleasant after all, though I
regarded their arrival at first as something more
than a bore, that is, when I returned from my
curtailed visit from Quondong.

Miss Brown was really very pretty, and by no
means the sort of girl Mr. Drummond's remark had
led me to expect. Perhaps she did laugh a little
more than was necessary, but she had such beautiful
teeth that it did not matter, and one forgave the
little twang for the sake of her bright eyes. The
other, Miss Blount, had at any rate a fine figure, and
was a jolly girl, good-natured, and quite willing to be
pleased,—almost did more than her fair share, indeed,
in the process. She sang, too, not so badly, though
in rather a spasmodic style, only letting out her
voice now and then in a way that was a trifle startling
till you got used to it. Hope said he did not like
it—too much of the minute-gun for his taste; but
then Hope was always hard to please. I used to
wonder if he ever enjoyed himself, he seemed to look
at life only on the seamy side.

One evening it was arranged there should be a picnic on the following Wednesday,—this was Monday,
—and that messages should be sent to our neighbours
at Ashwood and Quondong, asking them to join us.
As we were to be off duty on the chosen day, we had
to do double tides on Tuesday, and I never got home
till just before dinner When we were sitting on

the verandah afterwards, the black boy came round and gave Mrs. Creek a note. 'That's all right,' she said as she read it; 'the Grimes are coming, and will bring a Mr. Hall, as well as Scott and Hamley.'

'Have you any answer from the Drummonds?' asked Mr. Creek.

'By the bye, no. You got him paper along Quondong?' she said, turning to the boy.

'By Gar, I believe I forgot him altogether;' and Master Jacky, with a grin that showed his white teeth from ear to ear, produced the note of invitation— well wrapped up, I ought to say—from the bosom of his shirt, which served as pocket, and handed it over.

'Well, that is provoking,' remarked Mrs. Creek; 'but it is no use lamenting, we could not let them know now in time, could we?' turning to her husband.

'No,' he replied, 'it's out of the question; they must take the will for the deed.'

'I think I could let them know, if you care about it, Mrs. Creek,' I said.

'Thank you! Of course I should like them to come, but it's not worth the trouble.'

'It's not the least trouble; I could easily ride over on a bright night like this.'

'I don't see any necessity,' broke in Creek; 'I'm sure Drummond wouldn't thank you, and it's ten to one if Mrs. Drummond would care to come.'

'I'll chance that,' I said, and got up to go. Fortunately the horses were in a small paddock, to be at hand for the next day; so, taking a halter and a tin of corn, I soon caught old Billy, and, saddling up, started at once.

I could not but notice as I rode along what a lovely night it was—nothing broke the stillness but the curious 'gluck, gluck' of the frogs in the swamps; the sharp chirping cry of their brethren in the trees resembling far more the note of a bird than that of a reptile; the tinkle of a bullock bell; the sound of an axe, every blow of which rang out clearly.

The sky was absolutely cloudless, and though dimmed by the flood of silvery moonlight, myriads of stars could be seen faintly shining; Sirius still flashed and glittered, changing each moment as I looked from one vivid hue to another; the Southern Cross—that matchless constellation—gleamed brightly from the pale blue of the heavens. The shadows were sharply defined, but the melting light fell too softly for strong contrasts; the huge fallen logs, whole skeletons of long dead trees, though brought into perfect relief by the light resting on their barked surfaces, had nothing startling in their distinctness, but bore the same shadowy air as all around them.

But the strangeness of everything was what particularly struck me. Nothing bore the likeness that it did by daylight,—one seemed to look up long vistas where the trees overhead formed Gothic arches; on sloping lawns carpeted with turf smooth as velvet; on lakes into which the drooping branches dipped; on dark ravines walled in by steep rocks; grand avenues wound through wooded paths,—all was so changed, so unreal and yet so real, that it quite startled one.

The house, as I have said, was some little distance from the station buildings, and, as I rode up to it, the utter stillness, the hushed repose about the place, where the very roses that shone so white in the moonlight looked as if they were sleeping, made me think, almost for the first time, how late it was. I looked at my watch—nearly twelve. Well, I thought, it's no use stopping now, though I would have left the note at the station if I had thought of it before.

I tied up my horse, and going to the stables, tried to rouse the man who I knew slept there. Not a bit of use; I couldn't get the fellow to hear. I could not call out loudly, and I might have battered in the door with a paving-stone, supposing such a thing had been handy, without waking him from his slumbers. It would never do to go to the female quarters, for the most probable result of that step would be a series of squeals, and my being possibly potted by Mr. Drummond as a kind of colonial Tarquin.

I began to think I was doing an impertinent thing, and was a fool for my pains ; but I could not go back now. Perhaps the best plan would be to go round to the sitting-room,—the French lights were pretty sure to be open in this weather,—and I could leave the note on the table, and disappear without disturbing the sleeping house. I did so as quietly as I could, though I fancied my step, generally light, made as much noise as a buffalo's. I opened the venetian shutters, the hinges as I did so giving a squeak that made me turn cold all over, put the note down on a table, and stole out.

Just as I was coming out of the window, I found myself face to face with a figure, whose approach had been so noiseless and so unexpected that for the moment it regularly dumbfounded me. In an instant I recovered myself, and saw it was Mrs. Drummond. She did not recognise me, for I was in the shadow.

'Who is it?' she almost whispered, for she was evidently frightened, as the tremble in her voice betrayed, in spite of her struggle to command it. Then, as I stepped on to the verandah, she exclaimed, in the utmost surprise,—

'Mr. Verner! But what is it? Is anything wrong at Grettan?'

'I really must beg your pardon. I am not robbing the house, only bringing you a note from Mrs. Creek. We have a picnic to-morrow, and want you to join us.'

'And you have come all this way at night simply to ask me? You are good!'

'Not at all; only I hope you will come.'

'I could hardly refuse after this, even if I had wished. Where do we meet?'

'At the Downfall, about noon. Now, I had better say good-night. I'm awfully ashamed of myself for disturbing you at this hour.'

'I—I can't ask you to stay,' she said in a hesitating way. 'Mr. Drummond is not at home.'

'Many thanks,' I answered, feeling confused, I

didn't know why; 'I couldn't. I have to see to the things in the morning.'

'Thank you,' was all she said; but I would have ridden twice the distance to be addressed by her in such a tone. I could see she was not regularly dressed. She had on a long trailing robe (dressing-gown, I suppose), and over her head a light fleecy white shawl (what is called a cloud) was thrown. You can't imagine how childlike and pure her face looked under it. She was like the white roses that lay sleeping in the moonlight. When she put out her hand, as she did, and then withdrew it, to say good-bye, the movement stirred her skirts, and I saw the small foot was only covered by a slipper. It was not a very alarming object, that dainty little bare foot, but it sent a shiver through me, and I could not have met her eyes at that moment to save my life.

I had not much time for beauty-sleep after I got back; and I rather think I didn't bless Hope when he came stumping into my den, calling out, 'Hullo, Verner! do you know what the time is? There's the missis wanting you to help her pack; she won't take me at any price. Says I'm no more use than a fifth wheel to a coach.' But after I had walked down to the creek and had a good bathe, I was all right, and fit as paint.

We were lucky in the day, fine almost as a matter of course, but the cool breeze was by no means a blessing too often bestowed upon us. The place we had chosen was on the banks of the river, a grassy

nook, sheltered on three sides by thick scrub that
quite shaded us from the sun, while it was open to get
the breeze from the river. Don't run away with the
idea that a fine stream of water rolled below us.
There was none at all visible from this place, only the
broad empty bed covered with grass in high thick
tufts, with half-dead reeds and clumps of bushes, and
any amount of *débris*, great logs, broken branches,
sticks and withered leaves lying piled up in tangled
masses and curved ridges, as the last flood had left
them. Through this ran a narrow channel, 'pro-
miscuous like,' swerving now to this side, now to the
other. It was hard to picture the whole of this wide
space filled bank high with a rushing, swirling torrent ;
but the rubbish lodged among the branches of trees
growing in it told a tale.

The Ashwood people came up about the same
time as we did, Mrs. Grimes looking wonderfully
young (she was well up in the thirties) behind her
black lace veil, under which her dark velvety eyes and
white teeth flashed most becomingly. Old Grimes
was in a suit of nankeen that had been so often
washed that its colour was almost gone, while it had
so shrunk that his legs and arms appeared to have
grown since he began to wear it. The stranger did
not take my fancy much ; but apparently my senti-
ments were not shared by Mrs. Grimes, for his
attentions—and he was pretty lavish of them—were
received graciously enough. Hope went off, and I
caught sight of him and Hamley planted behind a fig

tree, and smoking like two steam-engines. Scott and
Hall did the amiable to the ladies, and I helped Mrs.
Creek. Miss Blount was good enough to come and
assist after a little, and took me in charge, telling me
where the things were to be placed, making me trot
about under her orders, so I was kept tolerably busy;
but I did not forget to keep a bright look-out on the
road that led towards Quondong.

No sign yet of the Drummonds. When we were
all assembled and the luncheon arranged, there was
some faint opposition on the hostess's part to our
beginning before the arrival of the missing guests; but
her husband pooh-poohed the notion of waiting.

'Nonsense, my dear; they could be in time if they
chose; and if they do come, they won't starve.'

I was not quite so sure of that, for I didn't think
much of Mrs. Creek as a caterer, and I certainly did
not like the idea of the Drummonds finding lunch
half over when they came—when they came? Suppose
they did not come at all! Perhaps the sky clouded
over just then,—I know the place looked as dull as
ditch-water for a few minutes,—and the view over the
dry bed of the river, where the air quivered in the
heat, and the flat beyond, sparsely scattered with gum
trees, whose scanty greyish-green foliage hardly
showed, had the dreariest air imaginable.

'Mr. Verner, you may sit down here,' called out
Miss Blount. But before I could take advantage of
her invitation, or rather permission, I heard the sound
of a horse's hoof, and caught a glimpse of Folly's

shining chestnut coat through the trees, and it was not long before I was helping her rider to dismount. 'Not pretty' had been the verdict passed on her the previous evening, when Mrs. Drummond was under discussion. 'Not proven,' I said then to myself, though I spoke out never a word; now I gave utterance, mentally, to a decided 'Not guilty.'

She wore her light grey habit, but in place of the shady straw hat she generally wore, she had put on a saucy little velvet hat that suited her fair hair and skin to perfection. She had a colour, too, with fast riding, and her soft hazel eyes and fresh lips were both smiling. Then her manner, simple, gay to playfulness, yet never overstepping the invisible bounds of good breeding, or losing its quiet dignity, was so different to that of the others; while her voice, with its modulated tones, fell so pleasantly on the ear, after the somewhat uncultivated accents of Mrs. Creek and her friends.

After I had found Mrs. Drummond a seat, I remembered Miss Blount's gracious offer, and the place being still vacant, took up my position by her side. She was not a silent individual, and had, besides, a very fair appetite. So between keeping her supplied with eatables and drinkables, and replying to her provocative speeches, I was not idle in mind or body. I managed, however, to see that my guest—for I felt as if I had a claim to her—was not neglected. I had no chance of saying much, but I glanced once or twice towards her, when my companion said anything particularly startling,—and she was rather given to uncommon remarks,—and we exchanged a momentary smile, more of the eyes than the lips.

We were certainly not a dumb party, and were so busily engaged eating and drinking, chattering and laughing about nothing, that none of us remarked the clouding over of the sky. We were not to remain long in ignorance, for soon there came a muttered growl of thunder, followed after one or two repetitions by a low rushing sound that betokened either wind or rain, perhaps both. Shelter there was none. Some kind of wraps were made for the ladies with what had been used to cover the things in the cart that carried the provisions, and I got Mrs. Drummond her cloud that she had brought with her, and had left fastened to her saddle,—I wondered as I carried it, was it the one I had seen her wear the previous evening,—to protect her hat, for the safety of which she was frankly solicitous. I wanted her to take my coat, but she would not hear of it. However, Mrs. Creek seeing it hanging over my arm, called out, ' If you don't mean to use that garment, you might as well lend it to me.' So I handed it over to her, catching as I did so a look of amusement in Mrs. Drummond's face that made me laugh at the discomfiture that my own must have betrayed.

Having made our preparations, such as they were, we awaited the coming storm. It did not keep us long in suspense. First came a gust of wind that bent all the branches in one direction, and then sent

them tossing and whirling in the air, blew the twigs
and dried leaves and bits of grass till they scampered
about like living things, and filled the air with the
noise of rustling foliage, and cracking, jarring
branches. The blast blew over. There was a sudden
stillness, almost startling after the late turmoil.
Some great drops of rain splashed down, and then
with a swish the shower was upon us. How it did
rain! None of your pattering drops, but regular
streams of water poured down upon our devoted
heads. Another minute and it was gone, and we only
heard its loud rushing sound, as we saw it, like a great
grey curtain, sweeping away over the tree-tops.

We were not much the worse. Even Mrs. Drummond's little hat reappeared from 'under the cloud'
safe from the threatened bath. Mrs. Creek gave me
back my coat, which I am happy to say had been of
no use to her. Mrs. Grimes took her handkerchief
away from her face, 'her skin was so tender,' was the
information she volunteered. I suppose it was, and
that the rain hurt it, for I saw a pink stain on the
white cambric. On the whole, the 'fair sect,' as Mrs.
Brown has it, came off pretty well; and though we of
the lower order of creation were wet through,—our
shirts clinging like loose skins, our unmentionables
defining our nether limbs more plainly than was
altogether satisfactory to the vanity of some of us,
our hats dripping,—there was nothing worth lamenting, and our plight only served to give fresh cause for
mirth.

But the luncheon! The cloth was soaking and splashed with sand, the dishes half full of water, the remains of the viands plentifully besprinkled with leaves and twigs and gravel, the bread a sop; and I declare that a piece of bread on my plate was washed white. Fortunately the inner man had been satisfied with the substantials, and the rain had not got into the bottles at any rate.

Very soon the sun was shining out of a sky of the most intense blue, made still lovelier in colour by the contrast with masses of snow-white clouds. The quivering leaves were sparkling as if powdered with diamonds, as a cool breeze shook showers of raindrops off them at each moment. Birds sang and gurgled most musically; for, though Australian birds have no continuous song, some of their notes are exceedingly rich and sweet. Not all, though, as we had good proof, for suddenly one solemn old feathered biped, sitting near us on a dead branch, lifted up his voice with a preliminary giggle, and then burst into a roar of chuckling laughter, so inharmonious and so utterly absurd in sound, that we all followed suit and roared in chorus. After this we got up the horses; and while some stowed away the things in the cart, the others saddled them, and soon we were nearly all mounted.

Just as we were about starting a song was suggested. The idea took. But first we were to have a stirrup-cup, and as a suitable chant to follow that operation, 'Drink to me only with thine eyes' was selected. What a group we made! We were now standing, having left the scrub, among some huge green trees whose smooth trunks were still darkened by the wet; the cart was ready, and formed a prominent object; all the ladies were on horseback, but some of the men still on foot.

I was by Mrs. Drummond's mare, resting my hand on her neck, lest the noise might frighten her, and stealing a look up now and then into her rider's fair smiling face. Old Mr. Grimes, with his hat off, his scanty red hair glistening with wet, his damp spare garments bringing his meagre limbs out in strong relief, his little eyes twinkling with pleasure, was singing away, glass in hand, with all his might. The carter, inspired by the music, and probably the bottle of beer, was joining in with a very shamefaced expression, but an uncommonly sweet voice.

All the others were doing their best. Mrs. Drummond contributed a sweet, if not over strong second, to which I added my mite. Miss Blount, one small, gloveless hand holding the whip with which she marked the time, took a capital first, though she did overpower rather Mrs. Creek's pure silver-toned soprano. Hope, whose forte was not music, was very busy doing something to Miss Brown's stirrup, and that young lady was apparently too deeply engaged with the subject of its being lengthened or shortened to attend to her vocal duties.

We had all, in separate directions, some little way to go; but when some one struck up 'The days when we went gipsying,' it was irresistible, and off we all went into a singing chorus. 'Isn't it jolly?' I heard Miss Blount say to Mrs. Grimes ; and the reply was, 'Yes, awfully ; but it wasn't quite so jolly when you *did* go gipsying, a long time ago.'

After this we really made a start ; and not too soon, for the long shadows showed that sunset was not far off. When Mrs. Drummond turned off, I, of course, prepared to accompany her.

'What are you thinking about?' called out Mrs. Creek; 'you are not going home, when Mr. Drummond does not return, you say, till to-morrow ; you are to return with us.'

'I really must not. Robert might come back to-night ; besides'—and she gave a meaning look at the already large party from our place.

'That's of no consequence,' replied Mrs. Creek, interpreting the glance. 'I can put the girls in one room.'

Mrs. Drummond still hesitating, Mrs. Creek said, 'Very well, if you won't come with us, we will go with you ; so take your choice.'

'Then really in pure kindness to you I must accept your invitation, for I don't believe my larder contains anything but the remains of the chicken I had for dinner yesterday.'

So she came back with us. I had never seen her in such spirits, she was the gayest of us all. She made Folly prance and curvet, and jump over the fallen timber, and finished with a race with Miss Blount on some straight-running that led to the house. Most of us joined in this, so it was a regular hurry-skurry. In the confusion and gathering darkness we came (almost without seeing them) on the milking cows, which were lying down placidly chewing the cud. Helter-skelter we dashed in amongst them.

Miss Blount's horse gave a great shy, cannoning against Mr. Hall's (who had returned with us) ; in trying to escape he jumped over a reclining cow, or rather he tried to, for the cow, alarmed, tried to get up just at the moment, and in an instant nothing was to be seen but any number of legs apparently, sticking up in the air, for the cow, the horse, and the rider all seemed to be on the broad of their backs, and all flourishing their limbs about at the same time.

As to thinking of any danger to Mr. Hall, not one of us troubled our heads in the matter. We regarded the affair as got up for our especial amusement, and appreciated it with complete unanimity ; and when the poor man, dusty and dirty, got into a sitting position and gazed around him with a most woebegone expression, it sent us off again into a fresh burst of laughter.

The fact is, the fellow was an utter cad, and we felt it would be a mere waste of sympathy to have any pity for an animal who left out all his h's. But no, I wrong him ; he used the right number, but, like the confession in the Prayer-book, that which he ought to have done, he did not do ; while he did do that which he ought not to have done. In reference to this failing, he tried us all fearfully at breakfast the next morning. In one of those pauses of silence that occur in a large party, his voice was heard saying,—

'I think it so dangerous to sleep on the bare ground, that I always take a h'air mattress with me into camp.'

'A hair mattress!' replied Mrs. Drummond, to whom he was talking, with a puzzled look. 'Surely that is very cumbersome?'

'Oh dear, no,' was the calm response; 'I only *h*-inflate it when it's wanted.'

I caught a glimpse of a look of horror on Mrs. Drummond's face. After that I dared not lift my eyes from my plate. There was a dead silence; the faintest suspicion of a giggle came from Miss Brown's direction. In another moment we should have broken down, when by good luck one of the youngsters dropped a plate, and we all broke out into a laugh that must have seemed perfectly idiotic to the real cause of our merriment.

I don't think I felt more amiable towards the fellow, as, a few hours after, I saw him going off with the rest of the visitors and Mrs. Creek towards Quondong. There he was, well mounted, and garbed in dazzling white, riding by Mrs. Drummond's side, and bending over towards her in earnest conversation; while I, scorched and grimy, and smothered in dust, was counting sheep in the yards.

I must say I was very glad they did not stop as they passed; and yet, as I caught a last glimpse of a lithe figure in a grey habit, I felt as if there was something almost unkind in riding by without a word of farewell.

The riding party did not return till late, for not only had they seen Mrs. Drummond home, but they had gone round by Ashwood, where they had left Miss Brown and Mr. Hall.

I expect the unwonted dissipation had something to do with it, but for some cause or other we were not festively inclined this evening. Music was tried ; Mrs. Creek would sing 'Some day,' and plainly expected me to join with the others in saying how much better she sang it than Mrs. Drummond ; but I didn't think, and would not be made to say so. It was very absurd, I know, that this trifle irritated me. I could not but acknowledge that Mrs. Creek had a finer voice, but its clear silvery tones had not a particle of expression, and beautiful as they were, never touched your heart ; and I felt not only that there was an injustice in giving her the palm in the rendering of a song the very *raison d'être* of which was feeling, but that there was a certain spice of ill-nature towards the rival singer in giving the award.

Then Mrs. Creek went off to her babies, and Miss Blount took her place ; but that would not do at all. She was tired, I suspect, and screamed like a peacock. The worst of it was, the others, taking advantage of my being installed as leaf-turner, cleared out, and I had to do the civil till I wished the girl at—well certainly anywhere but where she was. Then cards were proposed ; but a round game for love, when there is no one whose love you care about, not being enticing to people arrived at years of discretion, the idea fell through, and very soon we all retired to try the effects of 'Nature's sweet restorer' in putting us into a pleasanter mood.

One day I had rather a queer adventure. I was riding home from an out-station, when, a mile or two from the house, I met Miss Blount and Kitty. Without vanity, I think I may say the former was very glad to see me, for she was not at all fond of solitude, and the little girl went for nothing. On my own part, I was pleased enough. It's awfully dull riding by yourself mile after mile through the bush, where one tree is exactly like the other, and each gully and ridge cries ditto to that you have just crossed.

This is not a very complimentary way to speak of Miss Blount; but, indeed, though I could hardly fancy a fellow losing his heart to her, she was capital chaff, and good enough to take the trouble of entertaining into her own hands.

We plunged at once into a kind of mimic warfare that raged between us—the cause of our mock dissension this time being the comparative merit of our steeds—till we came to a crossing place over the river, about a mile from the house.

Here my horse, being thirsty, put down his head to drink, my companions riding on. Sepoy was very dainty in his tastes, and the shallow water crossed by the others being muddled, he sniffed disdainfully at it, and insisted on going to a place where the stream

ran clear. This took some little time. The others
had gone over, mounted the bank, and were disappearing out of sight, the land falling beyond. Sepoy,
having slaked his thirst, lifted up his head, champing
his bit, and shaking the wet off his muzzle. I was
about to follow the others, when I thought I heard a
voice calling me by name,—a man's voice, too,—so
there was nothing wrong with the girls. I looked
round, but could see no one, and gathered up my
reins for a rush up the bank, a favourite proceeding
of Sepoy's, hastened by Kitty calling out in impatient
tones, ' Do make haste, Mr. Verner ! '

But there could be no mistake this time about the
strange voice—' Verner, Verner, for God's sake don't
go !' Guided better by the sound, now my eyes
caught sight of a pale face peering round a tree not
far distant.

' What's the matter ? ' I said, staring in amazement
at the scared countenance from which the voice had
evidently proceeded. I did not go towards it at first ;
for if I had any ideas at all on the subject, it was that
my interviewer was a madman, and that it would be
as well to carry out the old adage as to discretion.
Sepoy, taking advantage of my inattention, now made
a move forward to follow his mates.

' Stop !' almost shrieked the owner of the head; ' I'm
Hall, I have lost my clothes ;' and in his anxiety
getting from behind the kindly shelter of the tree, it
was very evident that some awkward accident had befallen his garments, for not a rag had he on save a hat.

E

'All right!' I called out, turning my horse and going towards him; 'only get out of sight again, my good fellow.'

But my warning came too late, for a shrill voice (Kitty's) exclaimed, 'Oh, goodness gracious!' and I caught a glimpse of the little girl's figure—she had evidently turned back to see what delayed me—in full retreat. Quite sure now that the coast was clear, I could listen with a tranquil mind to the tale he told.

It seems Hall had stopped on his way from Ash-field to Grettan, at the Downfall, at the large water-hole close to where we had had our picnic. Here the water looked so deliciously cool as it splashed over the little ledge of rocks forming the miniature cascade from which it had its name, that he thought he would have a bathe. Now, a few days before, when indulging in a similar luxury, he had been stung by some large ants that had got into his clothes as they lay on the ground To avoid this danger, he strapped them together, and fastened them on to his saddle, and then hitching his horse securely to a sapling, proceeded with an easy mind to disport himself in the crystal stream.

So far so good. But when he came out again, no sooner did he approach his horse than the latter started back with an affrighted snort. Like a fool instead of standing still and speaking so as to re-assure the animal, he rushed forward to grab the reins before they broke; the natural result was that terrified still more at the antics of this strange object the horse plunged wildly, the head-stall gave way, and off he went, carrying the clothes along with him. He did not go very far, though, but wheeling round, stopped in his flight, and, with uplifted tail and expanded nostril, gazed at the cause of his alarm.

Taught discretion, Hall advanced more carefully this time, trying, by addressing him in soothing tones, to calm his fear; but in vain. No sooner was he almost within touching distance, than the horse would gradually back, give a snort, and, wheeling round, trot off again. Again he advanced, and in terms of dulcet flattery—'Whoa, good horse; good boy; coop, coop, come along; gently, old fellow; poor old boy'— strove to calm the truant steed.

But the result was another failure; and so it went on, the horse letting him approach to just beyond catching distance, and then at the moment he thought he had him, sheering off. Once he stalked him, and creeping up behind actually got hold of one of the legs of his trousers. The horse, startled afresh, started forward. Hall held on, and as the animal was not only stronger, but had a base of four to Hall's two, the man toppled over, and as he scrambled up he found himself in the possession of about as much of his nether garments as would encircle his ankle, and saw his horse disappearing in the distance, carrying away the rest of his attire in triumph. There he was, in a nice predicament. He tried at first to run after his horse, but soon pulled himself up with a barked shin and a scratched face, having tumbled into the head of a fallen tree. What was he to do? He wasn't very far from Grettan, for his horse had headed that way; but how on earth was he to make his appearance in such a plight? He shuddered at the bare idea (no pun meant). Yet he could not stay where or how he was.

He thought of our first parents; but thatching himself with branches did not seem a feasible plan; and as to using single leaves, the only kind that were at all suitable were those of the nettle tree in the scrub, and they certainly would not do, for as much as these leaves excel in size those of the nettle of our ditches, so do they excel them in the virulence of their stinging properties.

At last he determined to make his way to the crossing place, and wait in concealment there, on the chance of some one passing. He got to where I found him at last with no little difficulty, for his feet were cut by sticks and stones, and, indeed, I did pity him when he held them up for my inspection, for their state proved what rough usage they had had, although his rueful expression, and the surroundings in general, were so ludicrous that I could hardly keep my countenance.

Here, planted behind a big tree, he had waited, shivering with cold and stiff with fatigue, and almost wild with the attacks of mosquitoes, who came in crowds to partake of the feast so bounteously spread for them. The sound of our advancing horses had fallen like the sweetest music on his ear. Judge, then, his dismay when he caught sight of two female forms. Crouching behind the tree, he had gathered himself into the smallest space, not daring to move lest his presence might be betrayed, all his hopes of a rescue being lost in the fear of being seen.

When, however, I lingered behind, it seemed like a special interposition of Providence in his favour; and he was in such an agony of fear lest I should not hear him, that he could scarcely control his voice sufficiently to call out. Of course his troubles were to a certain extent over now. I could not give him any garments there and then, because I hadn't more than was absolutely necessary for myself, one's toilet in the bush being distinguished more for simplicity than abundance; but I rode back as quickly as I could, and returned with a led horse and wherewithal to clothe him, not forgetting something to comfort the inner man.

Nothing could induce him to face the fair females. Indeed, he was so utterly done up, and in such pain from his bruised and swollen feet, that bed was about the best place for him. So I gave him up my room, as it was on the verandah, and he could crawl to it without being seen, except, indeed, by one or two of the boys, who had evidently learned something of the affair from their sister, and whose looks were certainly not expressive of pity as they watched him hobbling along.

. . . .

When I made an agreement with Mr. Creek to take

me as a new chum, my services and a certain premium being accepted as an equivalent for the opportunities given me of acquiring a knowledge of station matters, of course it was for a fixed time. This time had now nearly expired, and though my present work was what is more usually entrusted to more practised hands,—naturally leading me to suppose that some little value was attached to my services,—Mr. Creek had so far said nothing as to my remaining, or rather, as I should say, as to my receiving any salary. He talked of plans to be carried out, and spoke as if I were to take a share in their execution, so I had no reason to conclude that he wished me to leave at the end of my term ; but he made no allusion as to any change in my position.

I, on my part, had certainly no desire to go—to do anything that might sever the pleasant relations that existed between me and the Drummonds ; yet, all the same, I had not the slightest intention of working any longer without pay. Not only did I feel that I was worthy of my hire,—and I don't see how any one who has his wits about him, and really tries to do his best, can be ignorant in that respect,—but I held it unfair to my father not to relieve him of the burden of my keep as soon as I could ; and the conviction that my inclinations led me to remain near Quondong, above all things, served but to make me feel the more keenly what was due to him.

So it came to pass that I was a good deal exercised in my mind on this matter. I shrank from speaking,

thinking that any proposal ought to come from Mr.
Creek, and because I dreaded taking a step that might
end in my having to leave this neighbourhood; yet I
fretted and reproached myself for remaining silent.

Things went on in this uncomfortable state for
some time; day after day went by; chances of opening the subject were lost, the present ever seeming an
inopportune moment; my period of pupilage had
come to an end, and yet nothing had been decided.
Of course I suffered for this shirking—one always
does. Had I spoken at once, as I ought to have
done, not only would I have been easier in my mind,
but I should not have been placed in a position that
gave others the right, as I could not but own it did,
to consider I had acted unfairly towards them. Not
that I had so acted, and therein lay the sting, for
surely never is an unjust imputation so hard to bear
as when you feel that, though guiltless, yet your conduct has seemed to give grounds for the accusation.

The whole affair was settled, as these long-pondered
affairs generally are, unexpectedly, and in quite a
different way to what I had supposed. I was spending,
as I so frequently did, the Sunday at Quondong, when
Mr. Drummond, turning to me in his abrupt way, said,—

'How much does Creek give you?'

'Nothing,' I answered.

'How's that?'

Then I told him how matters stood; and being very
full of the subject, doubtless enlarged considerably
on it.

'I think you are making a great mistake in staying,' he said, interrupting me after he had listened silently for some time. 'You are worth pay, of course, or Creek wouldn't keep you on; but it isn't fair to your father to give your services for nothing.'

'You would advise me, then, to ask for a salary?'

'Well, I don't advise you at all in the matter, that is your own affair; but I'll tell you what I'll do. I will take you on in Gardiner's place. I won't promise you the same pay, because you are not an old station hand like him, but I'll do what's fair.'

Seeing that I hesitated, for the idea of being actually at Quondong startled me into silence, he continued,—

'It's better than staying at Grettan even with a screw, with the sheep I have, and my management. Creek knows about as much as a black fellow about sheep; you will learn far more here. Of course, though you take Gardiner's place, you will be on a different footing. The fact is, I want some one I can trust to act immediately under me, and I think you will do.'

Then he stopped and went on smoking, not looking directly at me; but I could see that his sharp little eyes were watching me furtively all the same.

'It is very good of you,' I answered slowly, 'and I should like the billet.'

'Then why don't you take it?' he said quickly. 'The screw shall be (and he named a fair enough sum), and your quarters—at the station, though,' adding the last few words after a momentary pause.

'I should be only too happy to get it,' I replied;
'but I can hardly leave Creek so abruptly, and you
say Gardiner goes at once.'

'I thought you told me just now that it was over a
month since your agreement terminated?'

'Yes; I suppose had he wanted me he would have
spoken?'

'Not a doubt of it. I don't see any need for hesitation on that score.'

'Perhaps not; though I should not like to offend
him by accepting another billet before I had fairly
left him, or even spoken of leaving.'

'Then don't say anything about it; the agreement
is finished, and there's an end of it.'

The upshot of the matter was, I did take the billet,
subject to the condition that I should not incon-
venience Mr. Creek by leaving him hurriedly.

Mrs. Drummond wasn't present when this conversation took place. She had gone down to the station
to see a sick woman, and her husband and I were
waiting for her, sitting on a fallen log a little way off.

Nothing was said about it when she rejoined us;
and it was not till just before I left, and she and I
were alone together, that I mentioned that I was to
be one of the Quondongs.

'Did you or Robert propose it?' she said, with a
sudden harsh inflection in her voice.

'Mr. Drummond, certainly; even my impudence
would not have been equal to that.'

She did not say anything more; but her remark,

and the tone it was uttered in, took me aback not a little, for I thought she would have been pleased, and had secretly reckoned on a look of pleasure in her face when I told her.

I puzzled a good deal over her speech on my ride home; and between that and thinking how I should tell the Creeks of my new plan,—I need hardly say that I never for a moment meant to follow Mr. Drummond's advice,—I can't say that my meditations were exactly agreeable; and I began to regret that I had been so communicative, and so led to the offer being made.

The lights were out in the sitting-room when I got back, so my determination to have no more delays— for I could not but feel how much more pleasant it would have been to have spoken to Mr. Creek before —was useless. My troubles did not keep me awake, but they set me dreaming, and amongst other uncomfortable things I thought Creek would insist on taking away my clothes to prevent me going. My objection to this stripping process awoke me, and I found the foundation for my vision in the fact of Hope's kangaroo dog having planted himself on the end of my blanket which had fallen down, and whose descent he was assisting by some rapid turns preparatory to curling himself up in its folds.

I got through the affair during the day, and found it sufficiently disagreeable. Creek chose to consider himself an aggrieved person, and that I ought to have spoken to him before I made any agreement. Perhaps

I ought; but I thought also that he ought to have proposed something if he had wished me to stay on, seeing that he knew very well when my time as a 'new chum' came to an end. He did not say much, but his manner was nasty, to say the least of it. I was half-savage at the time, that I could not find any words in which to resent it and yet not betray temper; but I am glad now that my wit failed me, for a sharp retort would probably have led to a quarrel, and I should have much regretted such a *finale* to a period of, on the whole, pleasant intercourse.

I found, as soon as I met Mrs. Creek, that she had heard the news, and I felt it too, for though she treated my departure as a matter of no consequence (nor, indeed, was it), she contrived to say more unpleasant things during the short time I remained than was at all agreeable to listen to; so that, both hurt and annoyed at the curt, ungracious way Mr. Creek put aside my offer to stop as long as suited him, I was not sorry that my stay was to be of short duration. I have alluded before to the jealous dislike the Creeks had for the Drummonds, and it was this feeling that was at the bottom of Mrs. Creek's manner to me. She had always resented my being on such friendly terms with her neighbours, and now that I was fairly leaving Grettan for Quondong, she seemed to take it as a case of desertion to the enemy.

I could not flatter myself that she had any regret at my leaving on my own account, for I was not ignorant that I was not a favourite with her. Perhaps for that reason I was not drawn towards her. She was clever and amusing, a capital wife to Creek, who thought her perfection, and good-natured to the young fellows (myself included) at the place; but I don't think she was particularly sincere, or that her standard of honour was a high one; certainly her sense of truth was not, if I may judge from the tarradiddles she told now and then.

And whether it was that I unconsciously betrayed my estimate of her character, or for what she was pleased to term my fastidiousness, at any rate I was not exactly in her good graces. She gave me a Parthian shot as I was leaving, congratulating me on the difference I should find between their 'poor fare and rough-and-ready ways,' and the luxury of the Drummonds' house.

'But you see, Mrs. Creek, I am going to live at the station.'

'Oh!' with a tone of malicious surprise, 'are you to be counted amongst the men, then?'

'I suppose so.'

'I thought you were far too great a favourite with Mrs. Drummond to be sent down to the station.'

'Most likely,' I answered, 'she knows nothing about it. Naturally they would not care always to have a stranger with them.'

'It's fortunate *our* sensibilities are not so delicate,' she rejoined, 'as we have had to put up with having a stranger with us.'

I felt very much, at this retort, like the man who

never opened his mouth but to put his foot in it, and
that I had better keep mine shut and let my an-
tagonist retire with all the honours of war.   Perhaps
this small triumph mollified her ; for when we next
met she received me graciously enough, and we have
always been on very fair terms since.

.   .   .   .

I did not see very much of Mrs. Drummond.   I
never went to the house without an express invitation ; and, moreover, I had very little leisure.   My new
boss not only knew what was to be done, but he had
a knack of making others do it.   Finding that I was
pretty good at figures, he got me to help him with the
books, as well as the outdoor work—not the regular
accounts, which he managed entirely himself, there
being no book-keeper on the station, but for some
extra returns he was making out on a plan of his own.

I could not but be amused at the way he got me
to do them.   He began, as we were riding out together to a sheep station, to discuss them.   I did not
think much of his method, though I thought the idea
might be carried out with advantage; and being
naturally concerned in all that related to sheep, I was
much interested in the question, and ventured to
propose a few alterations, giving my reasons for these
changes.   Of course I only put these forward as
suggestions, not being quite such a fool, though I was
a new chum comparatively, as to be at all sure that
any notion of mine could be of any use to an
experienced man like Mr. Drummond.

After what I have said of him, you would hardly imagine he was the sort of person to let a youngster and a subordinate discuss, and in a mild manner even criticise a plan of his; but that is just what he would do. When he had a scheme *in petto*, he liked to talk it over with any one he met, and what's more, to listen to the remarks made on it. Out of these different opinions he used to form his course of action; and if he was not clever in originating, he certainly was in choosing the best from the various views he elicited—in making the wisdom of others work for his ends.

It sounds ill-natured, but I believe it was his thorough selfishness that was at the bottom of this unusual disregard of his own views; the intense hold that his interests had on him would not let him treat his own thoughts with any especial favour, so that he was never, as most people are, influenced unfairly by a scheme because it had been evolved out of his own internal consciousness.

But to return. After I had talked for some time, and had shown, I suppose, not only an interest, but some slight insight into the matter, he said, turning towards me with quite the air of *bonhomie* with which people generally confer a favour,—

'I tell you what it is, Verner, you shall make them out for me yourself. Put them into some shape to-night, and to-morrow evening come up, and we can look over the plan, and see if it will work.'

I think I did murmur something like an assent, but

I doubt if he heard me : he certainly never heeded. He seemed to consider that for the present he had done with the matter,—that it was out of his hands ;— for when I made some further remark on the subject, feeling, indeed, rather nervous at the responsibility, and desirous of more information, he made no answer, and began, almost before the words of my question were fairly uttered, to give me directions on another business. That done, he lighted his pipe, and smoked on without speaking a word till we reached the sheep station.

Here he broke out into a fine storm. The shepherd, a Chinaman, not expecting a visit, as he had only got his rations the previous day, had coolly brought home his flock quite early in the afternoon, and the wretched animals were yarded, to remain for some fifteen hours without food or water ; while the ruffian was comfortably stretched out in his bunk, and, a savoury smell proceeding from a pot on the fire, was evidently going in for an afternoon of quiet enjoyment.

You should have seen the boss's face as these things dawned upon him. He made one jump off his horse, throwing the reins to me, dashed into the hut, and the next minute out came, first the pot and its steaming contents, then John himself, followed by a shower of pannikins, damper, sugar, tea, and, finally, a blazing fire-stick ; after this emerged Mr. Drummond, with a very red face, and blowing like a porpoise. I fully expected he was going to follow up his attack, and was preparing to lend a hand in demolishing the child of the Flowery Land, who, having taken refuge behind a big gum tree, was loudly vociferating in the nasal high-pitched twang of our yellow brethren ; but whether he was explaining matters or breathing forth vows of vengeance, I can't say. I expect he got back, in his state of high pressure, to his mother tongue ; at any rate, the only words I could make out were, 'You savey.' But the boss never even looked towards him, but, taking the reins out of my hand, mounted and rode off, turning round after he had ridden a few steps to call out to me,—

'Just wait till the other shepherd comes in, and see if the sheep are all right. I expect that (adjective) scoundrel has lost some.'

As soon as he was out of sight the culprit ventured into the opening, and began picking up the fragments, with a smile that was childlike and bland.

By the time the other fellow had returned, and the sheep were counted, it was pretty late, so that, when I had got home and had something to eat, I didn't feel much inclined to tackle the returns. But I knew it was now or never, that the next day I should have no time, and I did not mean to lose a pleasant evening up at the house ; so I set to work, and once fairly at it, found my fatigue vanish, and was quite surprised, when I had done my task, to see how late, or rather how early it was.

When I went up in the evening I found a new arrival there, in the person of Miss Blount, who was making a regular round of visits in this part of the

country. Mr. Drummond had been speaking lately
of a visit he would have to pay shortly to a station
he was thinking of buying, and he had brought
the young lady over from Ashwood that she might
remain with his wife during his absence. I must say
I was glad to see her. She was so lively that she
seemed to set us going, as it were. Not that I had
much chance of benefiting by her presence on this
occasion, for the boss took me off almost at once to
his sanctum, and kept me grinding away till it was
so late that I began to think he did not intend to let
me return to the drawing-room. As it was, I could
only stay a very short time; and I cannot say that a
little chaff that I exchanged with the visitor quite
compensated me for the pleasure I had anticipated—
a pleasure that certainly was in no way connected
with Miss Blount.

But I was to see more of her, as well as her hostess,
than I had at all expected. The afternoon just
before Mr. Drummond left, the three rode into the
station yard as I too came in, though from an
opposite direction. So we stopped to exchange a few
words. An allusion was made to Mr. Drummond's
departure, and I said something about being glad Mrs.
Drummond would have a companion, but I wished
the house had not been so far from the other buildings.

'All the more glory for you,' answered Miss Blount,
'for having sole charge of two forlorn females.'

'I'll do my best, Miss Blount; but don't you think
we had better establish a code of signals?'

'Why? What do we want signals for?'

'How else am I to know the dangers you might be exposed to? Suppose a particularly large spider' (her especial aversion) 'put in an appearance, if you hoist a flag half-post high, then I'll rush—rush to the rescue.'

'I don't understand. Where are you to be?'

'Here, I presume,' I answered, pointing to my quarters.

Miss Blount stared at me for a moment, and then turned round short on Mr. Drummond.

'You don't mean to say,' she exclaimed, in the utmost indignation, 'that we are expected to stop up there by ourselves! Indeed, I will do nothing of the kind. I would rather sleep on a shelf in the store. Of course, I supposed Mr. Verner would be at the house while you are away.'

Mr. Drummond, rather taken aback at this unexpected attack, muttered something about his wife having often been alone there.

'More shame for you, then!' was the retort. 'But certainly I won't.'

Mr. Drummond, looking as if he felt convicted of having been neglectful of his wife's feelings, and yet hardly caring to give in, evidently did not know what to say. Mrs. Drummond, with an amused smile on her face, though she never raised her eyes, played with her reins. Miss Blount was unaffectedly in earnest in her protestations. I wished myself anywhere but where I was, while I mentally most heartily endorsed what the latter had just said.

After a short pause, and a look of inquiry at his wife which she would not see, Mr. Drummond said in a hesitating way,—

'Perhaps, Verner, Miss Blount is right. You had better go up to the house.'

So it was settled, and on the boss's departure I was installed as watch-dog. I can't say I had much cause to complain. I found my evenings pass very differently to what they usually did. Miss Blount and I were soon on our old footing of friendly war ; and though it was hardly fair of Mrs. Drummond to go over to the enemy as she did, still they were neither very remorseless foes.

Of course, now that I was to a certain extent in charge of the station, I was fully occupied all day, often having to be out on the run before my hostess and her guest had left their rooms ; but my evenings were always free, and I certainly did find them pleasant. I enjoyed being with Mrs. Drummond above all things, preferring her society to that of any one else ; but Miss Blount's presence in no way interfered with that pleasure ; nay more, I think it enhanced it. It took away all feeling of restraint, and somehow I always was to a certain extent embarrassed when alone with her, and she used sometimes then to put on a cold, indifferent manner that seemed to freeze my ideas ; but now we were all together, she had not a trace of it ; indeed, I think we all felt in some degree like children when the master is away.

We got up little concerts, with ourselves as audience. We played at whist, Mrs. Drummond and Miss Blount against dummy and me; such whist, where revokes and leading questions made startling variations in the game. We started a species of drawing-room tennis, till the ball was within an ace of bringing the lamp to grief; and one evening we had a dance. Mrs. Drummond was at the piano, when suddenly she dashed into a gallop. She did not generally play dance music well, but she was in the humour, I suppose, to-night, for nothing could be more spirited than her way of rendering the music.

'Really, it is too bad,' called out Miss Blount; 'it's positively aggravating to listen and be still.'

'Why are you still?' answered the player.

Miss Blount half rose.

'All right,' I said, jumping up, and the next minute we were pirouetting round the room; but naturally the place wasn't arranged for that sort of thing, and we found chairs and tables somewhat hard objects to come against. So we had to stop and clear the gangway, and on we went again. We stopped the second time by the piano.

'Go on!' cried Mrs. Drummond. 'I am not at all tired.'

I think my partner was quite willing, but I thought it was hardly fair to give the other all the work, we taking the pleasure for ourselves, so I daresay I lagged a little in starting, for she said,—

'We will have one more turn, Mrs. Drummond, and then I'll play.'

It was a very short turn, I confess; and then after a pause (for Miss Blount wanted the music-stool altered, and to take off her rings, and to get into position generally), with a preliminary crashing chord or two, she began her part, and settled down to a rattling gallop. But no, Mrs. Drummond wanted a waltz, and what do you suppose her guest chose?—'The Pilgrims of the Night.' But hymn tune or not, it makes a delicious waltz, and we began.

I have danced pretty often, and with a fair number of good partners, but I never had such a dance or such a partner. She had a perfect ear, and, lithe as a willow wand, she seemed to be one with the music and her fellow-dancer, turning to the slightest move of the guiding arm, swaying to the melody as if she was literally floating on the strain. My arm clasped her rounded slender waist, my breath stirred the soft hair on the pretty head that drooped towards me. I could feel the beating of her heart—I felt a wild desire to go on for ever.

Involuntarily I drew her closer to me, and held her hand with a tighter clasp. I looked down at the face that was so near, but she would not raise her eyes; I could only see the long lashes lying on a cheek tinted with the tender hues of a sea-shell, and as I gazed I utterly forgot myself, and whispered her name. Then with a sudden clash the music ceased, and quick as thought Mrs. Drummond had glided out of my arm and from the room.

'What has become of Mrs. Drummond?' exclaimed Miss Blount, as she turned round and saw only one of the performers. 'You were dancing a minute ago.'

'And we only stopped a minute ago, when you did.'

'Yes, I did that on purpose; people generally look so delightfully silly when pulled up with a round turn. Now I feel ill-used.'

'Thank you. I am sorry, of course, for your disappointment, especially after your admirable playing.'

'Thanks; but for my own part I prefer dancing.'

'I need not tell Miss Blount that I, too, prefer her as a partner.'

'No, you need not, for I should not believe you. But you, you poor boy, you are quite tired out. You are as white as a ghost. Mrs. Drummond,' she called out to her hostess, who had just returned to the room, 'it's really too bad of us; we altogether forgot that Mr. Verner has been out after cattle all day, and have nearly danced him to death.'

Mrs. Drummond made no answer. For myself I felt horribly guilty. I must have been mad to have ventured on such an impertinence, and I did not dare to face her lest I should read my fate in her eyes. I busied myself putting the music into the stand. I suppose I was making rather wild work of it, for Miss Blount, seeing what I was about, exclaimed,—

'Pray, don't put the music like that. One would

think you were "Buttercup" mixing the babies, the way you are jumbling everything up. We strive so hard to keep our belongings apart.'

'Never mind,' answered Mrs. Drummond, 'we can separate them to-morrow; let us sit on the verandah—this room is stifling.'

The tone of her voice reassured me; there was no anger in it—if anything, it was softer than usual. She was very silent the rest of the evening, leaning back in her chair, her hands lying clasped in her lap, and with a dreamy, almost sad expression in her face, that looked so white and still in the moonlight.

Miss Blount was in high spirits, and talked for all of us; and, of course, I did my best to keep up the ball, not that I felt particularly bright, and indeed answered her sallies almost at random, but I was restless and excited, and anything seemed better than dwelling on the folly I had committed. I had not dared to speak to Mrs. Drummond; but seeing that the moonlight seemed too bright for her, I got a little screen from the room and offered it to her. She took it without a word, without once raising her eyes, and after that I too grew silent. I suppose our companion found a solo rather slow, for, stifling a yawn, she got up, saying as she did so,—

'So many angels have been passing over the house in this last half-hour that there must be a regular procession of them. I vote to seek the balmy.'

The next morning I was obliged to be out early, and did not return till dinner-time; indeed, I was rather late, so that I was not a little surprised to find myself in sole possession of the house. They had gone out riding, the servant told me, but had said nothing as to where they were going, or any likelihood of being detained. As time went on I got anxious, and went out to see if I could get any information as to their movements at the station, for no one up here seemed to have any idea in what direction they had ridden; but as I was going out at the gate I heard the sound of approaching hoofs, and saw Mrs. Drummond cantering up. She was alone, and answered my look of inquiry by saying, 'Miss Blount found a letter at Grettan to say her mother is very ill. Fortunately, Mr. Creek was starting for town this afternoon, so she went off with him in little more than an hour after she got the news.'

'That was lucky. But did they let you ride back by yourself?'

'There was no one there. Even Mrs. Creek was away. Besides, Folly is as quiet as a sheep; and even I, stupid as I am in that matter, could not miss my way.'

'At any rate, you have not; that is the main thing.'

I think Miss Blount would have been flattered had she known how much we missed her. Dinner, instead of being the cheerful meal it had been, was as dull as a funeral. I seemed to have hardly an idea at command, and those I did get out were stupidity itself. Even my hands shook in the embarrassment, for my carving, never good, was to-night a miracle of clumsiness.

I had a wild duck to perform upon. Now this wretched little bird was a proof of how often our most coveted desires are only a mockery when gained.

Mrs. Drummond having expressed a wish to taste this particular kind, I had spent some hours in the early morning wading through a very muddy swamp in pursuit of it, and had counted myself a fortunate man when it fell a victim to my by no means unerring aim. Yet I ended by pouring anything but blessings on its head ; for, trying in my nervousness to carve with easy rapidity, my fork slipped, and away went the duck with a jump, as if alive, right out of the dish, sending a shower of gravy in all directions, and leaving me with the fork in the air, looking the biggest fool imaginable. As to the attendant Hebe, she first gave a little squeal as a great splash of gravy struck her full in the face, and then went off into a splutter of laughter that she had to run out of the room to hide.

One good thing, my little accident had the effect of setting us more at ease for the rest of the dinner, and the evening promised to pass with somewhat less of stiffness than it had begun. I don't know why I should have felt so stupid, for I had often to all intents and purposes spent the evening alone with her. Mr. Drummond frequently, when I was up at the house, went off to his den for most of the time.

I was sure now—indeed, I was sure since I gave her the screen—that she had forgiven me my folly,— possibly she had not noticed it ; but no, I did not care to take that view,—it was not this that bothered me. What troubled me now was, whether I ought to stop up at the house since Miss Blount had gone. It did not seem to me quite right to remain, yet how could I say anything? Moreover, I did not think she should be left with only the protection of the servants.

Naturally this state of uncertainty made me uncomfortable, and I can't help thinking she was debating the same question in her own mind, for she was unmistakeably embarrassed, and the temporary ease that had followed my carving mishap soon gave place to fresh restraint after we went into the drawing-room. She made hardly any effort to second my attempts at talking; got up several times and sat down again without doing anything save move aimlessly about the room; went to the piano, but after trying to sing or play, and failing decidedly in both, shut down the instrument with an impatient gesture; then took up some needlework, and, bending over it, seemed determined to become absorbed in her occupation.

I got a book; but if she didn't do more work than I did reading, her embroidery was not much the better for her devotion. I wonder how long we sat there, both silent and seemingly so occupied. I for my part, though my eyes wandered mechanically over the page of the book before me, hardly saw the words, certainly did not take in their meaning; while I heard every rustle of her dress, the very sound of her needle as it passed through the stuff she was embroidering.

I could not but think what a pretty picture she
would have made as she sat there, the light falling
on her bending head, with its shining tresses, on the
milk-white throat, on the soft curves of her slender
form ; a colour far more bright than the faint pink
that generally tinged her cheeks, gave her complexion
an unusual brilliancy, and made one notice more than
ever the exquisite purity and fairness of her skin.
Nothing could be more easily graceful than her pose,
drooping slightly over her work, or prettier than the
quick, deft movements of her small hands, and their
rounded, pliant wrists.

Gazing at Mrs. Drummond seemed a quite sufficient
and pleasant occupation. I only, it is true, ventured
a glance now and then, but these stolen glimpses
filled up the time in a thoroughly satisfactory manner.
The approach of a servant (Mary had a pair of uncommonly pretty feet, and the tramp of an elephant)
made Mrs. Drummond look up, and break the silence
that had lasted so long. Her remark was about
nothing in particular, but her voice struck me ; it
reminded me of the time when I rode over to ask her
to the picnic, and met her as she came out of the
French light ; it had a curious strained tone, as if she
could only steady it by a strong effort. But I am not
sure if it was not fancy on my part, for when she
spoke again, it sounded as usual.

My chapter of accidents had not yet come to an
end. As I was giving her a glass of water, my hand
in some awkward way touched hers ; either I, confused

at my blundering, let go the glass too soon, or she relaxed her hold ; at any rate the tumbler fell, both of us made a dart to save it, and only escaped as by a miracle from knocking our heads together. This set us off laughing ; and this fallen glass not only broke itself, but the ice that had formed between us.

Next morning things were as usual, and at dinner it seemed quite a matter of course that we should sit *tête-à-tête ;* that afterwards I should pour out the tea for her, as well as carry her her cup ; stand by her side as she sang, asking for and hearing all my favourite songs ; read to her as she worked. Both book and embroidery were the same as on the previous night, but I had no lack of interest now with her for a listener, to exchange sometimes a few words of appreciation or criticism, sometimes only a glance of sympathy ; while I think her embroidery was rather a sufferer.

In the course of the evening she told me she had heard from Mr. Drummond, who was to return in at most two days. A little while after this piece of news, that I can't say honestly rejoiced me exceedingly, she began to talk about a flower she had once seen on the border of a scrub, that had exactly the scent of vanilla. I remembered perfectly her speaking of it the day her husband had so curtly sent me to the bachelors' quarters at the station, and I proposed that the next afternoon we should ride in search of it.

Neither of us said as much ; but I am sure we both felt the search was not to be put off if we really

wanted to carry it out, for Mr. Drummond was not
much given to wasting his time in excursions with his
wife in search of flowers or scenery; and he took
good care not to let me be spoiled by idleness—for
which last I by no means blame him, quite the reverse.
By good fortune I had not much work the next day;
and if I had, I am pretty certain that for this once—
and I don't mean to say that it was such a very
unusual occurrence—duty would have yielded to
pleasure.

We had an early lunch, and started shortly after
two, Folly, as skittish as a colt, tossing her head,
arching her neck, curveting and prancing, pretending
to shy at every fallen bough; even Sepoy, usually the
most staid as he was the most trusty of steeds, indulged in a big jump or two, to show how much he
appreciated—imitation being the sincerest of flattery
—the graceful gambols of his equine companion.

Australian scenery does not strike at first, but its
beauty grows upon one. This, I think, is partly owing
to its depending so much on the weather, as it is on
the atmosphere its beauty mainly rests; for that on a
fine day is so exquisite, that it gives a singular charm
even to an ordinary landscape. So on this day, as
we rode along, our admiration was continually excited,
though it would have been hard by description to
justify our praise.

The air was so clear and limpid, the play of light and
shadow so lovely and varied, that a sunny glade where
groups of trees were arranged by Nature's carelessly

graceful hand, had the air of a vista in a royal park ;
a narrow gully in which banks of fern were shimmer-
ing in the sunshine ; the fringe of wattle covered with
their fragrant blossoms of paley gold along a water-
course ; a little valley winding away towards the hills,
the long blady grass with which it was overgrown
tinged with golden brown, and waving and swaying
before the slightest breeze, till you could almost
suppose some invisible hand was bending it down as
it passed softly over it; a group of gum trees, their
giant trunks white as milk and lustrous as satin, rising
straight and branchless for more than a hundred feet,
their shadowy foliage looking ghost-like against the
pale blue sky,—a score of such objects, trifling in
themselves, but made lovely by an atmosphere lumin-
ous with soft light that surrounded them, attracted
us at every turn.

Some of the views were indeed beautiful in themselves. There was one crossing place where, as we
rode down the steep bank, we were nearly shut out
from the garish light of day by some noble chestnuts
that grew in the channel, their pale green delicate
leaves only letting the sun glint down here and there,
enough to show the crystal clearness of the water, not
above our horses' fetlocks, as it ran sparkling along,
forming an ever-changing network of light and shade
over the sandy bottom. To our right the broad
lagoon spread out, perfectly still, reflecting like a
mirror the scrub that clothed its banks, and formed
perfect walls of the richest and most varied verdure.

Tinkle, tinkle went the little bell-birds, like fairy chimes ringing in the wind; then the long-drawn liquid note, ending in a sudden chirp, that has earned for its utterer the name of coach-whip, would be heard. And again, as we rode under a big spur that projected from the range as it rose up above us, clothed to its summit in unbroken forest, its crest came out against the sky as if carved, so clear was every curve, so distinct each ragged pine; but there was no sharpness or hardness, the wonderful transparence of the atmosphere was softened by the golden haze that floated over all, that filled each ravine, and lay like a veil on the wooded sides.

Involuntarily as we looked up our eyes met, and hers told me, a thousand times better than the most eloquent words, how the beauty of the sight touched her. But we were not voiceless as a rule. Mrs. Drummond, generally rather silent, was to-day as gay as a child; indeed, we were neither of us very far from girlhood and boyhood; and any one who had seen us racing over the big plain, and heard her ringing, musical laugh as she came in the winner by a few yards, might have supposed we were two youngsters out for a holiday.

One incident was hardly cheerful, though. At Cedar Crossing we went over the river again. This was a very different place to the first ford. The western bank was high, though the edge of a small flat; and as the bed of the stream was narrow, we seemed to be going into a dark trough as we rode down. The water was shallow, but black from the dense shadow of the trees after which the place was called, and with its sluggish flow gave it a sullen look. On the opposite side flood water seemed to have broken down the bank, and as we came out of this miniature ravine we found ourselves on a bare ridge, only a few stunted iron-barks being scattered over it.

There, on one side, were the remains of a hut, a couple of chained posts still standing, slabs lying about, the traces of a fireplace still visible. On the other side of the track was a small mound, not a blade of grass grew on or near it; the rains had washed away the loose earth, so that it looked more like a heap of coarse gravel than anything else. But no, there was no mistaking it, though not a post or a stone, not an attempt at enclosure, marked out this lonely grave. Mrs. Drummond gave a little cry, as our horses, jumping up from the water-worn ascent, brought us suddenly in full view of this dismal object.

'It's not a cheerful sight, is it?' I said, as we pulled up and looked down; 'nor is it connected with a pleasant story. A German shepherd lived in the old hut, and he used to make his wife work like a nigger. The poor woman was, it seems, in wretched health, but the brute thrashed her if she did not do everything he wanted; so, though she could scarcely crawl about, she managed for some time to get through her tasks. But one afternoon a boundary rider going up to the hut found the woman lying dead not far from it, an axe still in her hand.

'Horrified, he galloped up to the hut to see if any one was in. There was the shepherd coolly eating his supper. "Don't you know your wife is lying dead close by?" he called out. "Yes, I do know my woman is det, because when I came home there is no fire." "But you don't mean to leave her there?" "And why not? I don't vant a det womans in the hut mit me." Luckily Barker wasn't likely to stand that sort of thing, and as he was big enough to eat the fellow, he made him bring the poor creature into the hut, and the next day they sent out from the station and had her buried.'

'But how was it,' asked Mrs. Drummond, 'that no one interfered before? Robert could not have known.'

'Most assuredly he did not; the men, most of them at any rate, did, but the right of a man to beat his wife, if he so pleases, seems quite a recognised thing. The women talked a little, or rather a great deal at first; but as the brute was married again in less than two months, I suppose they thought that the fault lay in the woman for dying, not in the man's ill-treatment of her.'

We were not so lively after this, though we did not say much more about it; but I did not find any particular fault with the change, for Mrs. Drummond became almost confidential, telling me about her childhood and early girlhood. Her mother had died when she was very young. Her father was in India. So she had been brought up by an uncle, also a widower, a hard man, who showed no more affection to her than to his own child, a girl a little younger than she was. This child, who was extremely pretty, was

always being held up to her as a rival, against whose
superior charms she had little chance.

'I could not tell you,' she said, 'what pangs of
mortification I was made to endure about Ella's
superiority. I did think her quite lovely, but would
not have owned it for worlds, I felt so indignant at
its being so thrust upon me. I don't think I resented
the downright criticism of the old butler, "that I
could not hold a candle to his young mistress," half as
much as I did the taunts of the maids, that I should
never be married till Miss Ella had made me walk
behind her as bridesmaid. I often laugh at the plans
I used to form that I might escape such ignominy.'

'Surely,'—I began, but somehow could not find
words to express my surprise at her not being
considered pretty, quite forgetting my own first
impression. I suppose, though, I looked my thought,
for she frowned a little, and said coldly,—

'Oh, pray don't pay me compliments. I only speak
of the past, I am not at all humble-minded now ;' then
changing her tone, she continued, 'Was it not lucky
I met Robert? for I was capable of taking Blue
Beard, mysterious chamber and all ; and you can't
imagine,' giving me a saucy look, 'what a model
lover Robert was. Even old nurse, who snubbed me
on all occasions, had to own the power of my much-
despised charms. "It must be your fair hair," she used
to say, eyeing me wonderingly. I suppose she thought
my light tresses had some magical glamour in Robert's
dark eyes.'

'Is your cousin married?'

'Yes, and dead. I wish they had not made such mischief between us. Perhaps if we had been let alone we should neither of us have married so young. That sounds odd,' she added, colouring with a vivid blush, 'but I do think one hardly knows one's mind at eighteen; and possibly if Ella and I had been the friends we might have been, she would not have made the foolish match she did, throwing away all her chances, and then fretting herself into a decline because she had only got a mere mortal in exchange,— though for that matter I fancy no one is quite satisfied.'

But the flower—we were so occupied with other things that we had both quite forgotten the very object of our ride, and with true feminine ingenuity Mrs. Drummond put the whole blame of the oblivion upon me.

'Mr. Verner,' she said, 'where is my flower? You brought me out on purpose to let me show it to you, and you have never even thought of it.'

Of course I confessed my guilt, and humbly declared that if she would only give me some clue as to where it was to be found, I would do my best to get it; but that was just what she could not do. We were at the right scrub, of that she was sure, but her recollection of the situation of the plant seemed to be of the most hazy description. Half a dozen times she was certain she recognised the tree on which it grew; but when we rode nearer, the result of a closer inspection was not satisfactory, and at last she had to own that her memory had not retained any mark that might guide

her in the search. So, as it was getting late, we had
to turn back, and the question as to whether this flower
did or did not belong to a true vanilla orchid, is an
unsolved mystery to this day.

Mr. Drummond did not come home for many days
after the time he had named for his return, though he
knew Miss Blount had left, his wife having written to
tell him so. I have often wondered since how he
could have lingered. Had he become so accustomed
to my presence, as to be unconscious of the equivocal
position his wife was placed in by my being thus
alone with her ; or had he, if aware of it, such complete
trust in her as to be regardless of remarks ?

Under no circumstances, however, do I hold him
blameless. He must have known what would be said,
and for her sake, if heedless himself of the opinion of
others, he should have let nothing stand in the way of
putting an end to so unfair a position. Even to myself,
enjoying a most exquisite happiness in this close and
daily companionship with a woman always attractive,
and to me inexpressibly so, this dread was the one bitter
drop in my cup ; and I have sometimes reproached myself that I, on my part, did not put an end to it. And
yet how could I ; would not any such attempt from me
have savoured of absurd vanity and presumption ?

.   .   .   .

Almost as soon as he returned, Mr. Drummond sent
me out to his new purchase in charge of sheep ; and
when I came back, both he and Mrs. Drummond had
gone to town, where they were to remain some little

time. It was rather dreary work living up alone at
the house where I had passed such pleasant hours in
Mrs. Drummond's society, and I found how much her
presence must have sweetened my work, that now
wearied me at times almost beyond endurance. I had
a few letters from her ; and though I own she did not
excel as a correspondent, and that her short epistles
gave no idea of the writer, still I came to reckon the
day the mail man passed as the only one worth
counting, the rest being mere blanks.

It so happened that we had a very dry season, and
were getting anxious about the stock, as the feed was
fast being all scorched up. Of water we never feared
any actual scarcity ; but some of the creeks were dry,
and the river only ran as a thread where there was
usually a fair stream. The day the mail was due was
a fearfully hot one ; but a coppery hue on the horizon,
and towards evening a great bank of clouds showing
to the south-west, gave hopes of rain, and the promise
made us endure the heat almost with satisfaction.

I was at the station when the bag was brought in,
and I opened it with as much fear as expectation, for
on the two previous occasions I had been disappointed ;
but no, I was not doomed to that fate this time.
There was the welcome letter showing out from
amongst the others like a dove in the midst of
crows. Possibly to most eyes it might have appeared
like an ordinary envelope, but to me, as I have said, it
was something wholly apart. I did not read it at
once, putting off its perusal till I was alone at the

house ; and I had no time to waste if I wanted to get there dry.

A strong breeze, though only coming in gusts, was blowing ; the bank of clouds had surged up high above its former place, and was fast breaking and flying in great trailing masses right in the teeth of the wind, as if to oppose the long, low-lying, stream-like looking clouds that were advancing swiftly from the opposite direction ; a low growl of distant thunder would be heard now and then, and a venomous streak of lightning dart zig-zagging across the sky ; a grey vapour, too, under the clouds, now fast melting out of sight, told a welcome tale, and I saw with no little pleasure that the drought would soon be broken up.

The letter was as usual interesting to me because penned by her hand and dictated by her mind, though in itself not very much. But there was a postscript, and that did not lack matter, at any rate, for this was what was written in it,—

' Since I began writing, Robert has come in. He has had letters that will oblige him to go home at once. We leave on Friday so as to catch the mail steamer at Melbourne. I may not see you again, but I must—I will—write before we finally start. Good-bye.'

On Friday—this was Tuesday. If I rode day and night I might still be in time, for see her again I would if it were in the bounds of possibility. I started up, indeed, with some vague idea of setting off at once ; but if I had really entertained any such notion, the rushing sound of the rain that was now pouring down in torrents would have put it out of the question. All night long it kept on, now in one almost unbroken sheet of water, now dashed against the house by the fierce gusts of wind that shook and tore at the shutters, and flung themselves upon the walls with such force that several times I thought they would yield to the fury of the storm.

Towards morning the gale abated, and at daylight a narrow streak of greenish sky to the westward, that rapidly increased as a high west wind came up, showed that all chance of more rain was over for the present. I was up before dawn, and, rousing one of the men, sent him to bring in the horses. Very likely the noise of the storm had disturbed the people, for they all seemed sleepy as owls, and so slow in their movements that everything got behind-hand; and I was nearly maddened by the delay, knowing as I did that every moment was of consequence to me if I hoped to carry out my journey.

There was one crossing place that I especially feared, and cross it I must, or my ride would be only a waste of time,—the one near Grettan where Hall had hidden; but the creek was always rather slow in coming down, so that if I could only get to it quickly I might cross it without difficulty. At last I got off, riding a station horse, a mounted black boy leading Sepoy, to keep him fresh as long as possible. But a few miles from the crossing place my horse cast a shoe, so I had to mount Sepoy at once and send the other back. I got over the remaining ground at

a smart canter, but was too late. When I reached
the river, it was, as I feared, flooded. I can't say I
liked the look of it as it went tearing between its
banks, its turbid, foaming surface broken by the tops
of the submerged bushes, that were all bent down by
the stream, save when, now and then, a change in the
current would let them lift their heads for a moment,
to be dashed down again the next instant by the
swirling torrent.

Had I been obliged to go straight over, it would
have been quite madness to think of crossing; but
somewhat lower down the opposite bank shelved, and
fell back, moreover, into a kind of shallow bay, and if
I could manage to guide my horse sufficiently to land
there, I should be all right. If I were carried farther
down, it would be a case of *u p* with me, for not only
did the channel narrow beyond, making the water
rush along like a mill-race, but a huge flooded gum
had toppled over, and if I got caught in its head there
would not be much doubt as to the result.

But there was no time for hesitation. The flood was
rising still, and if I did not cross now, there was no
chance of reaching my destination before the steamer
left. I knew Sepoy was a capital swimmer, for he
had carried me more than once over rather bad creeks,
though never such a one as this, and I could trust
to his powers once more. The poor beast did not
seem to relish the idea himself; he went in very
unwillingly, snorting and turning round and refusing
several times, trembling all over, as he would lower

his neck, sniff at the water with neck extended, and then start back from the stream, that, rushing and tumbling along, made such a deafening din as to overpower every sound but its own.

Just as I succeeded in fairly getting him in, I caught a glimpse of two mounted figures on the opposite bank, frantically gesticulating and waving me back ; but even had I wished, it was too late now. No sooner was Sepoy afloat than he struck out at once for the other side. We were in the current almost immediately, and then return was an utter impossibility. It had not looked very inviting from the bank, but I had no idea what it was like till I encountered the full force of the stream. It seemed to seize upon my horse and myself and fling us along as if we had been two broken twigs. The rush and roar of the water, as it tore past in great swirling masses, the hurry and sweep of the swift, ever-changing current, now gliding in a smooth unbroken surface, now breaking and chafing against some obstacle, now whirling round in quick raging eddies ; the wooded bank, the trees on which seemed to be flying by me—these utterly confused me. I was stunned and half-blinded by the rapid movement and ceaseless turmoil. I did not seem to know where we were, or whither we were going. Dizzy and bewildered, I could only mechanically grasp the pommel of my saddle.

I had but so much sense left as not to interfere with my horse, who, I was conscious, was striving to make for the landing place I have spoken of. Whether he could have reached it I can't say. I doubt if he could have stemmed the force of the boiling flood; at any rate, the sight of the narrow channel, into which we seemed to be fast drifting, proved too much for my self-command. I tried to turn Sepoy's head too quickly with the rein; the next instant he rolled over, and I was under the water.

I had kicked my feet out of the stirrups before starting, so I was at once free from the horse. Instinctively I struck out, felt something touch my hand, and grasped it; it was the top of one of the flood-swept bushes. The current catching my extended body as I hung on to the branch, swung me suddenly and violently to one side. Luckily it wrenched apart my grasp, for I was flung out of the fierce strength of the rushing waters into a comparatively calm part, and a few strokes put me into safety. I scrambled somehow on to the bank, and then fell down. I expect I must have become unconscious, for I don't remember anything more till I looked up and saw Creek's face bending over me.

'Where's my horse?' I said, croaking like a raven with a sore throat, for I didn't seem to have my own voice at all.

'Not here, certainly, for he's in the head of the big tree, and as dead as a herring; the only wonder is you are not the same,' was Creek's answer.

When I got up the water seemed yet to be sweeping and eddying by me, and the roar still in my ears; but I was soon able to steady myself, and the stockman giving me up his horse, he going at my request to see if by any chance Sepoy could be saved, I rode on with Creek to the station, fortunately quite near, where I got a dry suit of clothes, and the cook set me up with a cup of half-scalding coffee. Mrs. Creek was not at home, much to my relief, for I by no means cared to face those sharp eyes of hers, or to evade the questions she would have had small scruple in putting as to why I was so eager to go on,—for go on I was determined to do.

Creek made some sort of remonstrance; but, of course, it was no business of his, and I don't suppose he ever troubled himself enough about it to find any motive for my determination. He lent me a horse, and told me I might take it on if I could not get a remount at Bishop's. He gave me one queer look as he shook hands when we parted, that I recalled afterwards with a certain annoyance, but said nothing after his first few words. I did get a fresh horse at the inn, and after a few hours' spell went on again, reaching town a little after ten on Thursday night. It was about time, for I was dead beat, and had almost to be lifted off my horse. I managed, though, to ask when the steamer was to leave.

'She doesn't go till Saturday morning,' was the welcome reply.

I could not eat, but I got a big drink of bitter beer, and turned in boots and all, for I woke up at dawn and found myself fully dressed outside the bed. A Turkish bath put me to rights; and as I had a

portmanteau in town, I was able to make myself
look fairly presentable. When I went to the hotel
where the Drummonds were staying, I was told that
they were absent, and would not return till the afternoon.   It was a bitter disappointment, but this unexpected reprieve of a day made it less hard to bear than
it would otherwise have been; and as I improved the
shining hours by falling fast asleep and remaining in
that happy state of unconsciousness for a considerable
time, it was not so grievous as I had at first thought.

When I presented myself again at the hotel Mrs.
Drummond was in, and I soon found myself in her
presence.   She gave a little cry as I entered unan-
nounced, for the waiter seemed to think that quite an
unnecessary ceremony; and though she never came
forward or said a word, I could not doubt that I was
welcome.   I don't know how I crossed the room, I
only seem to remember holding her hand in mine
and seeing my own feelings reflected in that agitated
face.   I daresay it was not many seconds that this
silent greeting lasted.   (There are occasions when our
old enemy is nowhere, and we measure by some other
standard than time.)

Then Mrs. Drummond seemed to pull herself
together, as it were, and I found myself sitting down
trying to talk on ordinary subjects, and not to be
bewildered by the sudden change in the face opposite
me.   Every trace of the expression that but a moment
ago, it seemed, had almost made me forget everything but how much I loved her, had vanished, and

neither in look nor manner was she more than friendly, scarcely that; for her eyes avoided mine, and when compelled to meet them without actual rudeness, there was something hard, almost defiant in them.

She told me what I already knew, that they did not start till the next day—and in all probability would never return to the colony, as the news received by the last mail did away with any necessity for again leaving England. I daresay she spoke about other things; but I felt dazed, and paid, I suppose, but little attention to what else she said, for I cannot recall the rest of our conversation.

While we were talking some strangers came in, and soon after Mr. Drummond and Mrs. Creek. The former gave me, for him, a cordial greeting; the latter began immediately to ask me the particulars of my adventure in the river.

'What's that?' exclaimed Mr. Drummond, looking at me in surprise; for from what he said on seeing me first, he had evidently thought I had come down on business, not knowing they were about to leave, and that I had made the journey in the usual way and time; and I had made no attempt to undeceive him, feeling, indeed, at that moment as if all and everything were a matter of utter indifference. 'What's that?'

'Hasn't he told you?' she said. 'Why, he was within an ace of being drowned. I have just got a telegram from Mr. Creek. Here it is, "River up— Verner nearly lost in crossing—Horse drowned."'

Who does not know that singular sensation when

you see everything at a glance, while at the same
time you seem hardly to have raised your eyes. That
is how it was with me then. I saw Mr. Drummond
dart one quick suspicious glance at his wife,—saw Mrs.
Creek's malicious smile as her eyes followed that look,
—saw Mrs. Drummond smiling as she went on talking
to one of the strangers. Had she heard? Surely
not; for even had she not guessed why I had thus
risked my life, she would have shown some feeling in
the matter. But she did hear; for after a little while
she turned to me and said, in a tone of complete indifference and rather flippantly, 'I think young men
imagine they have as many lives as a cat.' Her speech
did not need any answer; and if it had I could not have
given it, for something seemed to choke me.

I went away soon, and did not see her again that
day. Mr. Drummond asked me to dine with them,
but his wife reminded him that they were engaged to
dinner at Government House. But though I did not
see her, I did hear her again; for as I was mooning
about that night, restless and unhappy, the idea
struck me to make one of the staring crowd about
the gates that led to Paradise, and so perhaps catch
a glimpse of her. As I stood there hidden by the
shadow of the gatehouse, a carriage that was coming
out stopped, and a gentleman, getting out, said,—

'Thank you, but here is my trap. Good-bye! I
wish you a pleasant voyage. You must be uncommonly glad to return to the civilised world.'

'Yes, perfectly delighted, of course,' answered the

voice I knew so well. 'Life there has one advantage
—you have no time to think.'

'H'm,' said the stranger, as the cab drove on,
and evidently speaking aloud unconsciously,—'got a
crumpled rose leaf somewhere.'

I should not have had courage to go to their hotel
next morning without some excuse ; but, meeting Mr.
Drummond, he sent me there with a message about a
missing trunk that had turned up ; but I did not see
her, she was in her room, and I had to give the
message by deputy. It did not seem as if I had
gained much by my wild ride. It was almost a pity
I had not shared poor Sepoy's fate, I thought bitterly,
as I turned away from the door.

It was now ten, and at eleven they were to go ; and
long before the first bell rang I was down at the steamer.
I *must* see her again ; and though but a little while past
I had felt that the game was hardly worth the candle,
I would have swum twenty flooded rivers now, rather
than miss that last look. At the wharf I met Hope,
who had come down, he told me, with Mrs. Creek.

' Had a narrow escape, I hear,' he said. ' Must be
more careful another time, my lad. One might find a
worse fellow if one tried very hard.'

I thought the Drummonds would never come ; and
as I was roaming restlessly about, consumed with an
anxious fear that I should not have time to speak to
her, I came suddenly on Mrs. Creek, talking, and not
in a suppressed tone, to a friend. She stopped
abruptly as I came up ; and though the phrase 'over-

did it' had no meaning for me, I could not but fancy I was the subject of the conversation.

At last they came. Mrs. Drummond was deadly pale, but very animated. I don't think I ever heard her laugh so much or so unmusically. She greeted me with a smile, hardly addressing me ; but when it was time to go she suddenly turned to me as I stood silent by her side, put her hand on my arm, and said, with a break in her voice,—

'Take me on board.'

She did not remove her hand for the few minutes before the steamer started. There was a crowd round us, and she needed some protection against a chance push, for her husband was fully occupied with the luggage. She never spoke or even looked at me ; but I fancied she drew nearer, and that the hand on my arm trembled ; possibly my own heart throbbed too violently for me to tell.

Then the warning bell rang. All her friends crowded round to bid her 'good-bye.' Mr. Drummond came up.

'Now, Verner,' he said, 'you must be off. Just write a line now and then to say how Powell is getting on.'

I don't think any looker-on would have noticed our farewell. I took her hand and muttered some unintelligible words. She made no answer—never lifted her eyes. All she said was,—

'Robert, I have given Folly to Mr. Verner.'

Then she walked away.

.   .   .   .

VICTIMS OF CIRCE.

II

VICTIMS OF CIRCE.

——o——

CHAPTER I.

N landing at that lonely country station on the edge of a small straggling village, that had an embryonic look about it as if it had been prematurely born, and could never reach a full development, one looked instinctively round after some nineteenth-century signs and symptoms other than the railway line, and for the minute one's heart sank with a rush. Somehow, Arcadia in the flesh, as it were, right under one's nose, appeals but slightly to the modern mind, especially if this should happen to be a feminine one, and young—more or less. But the second glance round the corner dispelled at once all illusions of a life fitted to the needs of a simple primitive folk like the Arcadian. Fronting the station, a little to the right of it, a bold-faced public-house flaunted out its sign in one's very face; a red Presbyterian church, that had planted itself on a hillock above the public-house, gazed down eternally on its hereditary foe out of its two badly-glazed eyes through a greenish and sickly medium ; lower down the street was a mechanics' institute, one of the first growths in any Australian township ; then came the school, and beyond it the English church, looking rather proud and high-stomachy, perched up on a hill—for all it was out of plumb, liable to come down at any minute, and with a cracked bell ; but it had nevertheless a smack of arrogant aristocracy about it, that caused it to stink in the nostrils of the dissenting population.

Arcadia wasn't here, certainly, I thought, as I noted these several outcomes of Christian culture,—the public-house, the churches, and the schools,—and wondered, with tingling toes, if any one would come to meet me, or if I must try my chance of a buggy at the pub.

I went back to the platform and took a glance at my luggage. I was not altogether easy in my mind as to its safety. To the well-constituted British mind Australia is invariably connected either with sheep or convicts. If a rich Australian goes home and dispenses his coin as befits him, we give him the benefit of the doubt, and talk sheep ; if he is not quite rich enough, or sticks to his gettings, we make a wild effort to find out what his father or his more remote ancestor was sent out for. Like many customs, this is foolish, and without foundation in fact or in reason ; the man is probably as clean-bred as

ourselves, or a deal cleaner ; but one can't outrage conventions, it is the correct thing to dig into the fellow's
past unless he does his duty by our present.   As I
was counting my packages, I encountered the gaze
of a large fat man in a greasy coat, with big glazed-
leather eyes ; he looked rapacious, and had loose lips.
I always distrust that style of person.   I involuntarily
clutched a Gladstone,—I knew it contained a very
decent necklet of sapphires, and I had just paid a
heavy duty on it.   Then I turned on him the
virtuous but forbidding glance of a British matron ;
it was quite effective, he shuffled off with surprising
speed.   As it happened, he was only a parson out on
the prowl, picking up gossip,—not an uncommon type
in Australia.   God help the Church !

I looked up and down the station, yawning, it was
so dull and ugly, when suddenly I caught sight of
the back of a small woman, right up at the other end
of the platform.   It was a curious and notable back,
with a lot in it,—a sort of back that holds one's gaze,
and makes one turn it over in one's mind.   Presently
it was joined by another back, a big, broad man's
back.   The two fell to talking with vigour, and the
female back shrugged and swayed in a distinctly
seductive style.   She wore a Redfern gown—I could
swear to the hang of that skirt.   I was outrageous!
My friends had said, ' Bring any rags you have,' and
I had taken them at their word.   I was in worse than
rags—in things of two seasons ago ; they were too bad
for the voyage, but I thought they would just do for

the bush. To crown all, I wore a pair of snow-shoes over my boots,—it was cold travelling, and there were no foot-warmers to be got,—and my dress was short.

It was most galling. There was this woman, with varnished boots that absolutely blazed in the sun ; and her hat was Parisian, if ever back of hat was. ' I'll see the front of her,' I muttered, ' snow-shoes or not.'

I went hirpling up towards the pair with as haughty an air as I could get up under the circumstances. Just as I had got near enough to take in the length and breadth of the woman, she and her companion swung round simultaneously, and we stood face to face.

If I had met her on the Boulevards—stepping out of Debenham & Freebody's, or even in Fifth Avenue— I would have given her a full look, and as I passed on I would have held up my head with an air, and have given my fringe a twitch, she was as remarkable as that ; and no man living would have passed her without making a *détour* to pass her again. But here, in the bush, where ' we went in our rags ' (God forgive those girls !), she was a startling revelation, and sent of Satan to buffet the female flesh in undress— that is—

As for the man, he had a general all-right air ; he was just a clean, wholesome-looking young fellow, a gentleman every inch of him, of a type that one is liable to drop on in any corner of the globe. His look of extreme youth was perhaps his most prominent characteristic.

But the woman! she looked artless and blooming, and her dimples might have been filched from a baby; but somehow I saw, in her swift, comprehensive, amused glance at me, that the girl in that young person was dead, or perhaps had never lived.

She was fresh to look at—fresh and dainty and soft; but there was a certain sweet mellowness in her glance, —of a sort that always staggers another woman, and puts her at a disadvantage,—a certain air of ' having gone the whole round of creation' and taken it all in, moreover, that is peculiarly trying, especially when one has lived and also 'experienced' in one's own humble line: under that glance I might have been still looking out at life from over the nursery blinds.

This look, I found later, was not habitual to her; and why she let our acquaintance begin by it, I never could find out. Some sudden incontrollable freak of *diablerie* I believe it must have been. When we had taken each other in, they went to the south of the platform, I to the north. Suddenly the sound of swift-rolling wheels caught my ear, and I looked over the fence eagerly. A big lumbering waggonette was thundering up the hill behind two powerful horses. I could just catch sight of two girls' heads crow ed with brown deer-stalkers, and a middle-aged bonnet. Before I was half down the platform, my mother's old friend (whom I remembered quite well) and her two tall daughters were welcoming me, and apologising all at once. Then their eyes fell instinctively to criticising my turn-out, in an off-hand, good-humoured way, however, that had no offence in it. Meanwhile the dimpled young person was waiting a few yards off with well-bred ease for her turn ; and when I was sufficiently greeted the two girls went to her ; and somehow it hurt me to see Dimples bow and kiss those fair young things, with that touch of lovely stateliness about them. I wondered if she would kiss their mother, who I knew had always been noted for her calm, serenely-contented dignity. She did it ; she grasped her hand with a little deferential, worshipful smile and bend that must have been supremely flattering.

It told certainly. Mrs. Fleming invited her and the man straight off to tea next day.

The drive to the house was pretty in a way, with the low blue hills in the distance—and nearer, the dull green-covered hills, curving half round the horizon in monotonous, short, humpy surges. Queer hills they were under the glamour of the sunshine and the shade, which gave them colour, and varied the monotony of their broken, blunted curves ; when the deep blue haze, that only an Australian atmosphere seems able to produce in perfectness, was on them, then those hills were lovely and bewildering, full of mystery and delight. When the sun was off, and the haze in the valleys had gone grey, then the same hills were hideous, and it brought cold shivers down one's spine so much as to look at them, they were so cold and dead and unfinished. The life of these hills always seemed to come from the outside,—from the sun and the shade and the air,—never to throb in their own hearts. That day they were fine, however, and the fields, or paddocks, as they call them here, were pretty ; and so was the little chattering stream that broke babbling over big stones, and went whirling on under a bridge that had had time to grow a little lichen, more then can be said for most Australian bridges. And the house, that was charming,—low and broad and generous, set on a terrace-like hill, with great verandahs and ample flower-beds and borders, and a wide stretched-out waste of orchard and kitchen garden flanked with big petosperum hedges.

Everything looked abundant about that house, and big and ungrudging, and that's a peculiarity of any amount of Australian country houses.

CHAPTER II.

DIRECTLY I got inside my room I made for my dress - trunk, and plunged down to the depths of it and brought out a tea-gown. It was one of Worth's. When I was fairly in it, I felt for the first time, since I stepped on to that solitary station, the divinity of my femininity. I could hold up my head now, and face the world. I had in a manner lost my reputation, all owing to a pair of snow-boots and a dippy skirt, and I put myself on my mettle to win it back. We had a merry tea that brilliant spring day. I had so much to tell; and old Colonel Carew was just the man to tell anything to, with his fine, clear-cut, hale old face, and his twinkling, observant glance, and his big laugh, and bigger powers of catching a joke. I was just fresh from England, and as arrogant and patronising as any of my kind. I must have been vastly amusing to the family circle that first day before I had found my bearings. Worth did me a good turn, however,—only for him they would have despised me, as I deserved.

The next day Miss Dimples and the man arrived, and were presented to me. They were step-brother and sister, I found. He was a Mr. Pomfret; she, a Miss Ariell; and they certainly seemed wonderfully attached to one another. The boy couldn't have been a day over twenty-three; he had that slim, callow look so attractive to some women of experience. I felt much drawn to him, and I had arrived at that stage when a woman can afford to be kind to young men, with anticipatory pity for what is before them in life. It comes after living and suffering oneself,— when one feels secure of one's own ground, and can be helpful. For all practical purposes, indeed, men are no more than shadows to a woman in this phase of her life.

As for their admiration, that is quite another matter. That is a woman's right,—one of the essences essential to her well-being and development, and she has every right to receive as much as she can hold of the thing. Indeed, to go so far as to compel its giving out; it is hers by Divine right, and she is in duty bound to collect it.

So as Clive Pomfret's eyes appealed to me, and as I saw directly he was as weak as a reed, I made up my mind to be his friend; and indeed I had him deep down in a good hot discussion that had a slight flavour of ethics in it—boys like that sort of thing—before he knew what he was about, and we were already *bons camarades*, when suddenly the step-sister swooped softly down and scattered us.

'Clive,' she said, with an artless glance out of her big blue eyes,—were they blue, by the way, or grey, or green? I never found out, no more did any one else,—'they want you for tennis, dear, and I'll take care of Mrs. Vallings.'

We were on a garden-seat in the shadow of a Norfolk pine watching the players, and she sat down beside me in Mr. Pomfret's place. I looked pleased—I couldn't well look any other way—and prepared to find out her age,—a much harder matter than I imagined, it altered so. She was sometimes sixty and sometimes sixteen; she was never a girl all the same,—there was an unsound look of age and experience in that person that belied her soft girlish exterior, and baffled me.

She had an alluringly musical voice, and she spoke with much gesture.

It was a perfect day, cool and fresh and sparkling, with the sunlight embracing and glorifying all things, even the ugly gums, and yet with a touch of the frost in it that kept it clear and clean. Down in the scattered orchard the almond trees were shedding their vesture of pale pink, and the cherry plums were budding out in dazzling white, and the wattle bloom shone like yellow gold through the olive of the gums, lovely to look at, till the enraptured wretch takes out his sketch-ing-pad and colour-box, and dips about among his yellows to catch their bloomy gold. Then he finds them — well — diabolical ! — it is a slight term to describe the artist's sensations ; but I have scruples, a woman is so handicapped in this matter of adequate expression.

I felt rather bewildered that afternoon. The amazing amount of sunshine had something to do with this, I fancy—it always does stagger a newcomer. Of course one finds sunshine in other places,—in Southern France, in parts of Spain, and in Italy,— but Australian sunlight is quite original, and only flourishes in Australia. It is young and rampant and bumptious, and it is rather cruel, with the cruelty of young untried things. Then it is inexorable, and can neither pity nor revere,—and the only time it knows tenderness is when it hovers on the threshold of the horizon on its road back to the old lands. Ah, but it is magnificent in the pride of its youth !

One wonders sometimes if it will mellow and soften as time goes on, and history is made in this wonder-ful boundless land ; and hearts break, and the wind catches the tune of human sobbing, and holds it.

The land is so young to civilisation yet, so young

and debonair, that the sun and the air, the winds and the waters, forget how old and sad and terrible the world is.

Besides being bewildered, I was consumed with curiosity. This person was intelligent; I would question her. All my talk with the Carews was of the old world and old friends. I could get nothing in at all of the new. It is curious how these Australians cling to the mother-land.

'Tell me of those people,' I said. 'Who is that girl there playing with your brother, and that young man? he doesn't look as if a young country bred him; he looks as if he had just emerged from a provincial town at home, and out of a narrow circle, and came home to his tea always whether he would or not; he has a coerced air.'

'How funny you should guess!' She laughed gaily. I liked the laugh, it really did ring true. 'That young man comes from a large family who live near here, and they used to live in England near some very microscopical, yet so very select little town. They number about thirteen in all, and'—she cried, with a little dramatic gesture—'never sinned, not one of them, properly, in all their lives; they are super-excellent, so wonderful! They have been brought up between two straight rigid lines, and they have never, not any of them, gone outside of them for any purpose whatever. They read nothing more modern than Thackeray in English and Racine in French; and even in that their mother has scored out pages!

They wouldn't look at French modern paintings, and on principle the entire family only lives to protest against modern morals. They always use the best brand of words and thoughts, I even believe their dreams have an ethical basis and a theological bias, and they are such a devoted family ; they have little family ways, and little family quotations, and select high-class little jokes of a literary turn. Ah, they are charming and so *naïve!* But you see they cannot naturally judge by comparison, and they are just a little—ah, they are my dear friends ! I am a wretch, and should not say it—ah, but they are '—

' Intolerable, I should say,' I remarked frankly.

Where did this young person get her little French turns and twists and modes of speech from, I should like to know? Her shrugs were got on French soil, I felt quite convinced.

' Ah, Mrs. Vallings, I would never have said that,' she cried, the artlessness coming to the surface at a gush.

' She is afraid of herself,' I thought shrewdly. ' Highly as these people entertain her, she daren't let it all out.'

' Of course you wouldn't,' I answered placidly. ' You are of the neighbourhood ; I am a stranger, and quite free to speak my mind. But how, then, do these provincial people get on here—with those delicious Carew girls, for instance ? '

' Ah, you see, they are gentle-people, and up here the society is limited.'

'I see; they would have no show in Melbourne, just like England. Is nothing different? I came expecting to find simplicity and the free life of primitive times, and I find not a whit less convention and complexity, only in rather a more miniature, and therefore, perhaps, a more galling way than at home.'

'Yes, in some ways,' she cried, in an agitated way I couldn't account for, giving her hands a sort of wring. I looked at her on seeing this queer squeeze, and her eyes had tears in them, or at any rate some form of moisture, however it was produced.

'Upon my word,' I muttered, and waited. I felt I was about to hear something, so I waited in silence, and watched the Carews in their flannel frocks and red sailor hats, as pretty and statelily *chic* a pair as you would meet in a long day's march, and the immaculate young man, and Mr. Pomfret, who was for the moment talking rather absently to one of the Carew girls. He never looked quite at his ease, and from time to time his eyes strayed towards our seat and rested on Miss Ariell; she drew those glances, too, they didn't come altogether of themselves. I found this out by noting the queer incomprehensible way she looked at him sometimes for seconds at a stretch, then her gaze caught his, and with a start always on his side.

'Remarkable,' I thought, 'between step-brother and sister.'

At last she broke the silence with a gentle soughing

sort of sigh. I wonder how she learnt the trick—it was most effective.

'Yes, there are conventions here. Think! The country has been getting civilised now for more than a hundred years. Of course, conventions have had time to find a firm foothold, and the soil suits them, as you will soon know. Australian conventionalism, however, differs from English. It is not so consistent; it is stiffer, to look at, in some ways, and wants careful manipulation. But if one once gets the knack of that, it is quite an elastic, compressible thing, and gives to the touch like anything. One only needs courage to be charming. We all know that, all over the world. But charm judiciously applied can do anything in Australia. Ah, it is funny, this Australian rule of conduct. Ah, very,' she repeated, with a soft laugh that went well with the veiled mockery in her eyes. 'They think it is unbending, so straight, that the English article is nothing to it. But, dear Mrs. Vallings, it is really only rigid in spots, so to speak; and in the country, when it is dull, and nothing "on," before this wild, short, wonderful season of theirs gallops in, the conventions grow quite complaisant, and will put up with quite strange things,—so long, that is, as they are of foreign manufacture, and bring a new sensation; no home-grown vagary is tolerated. Now in England that never is. The duller the place and the people, the straighter and stiffer the sense of "conduct" grows. It spreads all over some people, I think, like a thin coat of enamel, warranted to crack nowhere, and to be quite impervious to exceptions. Do you not agree with me, Mrs. Vallings? You are not conventional, neither am I.

But I looked quiet and dignified, and as correct as my nature would allow. I made no reply. I had no notion of being claimed as a kindred spirit by this piece of artless impudence.

'Ah, but the people here are so good—so good!' she cried, completely altering her voice and manner, which with one dexterous twist gave one a distinct impression of suppressed tears. 'They have taken me into their circle,—and oh, so warmly, so full-heartedly! Ah, they are good!' she murmured.

I wondered what she was driving at, but I gave her her head and let her go her own gait; I was in no hurry. Her gestures and changes of voice amused me and kept up my interest, they looked so natural; and yet kept me wondering all the time how or where she collected and assimilated them. They had never grown up with her, I was quite confident.

'They are good, I am sure,' I said calmly; 'but it doesn't strike me that the fact of their taking you up is any particular proof of their goodness. Why shouldn't they?'

She threw up her little hands; they were pretty, plump little hands, but cruel.

'Mrs. Vallings, I am an actress.'

'Well?'

I had recently gone through the actress craze, and

I

had met them at every decent house. I was certainly
not crushed by the information.

'Ah, but I am not a great creature, with a world-
known name. I am only a poor little one, who hopes
and waits—waits, perhaps, for years' (the artless tap
was quite turned on now)—'and then—I ran away—
engaged as I was, too. My people were old-fashioned ;
the stage for them was the threshold of hell—and I
was so young—so young—not so much in years,
perhaps,' she cried (I think she noticed an uncon-
trollable flash of intelligence in my eyes), 'as in
experience. I was brought up with my sister in a
Parisian convent school' ('Ah,' thought I, 'that's
where you learnt your little ways!') 'under such strict
supervision ; and afterwards I lived for my dying
sister, and never went out. She died—and then—I
could not live then. I must have change and excitement—I could get neither in our narrow, refined circle.
I knew I could act. I felt it tingling in every
vein ' (she threw out her arms with a dramatic fling)
—'I had to go—I was a wicked girl. Ah, I went to
London—away from the man I loved. He was a
Captain Panton in the 7th Hussars' (she hid nothing,
this young person). 'Ah, look at his picture,' she
continued, extricating it from inside her dress.

He looked quite a decent creature, with nothing
to distinguish him from hundreds of his kind. I
wondered with an inward grin if he were a stage
lover.

Fresh suspicions always kept cropping up in my

mind as this woman spoke ; why, I couldn't tell.   She
looked and spoke (bar the theatrical turn) and seemed
straight, and yet I felt it borne in on me that she was
not.   I felt she was laughing all the time in her sleeve
at the whole batch of us, myself, of course, included.
I felt it quite distinctly, and yet it amused me to
laugh with her.

'Ah, Mrs. Vallings, he was noble and good ; and
oh, how he loved me !'

'But you did not break with him, surely—you
will marry him one day ?'

'Some day, perhaps.   I have offered him his
freedom, but he will not take it from my hands ;
he is too good, too true.   You see I must not go
home—I cannot stand the climate.   My lungs are
organically wrong—yes ; that is what the doctors say.
There is a great big hole just here,' she explained,
planting her hand on a part of her form that I always
used to consider covered the heart ; at least, I am
quite certain that was where the ambulance lecturer
put it.   However, Miss Ariell seemed quite confident
as to the site of the cavity, and no doubt she knew
best.   'No, I cannot live at home ; and Everard, poor
fellow, he must stick to his regiment—he may not
come into his property for years.   Ah, parting is
sad, sad !'   She stopped to sigh and pose a little.
'And such a parting as ours !   Who knows if ever we
shall meet again !'

'Oh, perhaps he'll come into the property sooner
than you think, and your lung will heal up, and you'll

be quite happy again,' I said cheerfully. 'Meanwhile, you seem happy with your step-brother, who is certainly most devoted to you.'

'Ah, Clive. Yes, we are devoted. My father married his mother, so we are much of an age.' (' Good gracious!' I mentally ejaculated.) 'We have been brought up together, and we are more to each other than many a full brother and sister. When my health drove me off the stage, he came to take care of me. We have bought a little house and place, and live up there among the hills. You will come and see us—lunch with us—with the girls on Monday?' she asked, in a pleading way.

'Certainly ; I should like to very much ; but isn't it lonely? Don't you both get very tired of it ?'

What possible motive could induce this young woman to live up among these hills and these dull woods with a step-brother, and no possibility, so far as one could see, of doing a stroke of mischief? As to the hole in her lung, her outward appearance quite belied the possibility of anything of the kind.

With these thoughts besetting me, I looked at her. She was in the very act of finishing a long and a most remarkable smile at the eldest of the good young people with baggy-kneed trousers. Was I dreaming or bewitched? I rubbed my eyes involuntarily, and looked again ; her expression was infantile, and the young man had his back turned to us.

'Tired of it? No; we are such friends, Clive and I. We have such a community of interests and hopes. Ah, he is a dear boy! We are never idle, and we never have ennui.'

'What well-constituted minds you must have. I should die of it,' I said dryly. 'I like my brothers very well. On the whole, I think we are a fairly united family; but to put up with one from year's end to year's end up there in those dismal hills—gur-r!—it would be the death of me. You certainly are a devoted sister and brother.'

I finished laughing and looking at her. She got pink, and the corner of her mouth gave one vicious droop, then it pulled itself together and spoke gaily,—

'Yes; I suppose we are peculiarly devoted. Many things have combined to draw us close. Some day I—I will tell you; I can't now,' she said, with a small break in her voice. 'Ah, not here—in this sunlight—before these girls, untouched by sorrow.'

I wondered if she acted as well on the stage as off. I found later she didn't—not by a long chalk. She was a most painful stick as soon as she touched the boards. Society drama was her *métier.*

Just then Clive came up. I saw him throw one quick uneasy glance on her, then he stretched himself down on the grass and began to talk.

He was a nice fellow, and full of a soft, gentle sort of fun; and without any doubt his eyes were entrancing, and they seemed strangely occupied with his step-sister. I felt sorry to see it. I wondered what his prospects were, and if he were worthy of one of those tall, fresh Carews, with their frank, off-hand ways, and their curious mixture of shrewdness and innocence. They had, both of those girls, ten times the *nous* and grasp of that gentle mother of theirs ; they could get to the bottom of a thing in the most direct and rapid way, while she never yet fathomed the ghost of a mystery without her husband's direct interference. Then those two were strong—strong and true. One of them might help this fellow— wanting in grit—to his manhood.

I was thinking vaguely on this subject—formulating a match in my idle brain—in the way of women who have done with that sort of thing for themselves. When I looked down on the boy, I caught his eyes turned on his step-sister with the pleading of love in them ; it was love, honest man's love, sure enough, if ever I saw the thing, and I may remark I know all about it quite well.

My match was nipped in the bud. I felt dazed. I went over to talk to the young man at whom she had smiled that long queer smile. He was standing watching her with a savage eye.

He was a good fellow when one dived down in him, but the surface was aggressively self-righteous and seemingly moral. He was the sort of young man of whom one felt instinctively that a downright good slip would be the salvation. As I watched his savage glances that day and her soft ones, and divers other

signs and symptoms, I felt quite a vicious sort of
satisfaction, and almost felt as if she would do a good
work in taking the young man in hand. She certainly seemed capable of being a liberal education to
him or to any other man.

CHAPTER III.

THE next week we spent playing tennis at each
other's houses, and drinking tea, and having little
women's picnics—all the men but Clive being about
their various businesses.

We amused ourselves quite well, however. Miss
Ariell was a constant contradiction.

By this time I knew all that was to be known of
her life, down to the minutest particular. I had
heard the tragedy from the first scene to the last.
It was a small domestic one, founded on a wicked
captain, and built up of a wonderful assortment of
shattered hopes and blighted hearts and rapid con-
sumption, — the pretty variety with pink spots and
preternatural brilliancy of eye, which the young
woman and Clive stood by with heroic tenderness
until the end.

It was quite a pleasure to think of the round, soft
creature, with those dimples, and a becoming shade
of sadness in those baby eyes, floating round in a

white apron,—she made quite a telling point of this in her narration,—and with a porcelain basin of broth in her hand to nourish the dying sister, who by the way appeared to have had a huge capacity for the liquid,—one was forced to wonder if so much can have been very good for her;—but then, as we all know, consumptive patients do have morbid appetites.

We learnt to know Captain Panton quite intimately in those days. The mention of this gentleman, however, seemed rather to upset Clive.

Two or three times, about this time, I noticed the two Carews coming back with flushed cheeks from conversation with Miss Ariell, and somehow it struck me as strange; why, I couldn't have said, for they were given to getting red—those two.

Miss Ariell certainly made good times for herself, and got a deal more than her fair share of attention, especially from the old colonel; indeed, she converted that fine old man into a species of domestic slave, and I saw it with an inward snort. She would send him on odd errands in an artless, deprecating way —for her slippers, or her handkerchief, or any of the dainty trifles she never moved without; and she always made him put on her spurs, or alter them whether they needed alteration or not, when she rode.

One day I went into the dining-room softly and suddenly, meaning no espionage, but my shoes were light, and I always do move noiselessly,—thanks to my heredity, I couldn't clatter if I tried,—and I found Miss

Ariell with her little arched foot poised on a stool, and Colonel Carew lacing her varnished boot.

Now this may have been infantine on the young person's part, but on the old man's it was undignified. The woman in me rose in protest against the situation.

I sat down placidly by the table and looked out of the window.

Nothing is so effective as quiet, silent, unobtrusive virtue, with plenty of staying power in it. I had not sat for more than three minutes, gazing out absently at the fading cherry blooms, before the guilty wicked red of the aged sinner had risen to the colonel's brow, and the twinkles had died in his kindly eyes. He doggedly finished up the lacing to the top, not skipping a hole, and winding the lace twice round the little ankle, and he chatted gaily all the time; and if he hadn't, I should have despised him to my dying day.

But when his task was done he slipped out like a shot, and went over to the garden to his wife, who was superintending the potting out of some rare plants, and he pottered about after her all the rest of that day.

As for Miss Ariell, she nodded her pretty laughing head at me with the merriest air of insouciance, and hated me a good deal more than before.

That very evening, after I went to my room, I heard a rustling in the passage, then a whispering, followed by a quick, soft knock on my door. I opened it, and found the two girls waiting in pretty soft white silk wrappers, and with their fair hair loose on their shoulders, the wonderful gold tips of it gleaming and sparkling in the soft light as if jewels had got entangled in the gold.

The girls snuggled down into two low basket-chairs, with big leaf-green cushions, the loveliest background to those golden veils of theirs, and seemed inclined to sleep.

The night was chilly, and a small bright fire burned on my big hearth, and we all drew ourselves close to it.

I put away my book, and watched the girls and the fire alternately.

There was something very attractive in their quaint wise old ways in conjunction with those fair young faces, and their sudden flashes of dignity, and the queenly airs they could assume on occasions, contrasting with their innocent girlish vanity and perennial pleasure in dress. Then the amazing untidiness of their ways and their reckless boyish habit of slang. Every turn and twist of them, however, was natural and unpremeditated.

I wondered when the silence would be broken by something definite.

We just mentioned the beauty of the night in a vague way, and with a passing remark on the croaking of the frogs and the chirping of the crickets; but as these sounds were always with them as soon as night fell, they were scarcely of sufficient import to bring those girls into my room at that time of night.

'Mrs. Vallings,' said Nancy at last, in her soft banana-fed voice, with the *soupçon* of twang, 'what do you think of Miss Ariell?'

'Yes, that's just what we want to know!' put in Mab, sitting up among her cushions, and twirling the golden tip of a great length of hair.

'I think she's a very charming person, and one I never dreamed of meeting in this part of the world.'

'I wish she had kept out of it—at least out of our corner of it,' said Nancy.

'So do I,' echoed the other.

I took a rapid glance at them.

'Why?'

'Why?—why?—I don't know exactly. Because she's not like other girls, that's why, partly. It isn't that she's more original,' said Nancy, in a quick way. 'She's not; but she's different.'

I looked at the girls. Nancy was sitting bent forward, watching the flames. Mab had straightened herself, and her sunny head, turned to red-gold in the fire-shine, was thrown back, and on both their faces there was a look of haughty, hurt maidenhood.

'It's the stories,' they both broke out together,— 'they somehow make us feel uncomfortable.'

I am not in the very least a mawkish woman, but I went over then and there and kissed those girls, one after the other, on their white, pure foreheads.

'The wretch!' I said, in a voice of smothered rage.

'Did you tell your mother, Nancy?'

'I told her one the other day, and she said she could see no harm in it. She said she would ask father; and that she considered Miss Ariell a sincerely religious girl, and incapable of any evil thought. She feared Ouida had been corrupting my mind. I read *Two Little Wooden Shoes* while I was staying at Aunt Grace's, and mother was vexed. I didn't know, or I shouldn't.'

'Miss Ariell has got our mother and father too,' said Mab. 'Haven't you noticed her little worshipful ways, and how she gazes up in my mother's face as if she was a Madonna or something, and runs to get her things. And she hides things in her eyes from mother that she shows us, I can tell you,' said the girl, nodding wisely; 'and then she discourses by the hour of us—the most idiotic things you ever imagined, she says. Oh, I heard her one day. Any one would have sworn we were a brace of angels. Mother swallowed every word of it, though, and Miss Ariell cried the whole time—she can cry like anything when she likes.'

'And religion,' cried Nancy,—'she's wonderful on that; and mother is so true and straight herself, she believes every mortal thing. We don't, I can tell you. Oh, we know too much. As for my father, he's bewitched; and the worst is, we don't quite know how she manages him. She does, though, like anything. He fetches and carries for her as if he was a boy; and yet one can't see how she gets him to do it. Catch him flying round like that for us! I believe it's a little in the way she drops her eyes and softens her voice whenever he's in her neighbourhood. He told mother that she's a charming creature, and a " most desirable person for us to form our manners on." '

' Ugh ! ' threw in Mab.

' The other day, when we abused her a little, mother said quite severely, " Your father, my dears, knows the world, and he approves her." Now—he may. But do you know, Mrs. Vallings, that Mab and I think the world father knows was dead and buried long ago, and that quite a new world has grown up since, and that he'd flounder about rather if he happened to plunge into it now. I don't think father is the man to fathom Miss Ariell,' she concluded solemnly.

' There's another thing I don't like about her,' began Mab breathlessly, before I had time to put in a word, ' she can talk religion to mother like a book, but she can be terribly blasphemous to us directly mother's out of sight. Now, I don't like religion thrust down one's throat, and I'm not fond of too much church, neither is Nancy—it doesn't seem to agree with us in quantities ; but I do think a little light religion helps a girl,' she explained quaintly, crossing her bare feet. ' It makes good seem better and evil uglier, and helps her to keep her feet down on the earth, and walk along it squarely and fairly the path she has to go, instead of kicking over the traces and landing you in a hole,' she concluded, with conviction.

'No, we don't like blasphemy,' chimed in Nancy. 'It's bad form in a man, and—well—its downright disgusting in a woman.'

'I don't think,' I said, after a pause, 'that Miss Ariell will tell you any more of these stories, or again blaspheme in your presence. I'll go and have a talk with her '—I spoke cheerily and lightly ; feeling the evil would slip off from these clean souls, and leave no trace, it seemed better to make no comment.

Both the girls suddenly blushed from their chins to where the soft gold line touched the white of their brows.

'We thought that too,—we tried to stop her,—but she is so persistent. We talk slang, you know—frightfully,' stammered Nancy, 'and — and we do queer things at times, and—and she said she was certain we weren't half as simple as we posed for, and that we knew—oh, lots of things.'

'Yes, that's what she said,' murmured Mab.

A sudden conviction came to me. 'I believe she thought it too, the fool!' I muttered half-aloud. It is possible to misinterpret some Australian girls—it has been done by wiser than Miss Ariell, and will be again, till the land and the people in it mellow; but these girls—a heart must be very foul or very false before it would do them this wrong.

'Look,' I said, 'both of you, don't worry about Miss Ariell. She is probably neither worse nor better than many other women. She is only very silly, and lets herself think foolishness and speak it. She hears things, and knows things, and instead of sifting out the evil and sticking to the good, which is sure to be there too, mind you—riddling the contents of her mind, as it were, from time to time. (See what wonderfully good fires we get from riddled ashes. An allusion an Australian girl can understand with good housewifery in her blood. That's where you have the pull over English girls, my dears.) Now, Miss Ariell stores up all this rubbish, and her fires get clogged with the dust and the dirt of it till they can no longer send up a pure, clear flame to heaven, and the smoke of them smirches herself and others ; but it makes her own throat smart worst of all, for she can't get away from it. Children, you don't know how easily that happens to women, or the infinite pity of it.'

Nancy caught my hand and held it against her smooth, shell-pink cheek. 'I believe you know a million times more things than she does, Mrs. Vallings. Your eyes look so deep and so full of things, often, and your mouth—it looks strong, as if you had learnt a great deal, and—as if it hurt you—hurt you—frightfully.'

'Yes, you do look like that sometimes, Nancy and I think,' said Mab, in a soft, breathless sort of fright.

'My little girls, whenever it is the lot of a woman

to "know things," as you say, it—well—it hurts—it
does hurt frightfully.'

Nancy's eyes filled with tears ; but I didn't con-
cern myself with them, I was thinking of myself. I
seemed to stand at the bar there, before these two
fresh young creatures, to whom the taste of the tree of
life was still a sweet mystery. I felt ashamed before
these girls. I—I forsooth—proud of my experience
for all it hurt—proud of it—oh, the petty pride—and
of the cut of my gowns. I, who knew, and had
seen. I—careless in my speech, too—picking up
as I went little silly flippant phrases and terms of
expression—nothing of harm in them, but light—
unfitting.

If you want to punish a woman of the world,—not
an evil or a befouled one, but just a woman bent on
the vanities and trifles and follies of a worldly life,—
put her, just for a little half-hour in the evening,
when the heart is soft and the trappings stripped
from her soul, under the straight gaze of two sweet,
pure, proud young maidens, and you may be quite
sure your punishment will follow.

Whether they understand the woman or whether
they don't, that doesn't matter a rap : she understands
herself for the minute, that's quite sufficient.

'You must go to bed, children,' I said. I fancy I
spoke a little faintly, from the girls' faces.

'Sit down,' said Nancy, 'you're so white.'

'We've tired you,' cried Mab ; 'and, do you know, I
can't feel a bit sorry. I came in—Nancy did too—

feeling — ugh ! — dirty. Now I feel quite white-minded again.'

' Your knowing things is such a comfortable sort of help,' added Nancy. 'Good-night—O dear, I am sleepy! Mab, come on!'

Little fools! I wonder if they will ever know the intensity of 'comfortable help' their last words brought me ; how they helped me to gather up the shreds of my self-respect and to huddle my nakedness up in them. They may some day, and be grateful they spoke them, when they are as old as I am, and ' know ' and have ' been hurt '—frightfully.

CHAPTER IV.

THE next morning I made a solitary pilgrimage to Miss Ariell's eyrie, and was struck by the way by many curious little arrangements in her *ménage*, which the conclusion of this story will sufficiently elucidate.

We had an understanding. I used the gentlest and keenest and most deadly of women's weapons, and I gained my point. In future the Carew girls need fear neither stories not blasphemy.

We parted friends, however, and Clive walked to the foot of the hill with me. What a well-bred, weak fellow he was. I would have given anything if I could

have carried him right away with me and saved him,
—from what I did not quite understand myself, and
yet from something that invariably brought creeps
to my spine whenever I thought of it. I know she
told him just how far to go, and that he daren't go a
foot farther for the life of him. When he arrived at
his limit, he pulled up and muttered something like
' cow '—what that animal could possibly want at this
hour of day I couldn't conceive ; however, I accepted
the excuse, and dismissed my poor escort with a
warm grasp of his long nerveless hand,—a feminine
hand, that no manual work could brown or make
sinewy.

That afternoon we called on the Flemings. There
was a queer little commotion as we deposited our
umbrellas and a fern basket in the passage. When
we got into the drawing-room, Mrs. Fleming had
draped an old white cashmere about her, and was
posing in the prim old lady-like way of a past age,
and the girls were grouped round her, with a book or
work on each lap ; and every one looked big with
colossal thought. One felt directly one was addressing no common flesh and blood article, but the very
best book persons ; and after a minute or two in that
suggestive room, one began oneself to experience a
sensation of cramp and half-suffocation, as if one
were getting gradually pressed together and shut in
between two cloth covers.

I no longer marvelled at the young men, but I
quailed as I thought of the first outbreak of nature

in the poor docked beings, and of its crushing, upheaving results to themselves and to their saintly relations. 'God help the whole lot together!' I mentally ejaculated, making one gasping effort to shed my book state and get back my comfortable carnal mind. It was in vain. I collapsed again directly, and just listened machine-like to Mrs. Fleming, who poured out upon me in a gentle stream a huge amount of information concerning books, the domestic animals, and her two sons. The eldest of them, Vandeleur,— 'always a family name ;' in point of family, as in all other points, the Flemings excelled,—seems to have been strictly virtuous, even in his long-clothes days ; as far as one could judge, he had never done any one wrong thing. And, upon my word, he must have been a good fellow in spite of it all, for he supported, he and his equally excellent brother between them, the mother and that tribe of young women, and pandered extensively to each of their several tastes,—and eleven individual tastes in one family comes expensive, as any family-man will tell you.

Directly we got out of sight of the house, we all set with a simultaneous sort of relieved chuckle to running, to get our limbs free again. Then we sat down on a stump, and aired our random thoughts with keen relish ; it was so delicious to throw off the mental and physical bandages, and to expand again and feel human. But on these two wretched male creatures with all their natural young instincts guarded and held in check and accounted as nought by a kind of foolish ignorant women who knew not what they did, poor souls, it was horrible to think of! Between our gay bursts of laughter I could have gone the length of crying for those boys.

I didn't get over that visit till I had thrown myself in careless abandonment on the big white bed in my room, and had drunk deep draughts of the fragrant Indian tea the girls brought me.

The next day I had to go down to town, to stay for a few days with some friends I had made on the voyage.

One evening we went to the theatre—to the beautiful Princess'. The piece was a melodrama, with too much colour and light and cheap sentiment. It didn't interest me, or perhaps I wasn't in the humour to be interested—I was bored. It was my doom to be placed between two as vapid young men as ever God put breath into. I tried to amuse myself with the people, and spent some interested time looking round, taking in the men and the girls and the dresses.

Taking them all round, the girls of Australia make a far finer show to the eye of a stranger than the men ; even in the matter of head shape they can give them points and win. This may, of course, be a merciful dispensation, the future of a nation resting so largely in its women ; but one feels sorry to see it all the same, and one wonders where all the grit, and the courage, and the adventure, and marvellous strength and patience and self-sacrifice of the magnificent old pioneers of this nation have vanished to. They don't reappear in the sons, seemingly. Could these qualities have worn themselves threadbare, from the very force and strength and vigour of them, in one generation—fail, as it were, through their own greatness? It is to be hoped not. Perhaps these young limp men, bumptious enough, too, with the twang rather spoiling the virility of their voices, hold more of the quality of their ancestors than their appearance would suggest ; perhaps, after all, they can throw forward quite their fair share of strength and grit and straightness into the ages. They'll have enough to do, poor souls, with the climate, and the evils bred of it all against them, and their pockets full of money.

We had good seats, right in front of the dress circle, and could get a fair view of the whole house. In the box to my right I had noticed for some time a lovely sea-green frock, and the tip of a white shoulder that shrugged from time to time ; and now and again I caught sight of the side of a man's brown head stooping towards the shoulder. When the curtain fell at the end of the first act, the light fell full on to the box, and suddenly the head belonging to the shoulder bent forward, and I saw Miss Ariell. I could not help it, I craned my neck round, like any schoolgirl, to find out by what name the dark head called itself,—it was shades too brown for Clive,—but it had retreated into the gloom. I couldn't get a glimpse of it.

'Do you care to come out ; it's melting hot? demanded one of my young men affably. The other.

hoarsely muttering 'cigars,' had fled the instant the curtain began to fall, and was no doubt at that very moment absorbing some liquid or another. It is amazing how much of that sort of thing they can do in this fiery climate, and yet retain whatever reason and liver Heaven has been pleased to bestow on them.

'No—yes,' I said, rather at random. It ended in my going, and boring my young friend a good deal. I could only manage to give him and his platitudes— which, to do him justice, he produced with marvellous ease and much good nature—just an atom of ear, the remainder, with all my eyes, had their work cut out for them in listening and looking for Miss Ariell and the brown head. I found them at last away in a corner, whispering. I could see the young woman distinctly, but nothing of the man but a dress coat and the flash of white linen.

'Do let us walk up and down,' I said, ' I am so tired of sitting.' The poor young man reached out his arm obediently, and we took a turn towards the brown head and the little black one which were close together in the shade of the wall. Ah, but I saw the profile plainly—unmistakeably! I took care to let no chance likeness mislead me. It was—it was Vandeleur Fleming. 'Good gracious!' I ejaculated, in a choked sort of way, I fancy, for my escort stopped and looked concernedly at me.

'Can I get you an ice or anything,—'tis a hot night for the time of year,—I'm sure you're thirsty?'

'No, I'm not,' I said, laughing ; 'but I have no doubt

you are. Leave me with Mr. Chaloner, and go, get
an ice or—something.'

I saw these two twice after that,—once at the
theatre again, and once having coffee at Gunsler's.
What a changed creature Vandeleur looked,—his own
mother wouldn't have known him in his well-cut
clothes and his general man-of-the-world air,—he was
no better to look at than any ordinary decent everyday sinner. Seemingly the liberal education had set
in. Now, what in the world was I to do?

It was certainly not my province to drop down on
the boy, and bring him *nolens volens* home to his
mother. As to attacking Miss Ariell on the subject,
she would have laughed in my face.

And yet—and yet, though in my heart of hearts I
felt there was a necessity for this experience, that
from the queer conditions of his life it must come,
yet my heart bled for the boy. Bubbling over with
foolish, frank, fond delight, he looked like a baby out
on the spree,—and so inordinately vain of it too, and
of himself. I would have helped him, but I had to
decide to let things go ; he must 'fare like his peers,'
and find the level of his strength. His false armour of
sunny self-satisfied righteousness would soon enough
prove its impotence and display its flaws, and
presently the scales would fall from his eyes and he
would see clear. As for his retribution, that was
assured when his mother would get to know—she
would be sure to, sooner or later, in this little place
where nothing is hid Then any known plan of tor-

ment ever offered to the public must be a fool to
the torments this boy would endure. Heaven knows
he would be thankful enough at the end of it all to
'range' himself and to return to the present paths of
righteousness!

Ah, it was inevitable; but I felt sorry all the same,
and perplexed.

I went back on Saturday, and was tired, and hardly
fresh enough even to look at the evening paper.

There was no one in my compartment but a horrid
old man in one corner, who snored and snuffled and
thrust out a hideous puce under-lip in a rhythmic
regular sort of way that struck one as predictive of
fits. I felt ready to choke him. People with such
habits should reserve their compartments.

The man attracted me all the same, and my eyes
would turn and turn again to that awful lip. I nearly
prayed for some one to come in and break the spell.

When we got to a small station about five miles
from Melbourne, to my delight and astonishment and
surprise, who should throw open my carriage door
and jump in but Vandeleur Fleming!

He still wore the worldly air; but he blushed
furiously as he took my hand, and he seemed to find
a difficulty in regaining his normal colour.

Then he plunged boldly into politics. I never could
quite get to the bottom of Victorian politics. I hardly
know, indeed, if they have a bottom. But that day I
listened to them quite placidly. They relieved my
young friend, and kept my eyes and thoughts off the lip.

As we were within two stations of our destination, Vandeleur pulled up suddenly, dropped politics as if they had stung him, and looked at me with two shy pleading eyes.

'Mrs. Vallings,' he whispered, with a side-glance at the lip, 'might I ask you not to mention—ahem—to my mother or—my sister and the—Carews that you saw us—Miss Ariell and myself—at the theatre? My people, you see,' he explained, with blazing cheeks, 'are so very—so—out of the world, as it were, so inexperienced, you see. They might misunderstand—you know—naturally—you see—but they might—might—in fact—blame—that charming girl. She, of course, though just as good and as innocent '—

'Good gracious!' I thought, 'the boy is even a bigger goose than I thought. What on earth is one to do? This alters matters.'

'But she has been differently brought up, and her stage life, you know, has—has—so to speak—enfranchised her.'

That word seemed to relieve him,—it was more like the family,—and he may have been feeling a little lost and aloof from it.

'You will comprehend me, I feel assured, Mrs. Vallings,' he went on, with a much bolder front and no stuttering. 'You know—ahem—that we MEN OF THE WORLD' (I gasped softly) 'do things every day—that—women—ahem—women such as my dear mother and sisters might misconstrue. Not—not that for a minute,' he resumed hurriedly, the hot blood rushing up again and flooding his face, 'I mean to imply that I would not as much as suffer one hair of Miss Ariell's head—Mrs. Vallings,' he cried, his voice thick with confused feeling,—' she's as safe in my hands—as—as she would be in yours,' he burst out. Then he muttered something. I think it was, 'God be my witness.' I wish the solemnity of the thing hadn't got so mixed up with the intense funniness of it, the incongruity gave one a hysterical sort of feel.

'My dear boy,' I cried, quite on the spur of the moment,—Vandeleur Fleming was the last young man in the world one would treat boyishly, for all his foolishness,—' it is certainly no business of mine to acquaint your family or the Carews with any affair of yours'—I paused and thought a minute, he was so young, so self-assured, so superior, so supremely idiotic; he certainly was years past his puppy days and his milk teeth, but Miss Ariell was the last person in the world to train him to the new diet. She would give him a moral dyspepsia that would last him his lifetime. All the mother in me came to the rescue. I would make one effort; but it was an ill thing to meddle in, and I always feel I did it badly. I began lamely.

'I am years older than you, Mr. Fleming. I have been about in the world, girl and woman, this many a year. We women pick up a good deal as we go, and we have what you great, strong, knowledgeable creatures have not' (that fetched him), ' we have intuition or instinct, and somehow I don't think Miss Ariell would ever quite suit you. To begin with, she's older'—

'Only ten months,' he broke in. 'I'm twenty-three, and she's a little over twenty-four.'

(She was thirty-five, if she was a day.)

'Indeed, that may be in years, but you see a woman's life makes such a difference,—experiences with us go for more than years,—and Miss Ariell has lived her life, I should think, more than most girls ; and, as you yourself said, her life has been so different from yours.'

'I said from that of my mother and of my sisters,' he remarked, with extreme dignity, and with an expressive pull-up to his shirt collar. 'The lives of young men, Mrs. Vallings, are, I take it—ahem— pretty much the same all the world over. Melbourne, I assure you, is behind no city of its size in the old world.'

'Oh, indeed, I never meant to imply it was,' I said humbly. 'I only feared that perhaps a girl like Miss Ariell, so used to the admiration of men, so used to constant excitement, might hardly be the wife to make you happy. Pray excuse me, I know this interference is an impertinence.'

'No,' he muttered ; 'most kind, I am sure.'

'It *is* kindly meant, but it is an impertinence all the same, and you think it is. But if an intuition once gets a good hold on a woman, and if it tells her any one younger than herself is in danger, there's no knowing the length she will go in obedience to this obstinate instinct to save him—or try to.'

'Danger? What do you mean,' he demanded sternly, quite ignoring the man with the lip, who was quite wide-awake, and taking us in at his leisure.

'I am perfectly convinced of the purity and honesty of your intentions,' I continued boldly enough, but I quaked inwardly, the boy was so wofully in earnest, 'but I am not by any means so assured of Miss Ariell. I fear she may lead you to do things you will regret later.'

'Ah, Mrs. Vallings,' he said sorrowfully, 'how is it the very best and noblest of your sex can so mis-understand their peers—their peers?' he repeated emphatically. 'Miss Ariell is as good a girl as ever drew breath. God bless her!'

I felt choky. I could have kissed the boy that minute; and then he turned ridiculous all at once.

'And even if there were danger, as you say, even if your hints had a germ of truth in them, and there were danger for me,' he raised his voice and stiffened himself, 'Mrs. Vallings, put my knowledge of the world aside, and even my common sense, do you think I have no religion?'

He raised himself proudly on his seat, crossed his hands on his knees, and glared at me.

We were just steaming into our station, where our assembled families and friends were standing in close converse, waiting to receive us. As I was collecting my packages, Miss Ariell came up to look for hers. She looked as artless as ever, and gave a start of surprise at sight of me.

'Ah,' she cried, 'dear Mrs. Vallings, how did I miss seeing you? I was in that horrid ladies' carriage, and nearly stifled. A great fat wheezy baby had bronchitis, and we couldn't open an inch of window. If I had only known—Mr. Vandeleur, were you there too?—Oh!'

Mr. Vandeleur got scarlet, and turned a suspicious glance on me; but I couldn't wait to see it out, as the girls were calling, and the horses becoming restive.

CHAPTER V.

WE did nothing worth speaking of for the next few weeks. It was the dull time, before the season when we were all to run down to town, and we just lounged along life in easy, restful bliss. The only thing that interested us very especially, was the growingly warm friendship between the Flemings and Miss Ariell, and the wretchedly dismal appearance of Vandeleur — which became visible to the naked eye about ten days after my return from town, and increased daily. I pondered on these things, and held my peace. There was one other thing that astonished us, it was the strange and morbid desire for solitude the step-brother suddenly evinced, and the bitter gruffness of his manner, whenever he came across any of his kind :

I would have given a lot to help either of the two unhappy boys. I liked them both in their different ways honestly and heartily, and I think they liked me. Vandeleur's glare soon changed to a look of rather pathetic trustful appeal that troubled my heart sorely, and made me curse my impotence to help him. Things had gone too far now, no human interference would alter matters one jot; he himself must pull *himself* up, or else—(there is an awful deal of truth in it) —' Better sin the whole sin, sure that God observes.'

Poor Vanny! I think even then he was losing his fresh first lovely young faith in the woman, and for her sake in all women.

It was a *stupid* everyday little tragedy, with excruciatingly funny points in it. And yet it brought a lump into my throat every time I brooded over it, which it seems to me I did a good deal in those days. The step-brother's condition troubled me nearly as much, and had the additional discomposing quality of mystery. Why he should lose flesh and forget his manners was a constant worrying puzzle to me, and gave me many wakeful nights. Indeed, I always will think that that horrid attack of neuralgia I had just then, was due solely to my restless, driving anxiety to get to the bottom of this boy's state of mind, which was enough to haunt any woman with a heart in her,—that and those horrid dusky shadows under his melting innocent blue eyes, and those queer, sudden, inexplicable sweeps of pain over that debonair young face.

There was nothing the least ridiculous in this boy's pain; no speck or tincture of sin in it either, as any fool could see,—which made matters worse. I would have given my right hand—although I have a remarkably good touch on several instruments; but, upon my word, I would have given it, and willingly—to have saved the youth in that boy's face; and yet one couldn't move fate for him by so much as a finger's breadth.

Once I had brought myself to the point of deciding to beard Miss Ariell in her own den, and to possess myself of the situation by violence. I went so far as to put on my best hat and my smartest jacket, and to sally forth in her direction; but when I got to the bottom of the hill qualms came upon me, and I sat down to reflect. Perhaps it was cowardly, perhaps it was wise, who knows? but I turned back and took off my things again—and came down to tea. I felt it borne in upon me with crushing conviction, that I should gain nothing by the step, and that she would score off me finely. And so the river flowed on towards the great sea, and I did not so much as try to stem its current by one thrown pebble.

The girls and I and Mrs. Carew were sitting one day on the verandah,—I think we were a little tired of one another that afternoon. The girls had a giggling fit on, about a visitor in the neighbourhood, a young fellow who struck me as being rather on the road to hydrocephalic idiocy, from the shape of his head and other symptoms. Perhaps, however, I was a little prejudiced, as I had heard him a few evenings before confiding in a young freckled person, with large salt-cellars in her neck, 'That Mrs. Vallings wasn't half a bad sort, hang it, but mossy, distinctly mossy.' Now, no woman of any pretensions to attractiveness likes to hear such things said of her, especially if she feels quite young still, and often looks it, moreover. But from a girl's point of view, no doubt, he had some attractions. He was great at tennis—had a fine moustache—a beautiful clean pair of legs—and quite £15,000 a year in the best station property.

Mrs. Carew was not interesting either; she was talking of her youth in general, and the size of her waist in particular—it was less than eighteen inches with no squeezing. I wonder how it is that all exhumed waists are of that slender make—and all due to nature.

The girls were still giggling; Mrs. Carew had left waists, and was on the religion of her youth, which appears to have been of a still better brand than the waists; and I—upon my word, I believe I was yawning, and dying for tea,—when a door out of the drawing-room was flung open in rather an agitated way, and the colonel appeared among us, puffing and very red in the face. He 'hanged' and 'damned' a chair or two, and at last settled down in a big basket one, with a cushion a shade paler red than his face, and began to fan himself with a big palm fan. I watched him, wondering what on earth made him so piping hot, the day was as cool and fresh as a daisy. He stirred about and creaked his chair in a queer uneasy way, and rubbed his brow in a perturbed style, that made me suspect his heat was more of the spirit than of the flesh. Then he once more 'damned' softly, and 'ahemed,' and looked at the girls in an unpleasant way.

'Isn't it tea-time, Henny?' he demanded at last, with a sternness quite out of proportion to the occasion. That Indian cook is a nuisance, and never boils the water. Can't you girls go and see about it? Let's have a decent cup of tea for once.'

I laughed softly at the foolishness of men.

'Run away, children,' said Mrs. Carew placidly.

'Why didn't you send them away, Henny? The tea is always excellent, I believe, Florence.'

He thought the girls wouldn't have a suspicion there was anything at all in the wind but tea.

'Shall I go too?' I asked, standing up.

'No, no, my dear Florence; no reason at all you should. I am, I must confess, rather upset. My dear,' he continued, turning to his wife, 'did you ever suspect anything wrong with regard to Miss Ariell?'

'No, indeed, I did not. I like her and her step-brother particularly.'

'I have just been speaking to young Swallow,—he's staying at the Rockes,—and, upon my word, if all or even a part of what he says is true, we've been let in. Let in—in a most disgraceful and unaccountable manner.'

'Good gracious!' said Mrs. Carew, and her hands fell limply on her lap. 'How?'

The colonel lowered his voice, and looked round carefully. 'She's married—married hard and fast—to a fellow, an actor fellow, called Sprague; and he's found her out, by Jove, and intends to claim her. A nice scandal for the girls!'

'But the step-brother?'

'My dear,' he replied, glancing at her with some natural scorn, 'he's no more her step-brother than I am.'

Mrs. Carew started and exclaimed. I did neither, I did not even wonder; I felt as if I had known it quite well all along. And yet just as surely as I knew and had known all along that the woman was guilty, so surely was I convinced of the innocence of Clive Pomfret; and yet I hadn't a vestige of fact to bring in proof of it, it was a mere theory; nevertheless I would risk ridicule and air it, this baseless theory of mine.

'I am certain, as certain as I sit here,' I said, with an air of the surest reasonableness, 'that the boy Clive is as innocent as a baby all through.'

'Good heavens, Florence!' they cried it out at me simultaneously, and the colonel lifted himself on his chair with both hands and surveyed me with strong dissatisfaction.

'Look here,' I said, with rather a feeble grin, 'how much will you bet?'

'My dear,' murmured Mrs. Carew.

'That "cup" has upset me,' I explained, laughing.

'Never mind, Florence,' said the colonel, sinking down again, and looking less like a wild beast, ' I'll bet you anything you like—though the boy may be weak—that he must have known the position of affairs. It is ridiculous to suppose otherwise ; and the idea of a man, a gentleman of birth and breeding, bringing a person of that character into my house— among my girls—why, it's outrageous—it's damnable! Pray excuse me. It's too much for a man,—one must swear.'

He jumped up and walked furiously to and fro in front of us, stamping from time to time. It did look worse than bad, one couldn't wonder at the old man's wrath, and yet I could have staked my life the boy was as much entrapped as we were.

'They may have been married : how was he to know of the Sprague creature ?' I pleaded weakly.

' Married !—a likely story. Why didn't they say so if they were. Step-brother and sister, indeed !'

' She may have had her full and sufficient reasons. That arrangement was of her making, I know.'

' You have a huge opinion of your sex's rascality, it seems to me.'

' Not at all ; but I have the very smallest opinion of a man's sense under certain conditions.'

' The fellow had plenty of brains. On everyday matters he was all there ; and he was a very fairly read fellow.'

' The very wisest of you creatures are just wax in the hands of a woman with her head screwed on the right way, and with no conscience : any man can be fooled, given certain circumstances.'

'Look here, my dear,' remarked Colonel Carew, with some asperity, 'generalities are the refuge of the reasonless : where are your proofs?'

'I haven't the ghost of one. But do faces go for nothing?'

'Not a damn,' muttered the old man.

'Yes, but they do,' I persisted idiotically ; 'and I put it to you, as a Christian man, if it is in the remotest degree possible that a boy with that face could bring a woman in Miss Ariell's supposed relation to himself in among a lot of innocent ignorant girls. It is beyond the bounds of possibility, I persist. Why, a man steeped to the neck in vice wouldn't do it, not to say Clive Pomfret. He may have lied and helped in a deception,—he must have,—but it isn't in him to do that.'

'Whether it's in him or not, he did it, that's enough for me,' snarled the colonel. 'Good God! to think of it,' he muttered, drumming on his chair elbow ; 'a nice story for the club. We've been let in—let in in a most disgraceful and scandalous fashion ! And to think of me, a man of my age and experience of the world,' cried the colonel,—his red turning to a danger-ous purple,—'being let in by a chit of a child and that woman, who really seemed quite straight. You thought so, my dear,' he stammered, turning rather pathetically to his wife. 'It's outrageous !'

'Here are the girls,' whispered Mrs. Carew. 'We

will have tea now, and we can talk it over to-night, dear,' she said kindly, looking up at the outraged man of the world.

We did talk it over. The girls were bundled off to their rooms at nine o'clock, to their infinite and most just disgust, bubbling over with reasonable curiosity as they were. Then we set to and talked till eleven, and to not the slightest purpose. During the talk I got into trouble myself. I was simple enough to betray my slight previous knowledge of affairs, and the conclusions I had arrived at ; and the colonel didn't like it—it hurt his sense of manly superiority. It struck him that somehow I had scored off him.

'Most unwise of you, my dear, most injudicious. These matters should never be dealt with by women, with their very beautiful and natural ignorance of the world. You should have come to me at once, and all this most deplorable scandal might have been averted.'

I wondered how, considering the circumstances ; but I thought it just as well to be silent. I saw a glint in Mrs. Carew's eye that told me that her belief in her husband's immaculate world knowledge had received a severe shock ; and I knew he would hear all about it before he got a wink of sleep that night, so I could afford to be magnanimous with an easy mind. Once or twice, as we were talking, I fancied I heard a light step on the verandah, but, as no one else remarked it, concluded I must have been mistaken.

CHAPTER VI.

WHEN I had taken down my hair for the night, and changed my dress for a loose white wrapper, I threw up my window and looked out, in a way I have had ever since the days of my childhood. It was a perfect night, cool and crisp and silent, with the moonlight pouring itself down in great waves of silver whiteness over mountain and plain. The moon does certainly know how to shine in these southern lands, and in no other land than Australia does it so completely transform the whole aspect of nature. Australia simply loses its individuality under the moon's rays; it drops its raw crudity of youth, and grows strong and great and grand with the strength and greatness and grandeur of virility, not with the cock-sure bumptiousness of precocity.

As I stood looking out, slipping involuntarily back to wander among the graves of old dead hopes and slain follies, that died hard in those old days, when life was so full and death so bitter, I was just preparing for myself a miserable and rather a mawkish *quart-d'heure*, when again I heard a little rustle, and the furtive tread of slippered feet, and I put my head out of the window to hear more distinctly.

My room was in a block of bed-rooms quite isolated from the house, and it had a separate verandah of its own; but it never struck me to be frightened. I think I was in too excited and absorbed a state concerning

man and selfish natures to take proper notice of outer
events.

I listened again, in rather a half-hearted way, and
the tread came nearer, and I could distinguish a black-
clothed figure advancing swiftly and softly. When
it saw me, it raised a white warning hand—a woman's,
from the size of it. I had no further time for specu-
lation; the walk changed to a quick noiseless run,
and the figure stopped before my window, threw down
its cloak, and displayed to my astonished sight Miss
Ariell in full dinner dress. 'Let me into your room,
quick!' she whispered, with a soft chuckling laugh.

I moved aside mechanically, in a whirl of passive,
silent, indignant amazement. I could not have got
out a word for the life of me. When she got in, she
pulled down the window and drew the blind, then
she ran to the door and noiselessly turned the key in
it, then she sat down in my most comfortable chair.
I saw her pause to select it—oh, the cool audacity of
that person! And then she broke out in a long
bubble of laughter that shook her from head to heel
with its low soft intensity, and she looked at me out
of those two untranslateable eyes of hers. I no longer
wondered at men, or blamed them for any depth of
foolishness. I believe I was in love with her myself
that minute, she looked so radiant and so lovely, and,
in the dim lamp-light, so young ; and the little mocking devil in her laugh only increased her charm a
thousandfold.

'Ah, I know you know all about it,' she cried softly.

'That duffer Clarence Swallow has it all over the place, just for mere spite. If you knew the love—and the sort of love—he made to me; but there was nothing either to like or to laugh at in the creature. I had to squash him at once. Look here; I'm going away by the first train to-morrow with my husband—yes, my husband. I'm married to him all right, and he's not half a bad sort, but you see he's an actor, and makes me work; and I can tell you an actor's life is a good sight harder than a stone-breaker's or a daily governess's; and, besides, the fellow's as jealous as a boy. I thought I'd take a holiday and give him one. But he didn't like it in all its points. Poor fellow, he makes his life a toil watching me! Isn't it idiotic? and such woful waste of time, too; as if a woman won't go her own way in spite of the watching of fifty men. Now this last affair was pure kindness on my part. I met Clive Pomfret on the Tasmanian boat, and I simply had to take care of the child. Mrs. Vallings, that boy's the greatest fool, and the straightest, honestest fool, I ever met in my life. Nothing would do him but to marry me!—marry *me!* Heavens!—and we went on a honeymoon, all quite correct. But for reasons of my own—I won't tell you them, they're too many and too complex—we were step-brother and sister; and we came up here—here, into this little hotbed of second-hand pigmy conventions—Oh, oh, oh!' she cried, shaking and gurgling—'and you saw how I was treated. You were the only mortal soul that suspected me, Mrs. Vallings. Why? do tell me.'

I looked at her indignantly. She gave another little laugh, and went on.

'It was the hugest joke. The boy's innocence—and the little coterie here, and its enthusiastic reception of me, and that wonderful Fleming family'—

'Yes, and poor Vandeleur,' I broke in angrily.

'Oh, that fool! I'm sorry for the other, very, though I assure you I have done my duty by him, for I've been disillusioning him like anything the last fortnight. But that Vanny—oh, that self-satisfied, virtuous ninny!—I'm not a rap sorry for him. Bless you, it'll be the making of him. I came here to-night partly about the creature. You never asked me, by the way, why I came, although you looked daggers, and bloody ones. Well, no matter, I suppose you can't, from your different make, see the joke in it all. I do.'

'Joke!' I could hardly speak for choking disgust.

'Joke! yes. Ah, you don't know anything about the spirit of acting on a person! I had quite a frenzy of it on me, playing half-a-dozen games at the same time, and mystifying the most intensely respectable and conventional audience in the whole length and breadth of the continent. Joke! it was a dozen jokes, and good ones, rolled into one.'

'Please continue,' I said, with much dignity. 'You informed me you came on Mr. Vandeleur's account.'

She laughed, and glanced from head to foot of me. I would have given a great deal to throw her out of the window. That was impossible; besides, I wanted to hear if in any way I could help either of these boys.

'How young you do look, to be sure,' she laughed insolently,—'in some lights, that is.'

I tried to freeze her with a look; but where was the use? she laughed again with her soft gurgling ripple.

'Oh, Van,' she went on lazily. 'Well, I had mapped out such a lark. Van and I were to be married to-morrow at 11.30 A.M. He has the licence this minute. I daresay it's under his pillow. O Lord!' —she collapsed again into a noiseless fit of mirth. 'You appear to have taken to him. He swears by you, anyway. You might meet him at the 11.30 A.M. train, and let him into the secret. My husband and I are going by the mail to-morrow at 2 P.M.'

'And Clive?'

'Oh, he ran up to town by the evening train on business I invented for him. When he comes back, I'll be on the high seas. You'll have your hands full with those two boys, Mrs. Vallings. How providential you should turn up just in the nick of time! Quite a direct interposition, I should say!'

'Have you no compunction at all, Miss Ariell; are you altogether heartless?'

She was perfectly silent for a few minutes; and gradually such a change came over the face of the woman as I never in my wildest imaginings could have thought possible. The mask of laughing, sardonic, devilish mirth dropped from her, taking all the sparkle and colour and light and youth with it, and a new face looked out at me—a terrible face, old and grey and wicked and sad, with the sadness

of death and with the corruption of the grave on it.
I shuddered and covered my face.

'Ah, you may well hide your face,' she hissed out
at me—her voice had altered with her face. 'Do you
know, woman, that I was once as good and as ignorant
—as ignorant, mark you—as those two yellow-haired
girls over there in the house? They're giggling there
this minute like two babies,—I heard them as I waited
for you,—and I was as innocent as these. Well, I came
to grief, by no fault of mine, through sheer idiocy, and
then men took me for a shuttle-cock, and played
their fill with me; and now my time is come, and I
am having my revenge. That's the whole story.'

'Why do you choose boys to carry out your revenge
on? That seems to me a poor mean game.'

'On the principle of an eye for an eye, youth for
youth. How old was I when they began their game
with me? But I assure you I have an atom of heart
still. It is wonderful, too, considering all things; but
I suppose a woman's heart is never killed outright,
God help her! I'm sorry for Clive; no one knows
how good the fellow is, and will be. Look after him.
Send him home, Mrs. Vallings; the boy must have
home life and good women about him to keep him
straight. Melbourne will be the ruin of him. Send
him home when he is fit to go. As for Vanny, that's
all calf-love. *He'll* be all right, bless you!'

She stood up and threw out her white rounded
arms with a gesture of utter weariness. I could have
pitied her, but for her conduct towards those girls.

'What devil made you tell those girls the things you did?' I demanded.

A flash of the old mocking malice crossed her face.

'What devil? The same old serpent, I suppose. There's been no special devil created for me, that I'm aware of—more's the pity! You think me a beast, of course,' she said suddenly—'all bad.'

'No, I don't,' I made impetuous answer. There was a worn, weary look on her face, and her hands dropped listlessly,—somehow she touched me; and good does get so intricately entangled in evil sometimes. 'No; I think there's a little sound bit in your heart still. Can't you give it a chance to spread?'

'No, I can't; it's too late, too late. Well, good-bye; we'll not see one another again. You've depressed me. I couldn't laugh now as I did when I came into the room, to save my life. Bah! the joke tastes flat. But I'm really obliged to you for these two wet eyes. Look after the boys, both of them. Good-bye!'

She opened the window and crept softly out.

'God help you!' I cried, as she was stepping off the verandah. 'Won't you try?'

'Can't be done,' she called back, with her mocking laugh. 'Thanks all the same.'

I saw her walk away under the brilliant moonlight into a dense clump of wattle, then she had gone out of my sight for ever.

Next day I went to the railway station at Spencer Street and met Vandeleur Fleming. I did my best for the boy, but it was a very poor and inefficient best. His suffering was as real and intense as if he had not had a ridiculous strain in him. As I foresaw, he found a very complete retribution in the bosom of his righteous family.

As for Clive, I have never been able to think of that boy's sorrow, much less speak of it. I have been the sole gainer in the whole miserable transaction, having come out of it the richer by two steadfast friends, who have done much to bring back the old fresh sweetness of life, and who make up to me for many past hopes and banished illusions. I see in those fair girls what I might have been, and pray God to keep them unspotted from the world.

THE BUSHMAN'S REST.

THE BUSHMAN'S REST.

———o———

IN the old days it had been merely a small hut, with stables at the back where Cobb & Co.'s coaches changed horses. But a diggings breaking out some eight or nine miles away, the owner had added to the building, and turned it into a general store and wayside public-house combined, greatly to the annoyance of the surrounding squatters, whose hands made it a resort whenever they had an hour or two, as well as upon every high day and holiday.

It was called 'The Bushman's Rest,' and did a good trade with travellers and station employés, who often put up there for a night instead of camping out in the bush.

The man who kept it was named Burgiss. At one time he had been a driver for Cobb & Co. on that very road, and a very popular driver too, but drink, the universal curse of these colonies, had overtaken him and totally unfitted him for the position; so, with the little ready-money he had managed to save, he bought out the original proprietor, and with his wife took possession and started the joint business. For a hundred miles and more the place had a notoriously bad name—every one on or off the road knew it ; and though none could exactly define the reason of its bad reputation, all felt that it was not unfounded. Burgiss was by birth a colonial. Who his forebears had been, history sayeth not, though it was hinted by more than one of his mates that Burgiss' father had been—

> ' One of that patriot brood
> Who left their country for their country's good.'

He had been at one time rather a fine-looking young fellow, and, before he lost his nerve, what bushmen call a smart hand among horses. Indeed. when a youth he had been a jockey for Mr. De M——, one of the largest owners of racehorses in the colonies. His wife was a barmaid in a West Maitland hotel when he met and married her, but since her marriage she had fallen into ill-health, and at the time my story opens was totally incapacitated from attending to the house, and in consequence they had determined to engage a housekeeper to take her place.

Now it chanced that Mrs. Burgiss had a friend in Sydney, a Mrs. Holland (wife of a solicitor), who had also been a barmaid, but had risen considerably in the social scale, owing to her marriage. To her she wrote, telling of her illness, and begging her to engage and send her up a housekeeper of good appearance and address—some one, in short, who could be trusted to take entire charge during her absence, for it was purposed that Mrs. Burgiss should go to Sydney for medical advice and treatment directly the new housekeeper arrived.

As soon as Mrs. Holland received her friend's letter, she at once drove to the depôt, a large number of immigrants having arrived only the day before.

After interviewing a great number of girls, and finding none who would suit in the double capacity she required of them, she was about to leave the place to try elsewhere, when her attention was arrested by a young woman who entered the room at the moment, crying bitterly. She was a tall, handsome girl to outward appearance ; and, notwithstanding the veil she wore over her face, Mrs. Holland noticed that she was decidedly prepossessing. As she seemed to be in great trouble, Mrs. Holland inquired of the matron the cause.

'Well, poor thing, she expected friends to meet her, —an aunt, I believe,' was the reply. 'And when she got here, the first newspaper she saw contained a notice of the death of her aunt. She came out second-class, but made friends with some of the girls on the ship, and asked to come with them here, as she had no friends to go to, and no money to speak of, poor young thing. She has other friends in the colony, but she don't know where to find them, even to send them a letter.'

Mrs. Holland thought for a moment, then she said, 'Do you think she would take a situation ? I really think she would just do for the place I mentioned, if she could be persuaded to take it.'

' I don't quite know, ma'am, what her plans are, or if she has made any yet, poor girl, but you can speak to her yourself,' the matron replied ; and, calling the girl over, she explained to her what Mrs. Holland was there for, and what she required. A pound a week, full charge of the house, her own mistress, and nothing menial required of her, it sounded very suitable,—the very thing, in fact, that she wanted in her helpless position. As there appeared no chance of finding her friends, it would be foolish to miss so good a chance of securing a home and a living.

Mrs. Holland was more than ever struck with her appearance when she raised her veil. Her complexion was beautifully fair and clear, eyes dark blue, and innocent and trusting as a child's ; in short, Ellen Dunne, for such was her name, was a very lovely English country girl, far too beautiful and pure-minded to be homeless in such a country as this.

The preliminaries were soon arranged, and an agreement drawn up ; and before she well knew what she had done, she had signed it, thus pledging herself to a six months' contract. However, once having determined upon accepting the situation, Nelly Dunne was not going to let herself look back or repine over the inevitable. She was alone, friendless, and without sufficient money to keep her more than a week or two, so felt inclined to congratulate herself upon her good fortune in having found a home so soon.

So one morning very early, before the great heart of the city began to move, she found herself and her modest belongings in the coach, *en route* for a town with a strange outlandish name, where she at last arrived just at dark, tired, dispirited, lonely, and very sad.

Imagine, reader, if you can, a young girl coming all the way from England alone, expecting to meet friends, kindly and loving, who would cherish and protect her at her journey's end. Then to meet no one save strangers, who knew her not nor wanted her ; to live three days constantly on the watch for a familiar or kindly face, to hear a step and run to meet it hopefully, and to find only the cold vacant stare of an utter stranger. At last she thought she must have forgotten her aunt's appearance, and so had perhaps missed her among the crowds that on the first day thronged the ship in search of friends. Then she sallied forth into the streets of the great strange city, in the vague hope of recognising the loved face among the countless thousands who passed and repassed.

It was during one of these wearying walks about the city that she entered a pastry-cook's and asked for a drink of milk and a bun, more for the sake of the rest than because she was hungry or thirsty. She bought a few cakes to take back with her, and these the woman wrapped in a piece of an old newspaper. Going slowly along, for she was heart-sick and weary, her eye caught the name of Marston,—it was her aunt's name,—and she read,—

'At Newcastle, on the 5th inst., Mary Ellen Marston, widow of the late Rev. Edward Marston of Hinton, aged 50 years.'

She turned the paper over; it was a month old. Yes, her aunt was dead. Then there could not be two Mary Ellen Marstons, widows of clergymen, and of Hinton too,—she remembered that was the name of her uncle's parish. She did not faint or scream, she only felt a numb despair come upon her, and a feeling of utter desolation. What was to become of her? She could not stop on board the ship much longer; indeed, it was only through the courtesy of the captain that she had been allowed to stay so long. Mechanically she walked on, seeing nothing, hearing nothing around her, till suddenly a hand grasped her arm, and a voice said cheerfully, 'Why, Miss Dunne, I didn't know you!' It was one of the immigrants, a young girl whom Nelly had spoken to several times on the voyage.

'Did your friends come for you yet, miss?' she asked kindly.

'No, Alice; my aunt is dead,' was the reply. 'I have just seen her death in this piece of paper;' and, as she pointed to the notice, her strength gave way, and she began to cry weakly.

'Ah, poor soul! I am sorry for you; but what will you do now?'

'I don't know, I am sure,' was the hopeless answer.

The girl stood for a moment thinking, then she said,—

'Will you come along to the depôt and see the

matron there; she is a real good sort, and maybe could think of some way to help ye.'

Without more ado she turned with Alice and proceeded to the depôt. Her story was soon told, and, under the advice of the matron, she determined to take her chance with the other girls who were in search of work. We know the rest. She had only just returned to the depôt from having bidden farewell to the captain and officers of the ship, when Mrs. Holland noticed and engaged her. This was Nelly Dunne's position. Think of it, you among my fair readers who have home friends and kindly voices to welcome you always.

When she found herself at the hotel, whither she had been conducted by the driver of the mail-coach, who had received instructions from Mr. Burgiss to bring the young woman along, she sat down on the small trunk which contained all that was left of her worldly possessions (for she had been obliged to part with some of her things to enable her to buy a few necessaries for her journey and her new situation) and cried as though her heart was breaking. Was this the grand free life in sunny Australia of which she had heard so much, and the glowing accounts of which had made her discontented with her humble village home?—that home which now, as she saw it in imagination, looked so lovely, so happy, so different to her present surroundings. What would she not give for the privilege of returning to it, of even only telling those she had left of her sore need of

their help and pity! However, she was tired, body
and spirit; and youth, thank God, does not fret long.
She drank a cup of tea, and ate some bread-and-
butter, then went to bed, and, strange to say, slept
soundly till they called her at daylight to prepare for
the journey before her, which in the days I am writing
of was an ordeal for any woman, however strong.

The driver of the coach, though a rough, coarse-
spoken bushman, had a tender heart, and sympathy
for all young women who travelled with him. He
was a widower with one child, and that one a crippled
daughter sixteen years of age; but oh, such a sweet
young girl, full of hope and love! Her affliction was
all the more sad, that it had not been of long standing,
but was the result of a foolish wager on the part of
her father, who had sworn that she, a child of twelve
years of age, could drive a pair of half-broken horses
over a certain piece of road. The child was terrified,
but dared not disobey, so drove them, the result being
they ran away. She was dashed against a tree, and
had her thigh broken and her spine injured, while
one horse was killed and the other had to be shot,
and the vehicle was smashed to atoms. Agnes had
ever since remained an invalid; and for her sake her
father was gentle and pitiful to all young women,
though still remaining outwardly coarse, hard-featured,
and rough.

When Nelly came out that morning, heavy-eyed
and sad-looking, Bill the driver, as he was called, was
very gentle with her, even whispering a word or two

of encouragement as he assisted her to the box-seat beside him.

I need not describe the journey in detail. No doubt most of my readers at some time of their lives have taken a journey by coach. Every ten miles the weary horses were taken out and fresh ones substituted. The heart of the lonely girl grew heavier and heavier as she was borne farther and farther away from civilisation, into what seemed to her the heart of a wilderness.

She had heard and read many tales of station life, and the difficulties often to be encountered in reaching these far-off homes, but nothing she had ever dreamt of approached at all near to the terrible roads and wild bush which they were passing through. She could hardly realize that these vaguely defined tracks which the coach followed were a high road. As they wound round and through the trees, lurching over stony or boggy ground alike, she grasped Bill's arm, and looked the fear she had not power to express.

When engaging her, Mrs. Holland had told her that the place she was going to was a station. Possibly she spoke in all sincerity, and as she had been led to believe, for it is the custom for people who live in the bush, even if they only possess half an acre and a couple of cows, to speak of their place as a station. Any one who owns a few head of cattle and sufficient land to run them on, is a squatter in his own opinion, and when away from home will frequently enlarge upon the capabilities, beauty, value, etc. etc., of his run. So it is quite likely Mrs. Holland spoke in good faith.

All up the road the young stranger's beauty and refined appearance attracted admiration, and at each stopping-place she was beset with unwelcome attentions from the men who lounged about the bars; particularly after it became known that her destination was the notorious 'Bushman's Rest,' for they argued that (to use their own words) 'she couldn't be much chop, or she wouldn't go there.'

It was well for Nelly that she did not understand their rude jests and coarse wit, or her sensitive feelings would have been shocked twenty times a day.

It was nine o'clock at night when the four horses pulled up before the door of the wayside inn which was to be Nelly Dunne's home for a time.

'Here you are, safe and sound, wind and limb,' said the driver; 'and I guess you ain't sorry neither, miss?' he added kindly, as he looked down upon the tired face of the girl beside him from his superior height.

'Is this the station?' she inquired simply, staring round her in bewilderment, and wondering where the house was, for she recognised directly that this was a public-house before her.

'This is "The Bushman's Rest," miss, and here comes the boss. Now then, steady while yer get down, or ye'll fall. I guess ye're a bit stiff after all the sittin'.'

She descended from the high seat, and, while they

unstrapped her box and took out sundry parcels from the coach, she looked round her on a scene the beauty of which could not but strike one so unaccustomed as she was to such wild, grand scenery. The moon was at the full, and hung in the cloudless heavens like a great white globe, lighting up the surrounding country with its clear, weird light. On all sides rose hills one above another; even the house stood upon one. The road along which the coach had just come continued its winding course down into the valley below, from whence stretched several miles of perfectly level country. In the distance, to the left, a river was visible, looking strangely white in the moonlight. For the moment the girl stood looking upon it all lost in admiration at its beauty, her spirit having flown away to another scene of which this reminded her a little; and it was with a great start she came back to the present, when Mr. Burgiss touched her arm familiarly and begged her to walk inside.

'S'pose you're dead beat?' he said, conducting her to a room behind the bar, from whence she saw the driver and two or three men drinking.

She sat down on the nearest chair, saying as she did so, 'Yes, I am very tired, I wish this was the end of my journey; but I suppose it is not far now?' Then, looking up eagerly, she inquired, 'Is Mr. Burgiss here yet to meet me?'

Mrs. Holland had told her that she supposed they would meet her at the coach, so naturally she concluded that there must be some distance yet to go

that this wayside inn was her destination never for
an instant occurred to her. So her surprise can be
better imagined than described, when to her query
her companion said with a laugh, 'Why, bless you,
I'm Burgiss.'

'You!' she exclaimed, in wide-eyed astonishment;
then, looking round her hurriedly, 'There must be
some mistake, I think. I am Miss Dunne; I was
engaged in Sydney by Mrs. Holland to take'—

'It's all right; yes, I know all about it,' he replied,
interrupting her abruptly. 'Mrs. Holland—she's a
friend of my wife's—engaged you to be housekeeper,
barmaid, and general help while my missus goes down
to see the doctors. Oh yes, it's all right, miss, you're
on the right track.'

All right, indeed! it was all wrong; in her amazement she had risen from the chair; but when the full
meaning of it all burst upon her she sat down again,
trembling in every limb, and white to her lips. But
Ellen Dunne was a brave girl, and though her heart
was so full she was afraid to trust her voice. She
gathered at once the full meaning of the mistake, her
position and helplessness. She had signed an agreement to do the work of housekeeper and general help
—lady-help had been the term used by Mrs. Holland.
Certainly she had said no word about a bar, or about
her having to wait behind a bar. And Nelly felt her
blood run cold at the mere idea; for, like most girls in
her position, she had been brought up with a holy
horror of public-house bars, and more than all of bar-

maids. Yet here she was, without money or friends, in the wild bush, at a low public-house, the like of which she would have shuddered to enter at any other time. What was she to do? Hastily viewing her position, she determined that her only course was to put a good face on the matter, and bide her time, till she could see a way out of her difficulties. So, swallowing down her tears and disappointment, she begged to be shown to her room, saying she required nothing to eat, but would like to go to bed if she might.

'Oh yes, the best thing you can do,' was the reply from Burgiss, who had been standing at the door apparently gazing out into the night, but in reality watching Nelly. 'You needn't see the missus to-night,' he continued, 'she's had a real bad day, and ain't up to talking to-night.' He led the way along a dirty passage which smelt strongly of stale liquor. On either side were rooms, through which she could see either untidy beds, or else tables with gaudy cloths upon them, and chairs with elaborate crochet antimacassars over their backs ; these were the rooms —parlours, Nelly supposed—wherein the men drank, and with which she would have to become acquainted as barmaid and waitress.

The weary girl followed, wondering whether her room was quite away from the rest of the rooms, and whether she would be able to make any one hear her in the night should she need help. To her dismay, they crossed a sort of yard, where half-a-dozen low-looking men—some of them half-tipsy—were smoking, talking, and laughing loudly round the stables ; then up a flight of ladder-like steps, and she found herself in the most squalid, poverty-struck apartment it had ever been her lot to enter.

'This is your camp ; it's a bit rough, but yer won't need to be in it 'cept of nights,' her companion remarked, as he set the dirty candlestick he carried down on a packing-case, which did duty in the double capacity of dressing-table and wash-hand stand.

With a look of real dismay, which could not but be noticed by the man, it was so utterly blank and frightened, the miserable young girl sank down upon a gin case, which was the only seat in the room, and the next moment she had fainted dead away.

No whit alarmed, Burgiss laid her flat upon the floor, and hastened away for some water and a glass of wine. He was gone some minutes, and when he returned she had revived somewhat, and was sitting up leaning against the wall, crying bitterly.

Burgiss was not unkind : he was a rough, coarse man, mean and grasping by nature, and drink and his associates had not lessened those qualities. The life he led tended to make him what he was (excuse the word), a blackguard ; but still deep down in his heart there was a soft spot which was very rarely touched, but which now made him pity this young creature so strangely brought into his disreputable home, for that it was disreputable none knew better than the master thereof. Kneeling down beside poor Nelly, he said coaxingly, and very much as if he were addressing a favourite mare, 'Come, come now, cheer up a bit, and don't go to spoil those pretty eyes. Gently now, gently now, old lady, what's to pipe yer eye about?'

Had poor Nelly not been in such dire trouble and distress, she must have laughed at this strange address and manner of consolation, for Burgiss had possessed himself of one of her hands, and was stroking and fondling it in an absurdly comical manner.

After a while she dried her tears and rose from her lowly seat on the floor, saying as cheerfully as she could under the wretched circumstances, 'I am better now, thank you, sir.' She hesitated slightly over the word 'sir,' wondering whether she would be expected to use it upon all occasions. 'I will go to bed now, and in the morning, no doubt, I shall feel better. Thank you for being so kind to me just now, it was very stupid of me to faint. I don't know what came over me;' and, quite forgetful of her new position as servant to this man, she held out her hand to bid him good-night. But evidently Burgiss saw nothing extra-ordinary in the offer of her hand. On the contary, he seemed pleased; and before taking the offered hand, which in reality, if the truth were known, looked too white and pretty to be grasped off-hand, he rubbed his own horny palm down the side of his trousers, saying apologetically, 'They ain't real dirty, yer know, but I was helping Bill to put the hosses in;' then, taking it very gingerly, as if fearful of hurting her, he shook it stiffly and awkwardly, as he returned her

good-night, then sprang away down the ladder
at two bounds, mentally voting the new girl a
stunner.

Left alone, Nelly Dunne gazed round her in dismay
at the appointments of this her future apartment.
Never, even in the poorest cottage home in her
father's parish, had she seen so poverty-struck and
unwholesome an apartment. The bedstead, or what
did duty for such, was a rough stretcher evidently
made on the place, as also had been the mattress,
which made a peculiar crackling sound when she
pressed it. The mosquito nets, which hung above
from a nail in one of the rafters, were on their last
legs, evidently past mending even, besides being
filthily dirty. In one corner was the packing-case
already alluded to, and on it a tin basin like those
usually used in bush kitchens for setting the bread in.
This too, upon examination, she found to be in a
dilapidated state, a piece of rag stopping up a good-
sized hole in the bottom. There was no jug, no
receptacle for water at all. Beside the bed a box
stood on its end, having at one time done duty as
stand for a candle, as was apparent from the quantity
of sperm dropped all over it and on to the floor beside
it too. There was no cover on this box, nor was
there any on the packing-case either. With the gin
case on which she had sat down, this concludes the
inventory of her bedroom furniture. Was it any
wonder that the lonely girl felt utterly and supremely
wretched? for, though never accustomed to luxury in

her English home, it had been as comfortable and pretty as clever, loving hands and moderate means could make it. There was no water in the room, and she wondered if it would be possible to find any if she went down into the yard ; at any rate she must try, she had not had a wash for nearly twenty-four hours, and could not go to rest without getting rid of the grime and dust of her long journey. Taking the basin, for lack of any other receptacle that would hold water, she descended to the yard. The moon was shining brightly as day, lighting up every part of the establishment distinctly, particularly the squalid back premises, with its array of half-ruined outhouses and dirty pig-sties, the occupants of which greeted her approach by a series of grunts and snorts. After a few seconds spent in peering here and there in search of a pump or tap, she spied a tank close to the main building, and to this she at once turned her steps, filled her basin (which, by the way, leaked wofully in spite of the rag plug), and was on her way back to her room, when she almost ran into a young girl carrying an armful of dry clothes, evidently just from the drying ground. The two met in the middle of the yard, and Nelly, pleased to see one of her own sex, said civilly,—

'Good evening!' then, with a smile, 'You see I am making myself at home—there was no water in my room.'

But the other girl made no reply whatever, only staring insolently at her. Nothing daunted, however,

N

she made some other trifling remark, and asked for a bit of soap.

'There's some down in the wash-'us,' was the ungracious reply, as, pointing carelessly over her shoulder to indicate the direction of the said 'wash-'us,' the girl disappeared, leaving Nelly, if possible, more disheartened than before.

She set her basin of water down while she went in search of the soap, which, after a long hunt among tubs, buckets, and kerosine tins, she at last found. After washing her face, neck, and arms as best she could in the small quantity of water she had managed to get as far as her room, and drying them on her pocket handkerchief, for towels were evidently an un-thought-of item in the appointment of her chamber, she undressed wearily and crept into her comfortless blankets, for sheets, too, were considered unnecessary luxuries, apparently. And there, in the silence of the night, she cried herself to sleep, wondering whether she would ever be able to live through the time she had engaged for.

Another and very different scene was being enacted this same evening, a few miles from 'The Bushman's Rest' on a station which I will call Morven Plains.

The mail-bag had not long arrived, and in the comfortable bush room two young men were seated on either side of the table, intent upon their separate correspondence. They were cousins, and joint-owners of the station ; their names, Herbert and Paul Wright. Herbert, whose letters had not been very numerous or voluminous, had finished reading them, and was engaged upon the English papers, which he turned and twisted at intervals, making them crackle and rustle in a manner truly irritating to himself as well as to his silent cousin.

Paul Wright held before him a closely-written letter, which every now and again he crushed convulsively in his hand as if he would read no further; then the next minute smoothed out again, and read on. All this was unnoticed by his cousin, until a muttered oath escaped, and made him look up quickly from his paper, and exclaim,—

'Halloo! what's up, Paul? Bad news, eh?' But, receiving no reply, he returned to his paper, and after a short time rose, and, carelessly bidding his companion good-night, left the room. For a while the other read on; he had mastered the contents of those delicate pink sheets at the first reading, but yet he returned to them again and again, reading every word deliberately and carefully, till all were impressed upon his brain like a well-learned lesson. After about the twentieth reading, he crushed the letter in his hand and sat buried in thought for more than an hour, from which he roused himself only to pace restlessly up and down the room, much after the manner of a wild beast confined in an iron-barred cage. From end to end of the long bush room he walked, and one could, with very little imagination, fancy him a wild beast labouring under suppressed though impotent fury. Having to a certain extent walked down the evil spirit that possessed him, he once more threw himself into his chair, smoothed out the crumpled letter, and began another perusal of its disturbing contents. It ran as follows :—

'KELLMINGTON, SOUTH WALES.

'MY DEAR PAUL,—A painful duty is left me, and I hardly know how to enter upon it, for the words I am forced to write you to-day will, I know, come upon you with a great shock, and also be a cruel disappointment, I fear. I should have told you before this ; and perhaps you will blame me, or even call me hard names, but I trust you will always believe that I have acted for the best, and with a strict sense of the duty I owe to my mother, to you, and lastly to myself.— You told me in your last two letters that you had had some spells of ill-luck since you bought into the station ; that the seasons had been against you,—your losses at one time heavy,—and that you feared I would have to rough it if I were to come out to you in the present state of affairs.—Now, my darling (for such you must ever be to me, whatever happens), I have thought it all over calmly and dispassionately, looking our position in the face, and after mature deliberation I have come to the conclusion that I would be acting most selfishly and against your best interests, present and future, if I kept you to this engagement any longer. You may not be able to come home for years, and my mother will never consent to my going out to you unmarried. So, Paul dear, though it breaks my heart to write it, or indeed even to think of it, we must part. I give you back your freedom. I set you at liberty to choose another for the wife you need to help you to bear your troubles. Do not think too hardly of me ; believe me I am acting more for your good than my own. And, Paul darling, you know I am not a free agent. My mother and Uncle Dick both claim my obedience ; the latter constantly tells me I must marry money for all our sakes. Your cousin is constantly here, and we meet him out a great deal more often than of old.—He has asked me to be his wife, and I fear that uncle will insist on my answer to him being a favourable one. You know where my heart is, and who owns it. Dear Paul, try and forgive me if you can ; and still with fondest love, I am, and always will be, yours at heart, MAUD.'

With a curse he folded the letter up and put it into the envelope ; then unfolding another sheet of paper, he read a printed advertisement which was pasted on to the middle of it, and which read as follows :—

'On the 11th inst., at St. Luke's, Kellnington, by the Rev. Samuel Bryce, Sir Philip Wright, only son of the late Algernon Wright of Mallons Park and the Old Hills, Derbyshire, to Maud Derrington, only daughter of the late Sir Astley Havers, and niece of Mark Hanbury of the Priory.

He read it over and over again as if he would fix it

on the tablets of his memory. As he did so, a thought seemed to strike him, and once more he unfolded the letter and looked for the date; but it bore none, and with a smile he turned to the envelope, the post-mark of which was dated the 10th June, only one day earlier than the advertisement he had just read. Then she had only written to break with him the day before she wedded his cousin. With an unnatural laugh that rang through the room, he turned and began to pace up and down, his thoughts finding vent now and then in muttered words and ejaculations.

'Ten blessed years of my life wasted on a woman —and such a woman! And now I'm thrown over for a puppy, just because he has money that should by right be mine. And I am a beggar, doomed to live the life of a dog in this God-forsaken country. Money, money!—woman's God. Oh, Maud, Maud, it can't be true; you were such a bonny darling, and you were mine! You did love me, or else you lied damnably. Good God! is there one woman in all the wide world capable of an honest attachment? And Philip's got her, my own cousin, and the only man I ever hated. I hope she'll grow to hate him; and she will, if she's the woman I take her for, as sure as there's a God in heaven. Philip, with his refined vices and his low estimate of the sex! Well, I could hardly wish her a worse fate than tied to my polished sensualist cousin. And Maud's son, if she have one, will stand between me and my birthright; that is all he wants, an heir. I can see her future as plainly as though it were written before me. He'll begin by neglecting her after the novelty of owner-ship has worn off, then possibly he'll ill-use her—he's quite capable of it ; and serve her right, the false-hearted jade. Damn her—yes—damn her—damn him—and damn them both !'

For hours he remained alone in the room, walking to and fro, thus giving vent to the thoughts that filled his angry mind, till the chill breeze, when the night and morning met, blew in through the open window and caused him to shiver. Pausing in the centre of the room for a moment, he turned towards the sideboard, where stood a pocket-flask of brandy, opened that evening to give a glass to the mail-boy when he brought the letters. 'Shall I have a taste of the old stuff,' he whispered half-aloud, 'to drink damnation to her and him ?' For a few seconds he stood, hesitating on the brink of temptation ; and it seemed as if his good angel would win the battle. From the sideboard he glanced towards the mantelpiece, where stood a hand-some cabinet photo of his old love. The effect was instantaneous : he broke into a mirthless laugh, and strode towards the bottle, saying, 'Yes, I will ; your influence is at an end, madam ; we'll drink to the dissolution ; what matter now how soon I go to the devil ?' Thus apostrophising the picture, he poured out half a tumbler of the spirit, added a slight modicum of water from the filter close by, and raised it to his mouth, as with mock politeness he bowed to the senseless photograph. But ere the spirit touched his lips, he put it down and shuddered violently, as though the smell of the liquor turned him sick. 'Seven years since I made a beast of myself,' he murmured ; then took another turn or two up and down the room, each time he neared the glass looking eagerly, almost greedily towards it. Oh for some kindly hand to take that glass away, some womanly influence to save him from himself! He paused before the tumbler, stretched out his hand, and then drew it back ; and as if reasoning with himself, he said, ' Why should I not have a taste of the stuff? Just a glass to put heart into me—I needn't get drunk. And even if I do, every man gets drunk once in a way. I'd like a taste of the old madness, I've nearly forgotten what it's like. Yes, I've kept straight seven long years for her sake. Oh, Maud, Maud, you could have made a good man of me, but now '— He leaned heavily against the sideboard, and presently through the fingers of the hand with which he had covered his eyes the tears trickled slowly, while his chest heaved with the sobs he at last gave way to. What sadder sight can be seen or imagined, than that of a strong man tempted by his besetting sin vainly struggling to get the better of the devil that possesses him! And saddest of all is the sight when that devil is drink. In a few moments he regained the mastery of his feelings. ' What a fool I am,' he muttered, ' to be so upset because a woman has thrown me over for another fellow. I must be terribly out of gear, likely as not a nip will do me all the good in the world ; anyway I must have something to steady my nerves, so here goes ;' and, seizing the glass, he drained the contents at a draught, as if he were fearful of changing his mind again.

The effect was magical, the spirit acted almost at once. In less than ten minutes he was a different man ; he laughed as he sauntered from one part of the room to another, examining books, pictures, ornaments, everything, in fact, that was there and caught his eye. He sang snatches of song, threw himself first into one chair, then another—in short, behaved like one labouring under some powerful influence or excitement. He seemed unable to keep still, the demon of unrest possessed him. Once more he took out the all-important letter and read it through, laughing loudly at certain passages. Then the impulse seized him to learn it by heart, repeating the words as he paced to and fro. When he had mastered it, and could repeat it word for word, he tore the letter into pieces and threw them savagely into the fireplace. Then he walked to the window, and drew aside the blind to look out over the moonlit plains. 'What a glorious night for a ride across country,' he muttered. 'I've a great mind to go over to the " Bushman's ;" there may be a choice spirit or two there to cheer my loneliness. I can't stop here doing nothing, that's certain ; perhaps another nip may decide the question.' Ever since the first glass of spirits had made the blood course through his veins, he had been craving for another ; at the same time he

had been mentally pushing it away from him, fearing
to give way—fearing to acknowledge to himself that
the old man was upon him with all the intensity
of a long drouth. The restlessness, the pretence of
occupying himself with Maud's letter, all meant the
same thing, and the whole time he was using his
utmost strength of will to overcome the craving. He
walked to the table and laid his hand upon the bottle,
took up the glass, and was about to pour out the spirit
—'No, I won't,' he said, and set the bottle down.
Then with a sudden impulse he took it up, and,
approaching the window, flung it out far into the
garden. It fell with a thud, but did not break, and
he turned irresolutely from the window. 'I wonder
did it break?' he muttered; 'didn't sound as if it did.'
He stood in the middle of the room. 'Shall I go and
see? Yes; if I leave it there Jacky will get hold of
it—better see and break it.' He went out through
the French-light on to the verandah, still debating
with himself as to whether to go or not; on the steps
he paused, his attention arrested by the peculiar cry
of a passing night-bird. He walked to the tree on
which it had lighted, and peered up among the
branches, just as the bird rose again and flew away
into the night. As he turned, his steps mechanically
took him in the direction of the flask. He could
see it lying upon a tussock of grass, the moonlight
glinting upon the glass. He picked it up and walked
slowly back to the house, as if guided by a will
stronger than his own. Up the steps and along to

the French-light he went, nor paused till he stood beside the table and held the tumbler in his hand. Without waiting now, he poured out a small quantity, added a little water, and drank it greedily. He had ceased to struggle (mentally) with himself. Virtually he was vanquished, his devil had got the upper hand, and Paul Wright knew it. Without moving from the table, he now poured out nearly another glass of brandy, diluted it slightly, and drank off the draught as before. A fourth glass followed that. 'I may as well finish the bottle now I've gone so far,' he said, holding it up to the light, 'there's barely another nip.' This he poured out quickly, and drank without a drop of water, and then threw himself into the only easy-chair the room contained. Very soon he began to nod ; but, rousing himself, he took up the lamp and deliberately proceeded to the storeroom, returning in a few minutes with a fresh bottle, intending to leave it unopened on the sideboard. But the evil spirit within him was not satisfied even yet ; and Paul Wright, having given way so far, was no more capable of holding back, or of saying, 'Hold, enough!' until that devil was appeased, any more than he could have arrested a fall in mid-air.

He drew the cork clumsily, being very unsteady by now, though not yet actually incapable, then poured out half a glass, and drank it. By the time he had had two or three more small glasses, the fiend was satisfied, and he was quite drunk, could barely stand,—a fact that seemed to amuse him.

'I'm drunk again,' he said. 'Richard's himself
again!—drunk, drunk; it's fine to feel drunk. I'd
forgotten what it was like; I'll get drunk for a week,
'stonish old Herbie; what a joke!' and with the last
words he fell in a heap upon the rug before the fireplace, and lay in a drunken stupor till Herbert, coming
in at daylight to see the time, stumbled over his
prostrate body.

'Good God! he's broken out again. What can have
set him off?' was the exclamation that broke from
him, as, glancing round, he noted the flask and bottle,
one empty, the other nearly three-parts full. Without calling assistance, he shook up the senseless man
and managed to get him to his bed. Then, locking
up the remainder of the drink, he put the key into his
pocket, and went out to his morning work, feeling
very low-spirited at the turn things had taken.

Though Herbert Wright had never before seen his
cousin in a state of intoxication, he had frequently
heard of his excesses when a younger man; and Paul
had himself told the story of his giving it up for the
sake of the girl he had loved ever since she was
fourteen.

He had drunk so heavily while at college, that
finally he had been rusticated by the authorities.
It had prevented his entering the Church, or indeed
any other profession; and when his friends could do
no more for him at home, for he drank himself out
of every situation they put him into, they seized
upon the fatal expedient of sending him to the

colonies, there to recover from his besetting sin, or else to lose himself in a country where he would not be a constant eyesore and heartache to every one belonging to him. When parents or guardians send a young man cursed with the craving for drink to the colonies to reclaim himself, they literally and metaphorically present him to the seven other devils of whom we read in Scripture, who were supposed to be worse than the sinner himself. In short, they simply throw him away to go his own road without let or hindrance.

A young man who comes to the colonies having the besetting sin of intemperance inherent in his blood, is as helpless and as sure to come to grief as a walnut-shell set afloat on the Pacific Ocean.

For three years after his arrival in the colonies Paul Wright went steadily down the social ladder. Then an uncle died and left him a few thousands, which necessitated his taking a trip home.

It may seem well-nigh incredible that a man of twenty-seven should fall in love with a child of fourteen, but stranger than that has happened, and is happening every day we live.

Paul had met and loved Maud Hilton when she was in the schoolroom. When he returned to England, Maud was on the point of coming out, and did come out too. They were thrown together in a country house for a fortnight (during one of Paul's rare turns of cessation from drink), and at the end of that time Paul proposed and was accepted by the young lady, but scornfully rejected by her parent and guardian,—a matter that gave Paul very little anxiety when he knew that Maud loved him, and was prepared to wait till he had proved himself worthy and able to keep a wife.

After a year at home he returned to the colonies, bringing his cousin Herbert; and the young men bought Morven Plains with the few thousands they had. From the day of his engagement Paul was a different man, and gave up drink entirely; not even would he touch a glass of wine, knowing the fatal disease that he had within him.

Seven years had passed since then. Several times he had begged Maud to come out and marry him; and doubtless she would have done so but for her mother, who was an invalid now, and was as greatly averse to her daughter's marriage with Paul as ever.

Paul had determined to go home for her at the end of the year, in spite of bad times; and no doubt it was the knowledge of this determination that led to her writing the letter we have seen, and which had such terrible results.

As Herbert Wright rode about that day, he constantly wondered what could have caused this outbreak in his cousin after all these years. 'Can Maud have played him false?' he wondered; and wondering thus the one cousin rode about in the fresh bright day, while the other lay in a drunken sleep on his bed alone.

A week had passed since the new housekeeper

had begun to reign at 'The Bushman's Rest,' and already her presence was beginning to effect a change in the whole house. Rooms that had seldom, if ever, been cleaned before, were turned out, scrubbed, brushed, and put in order. The meals presented a different appearance,—were no longer flung on the dirty tablecloth, and flung off again.

Now, though coarse, the table-linen was spotless, and the plates and dishes no longer greasy; flowers were to be seen in the vases that stood on the mantels, the windows were clean; and, in short, a wonderful change had come over the house, owing to the presence of the young girl who had so strangely come there. Nelly was not afraid of work, in it she found the only distraction from miserable thoughts; so, with the help of the one other woman on the place, the girl she met the night of her arrival, and who had proved to be a young half-caste who had taken refuge there from the persecutions of her tribe, she worked from early morning till late at night, winning golden opinions from her master. There was only one thing Nelly had stipulated for, which was to be exempt from waiting upon the bar or parlours attached to it.

Before Mrs. Burgiss left (which she did the day after Nelly's arrival), the girl had won a promise from her that she was not to be asked to serve drinks to the men either behind the bar or in the rooms. And Mrs. Burgiss had consented to her request in an off-hand manner, merely saying contemptuously, 'Oh, you'll get over that nonsense by and by; better than *you* have had to do it before now.'

The day after her arrival, during the afternoon, Paul Wright had ridden up to the house, dismounted, and had given orders to the boy who took his horse from him, to turn it into the paddock, and, to the great surprise of the whole household, he had remained there ever since drinking heavily. It was very seldom that either of the Wrights passed an hour at the 'Bushman's,' unless it was with the object of catching the coach on its way down country. For this purpose they had once or twice ordered a room for a few hours. But Burgiss knew that they were among his most bitter opponents, on account of being constant sufferers through the proximity of his house to their shearing shed, which the men often left on Saturday evening, to return heavy-eyed and incapable on Monday.

Hence his surprise at Paul's strange proceedings. At first he was inclined to think some ruse was intended to bring about the loss of his licence. But when he found that he only stayed there to drink and sleep, and sleep and drink again, he determined to encourage so good a customer, and laid himself out to do so.

When Paul wakened from the drunken stupor into which he had fallen after being placed on his bed by his cousin, it was nearly two o'clock. Herbert had not returned from his ride, and there was not a drop of spirit of any kind available; for, as we know, he had taken the precaution to pocket the key of the storeroom when he put away the remainder of the whisky. Paul woke with a burning thirst upon him, and an irresistible craving for more drink. He was like a madman ; all efforts to fight against his craving had now left him, and his one thought—the one idea that now possessed his brain—was to get more drink. The old housekeeper made and brought him a cup of tea, and with tears in her eyes begged him to drink it ; but he turned from it roughly and rudely, and demanded the key of the storeroom.

'Mr. Herbert has taken it, I think, sir,' was the reply.

'Then tell Jacky to run up my horse and saddle him at once,' was the next order ; and in less than half-an-hour she saw him stagger from the house, and, after several ineffectual attempts to mount, he finally scrambled into the saddle, and, to the horror and terror of his faithful old servant, galloped away through the bush.

'Follow him, Jacky,' she said to the black boy, 'and see that he don't come to any harm.'

Jacky did as he was instructed, not returning to the station till late in the evening, when he informed the anxious household of their master's whereabouts.

The next day Herbert rode over and endeavoured to remonstrate with his cousin, and begged of him to return home ; but to no purpose. He either could not, or would not, be stopped in his mad course now ; and very sorrowfully Herbert Wright rode home again,

O

leaving him to his fate. For the first two days he merely sat in one of the parlours by himself, calling for drink after drink, until, completely overcome, he sank into stupor, and so was conveyed to bed by Burgiss and one of his men. After a while he became violent, occasionally breaking and destroying glasses, decanters, anything, in fact, that came in his way while drunk.

Though never before brought in immediate contact with drunkenness, Nelly had heard and read a good deal about it and its fatal effects ; so it was with very great sorrow that she observed the hold it had taken of this fine young fellow. Instinct told her he was worthy of a better fate. That he was a gentleman she had heard from those in the house, even had she not discovered the fact for herself from his manner and address when sober, and therefore she all the more deplored his terrible conduct and dreadful language when under the influence of drink. Seeing him day by day falling lower and lower, becoming more imbecile and sottish every hour, she pitied him from the bottom of her tender womanly heart, and whenever circumstances threw her in his way, tried to say a word or two of warning to him. She had very soon learnt the nature of much of the business done in the house. Her attention had been drawn to several cases of what she called dishonesty—such as cheques abstracted from the pockets and swags of sleeping men. Though she had not actually seen it done, she knew it was so ; and the iniquitous charges made for a few nights' lodging, items charged for that never were ordered,—these sort of doings soon opened Nelly's eyes to the kind of house 'The Bushman's Rest' was, and made her long the more for the months to slip by till she could be free to leave. She had felt drawn to Paul Wright from the first, on account of a fancied resemblance he bore to an old friend in England whose brother had married her only sister.

Day after day passed, and still Paul remained at 'The Bushman's Rest' drinking. He was seldom sober for more than an hour or so at a time; it seemed as if he could not keep from the drink long enough to put the craving from him. One evening, when he had been about ten days at the house, she was standing leaning over the low paling fence which enclosed one side of the vegetable garden; she was at the very corner, and overshadowed by a thick vine of creepers which shut in the whole end of the verandah. It was quite dark, there being no moon, and the hour was late. Nelly had wandered out to think, for complications in her position were beginning to distress and alarm her. That very day she had been grossly insulted by a teamster who was camped within a short distance of the house; and it was not the first time such a thing had occurred, though she had not been yet a month there. The poor girl was utterly miserable, and so deeply engrossed with her own thoughts, that she did not hear footsteps on the verandah immediately above her till her attention was arrested by the following words :—

'You're too blooming soft; there's Burgiss lambing him down fine, why shouldn't you and me have our whack at him? I tell ye he's got better nor seventy notes on him. This very evening I seen Bill the driver hand 'em over when he came. And by the same token, I 'eard Bill say, "You'd best let some one keep it for yer, Mr. Wright, ye'll be losing it when ye're a bit on." But the other chap only laughed, and said something 'bout the best man could keep it.'

Nelly listened breathlessly for the continuation of the conversation; her heart was beating so loudly that she feared its being heard. After a few minutes, during which she could gather that one of the men, perhaps both, were filling their pipes, she heard the match struck, and the odour of strong tobacco was borne to her on the night air. After a few preliminary puffs, the conversation was resumed.

'What's yer dodge?' asked the man who had not yet spoken. 'I don't care about too much violence, it don't pay.'

'Whose agoin' to use violence?' said the first speaker, expectorating freely first. 'I've got a plan cut and dried. I've a bottle of sleeping stuff; it's easy to drop a few drops of that into his grog, even while ye're a-talking to him, and come back in half-an-hour to find him as quiet as a hinfant; then just whip open 'is coat, and ye'll find the notes in a inside pocket, or else in his trouser pocket, I dunno which he favours for keepin' of his cash.'

'Can't we do it without this stuff? He mightn't never wake, yer see, and that'd be arkerd for us.'

'Do without the stuff? No, we can't, it ain't safe,' was the reply. 'He's a stiff 'un in a row, and as fly as a fox even when he is drunk,—keeps his pockets buttoned, in case o' accidents. I seen him do it many a time the last week, and I heard him tellin' Bill'—

There was a long pause, as if both men were considering the matter, then at last the other said,—

'Oh, all right, mate; I'm with yer, and the sooner we get about the business the better and the quicker it'll be over. Here, where's yer sleeping stuff?—come on.' And both speakers moved away beyond hearing; but not till Nelly had gathered their full meaning, and also recognised both men. One was the bullock driver who had attempted to kiss her that morning; the other, a young fellow who had arrived to join him in the down coach the day before.

I have already said that Nelly felt a strange interest in Paul Wright, confirmed drunkard though he appeared to her. She was grateful to him for many little attentions he paid her. Whenever he was sober for an hour or two, he would usually find his way into the little parlour where Nelly sat with her work or the accounts; and though she instinctively felt that he looked upon her as no better than a superior servant, she had too much common sense to resent it, for she reasoned, what does he know of me or my history? Two days before, he had knocked a tipsy jockey off his chair at the breakfast table for addressing a rude remark to her. Was it any wonder, then, that her starving heart grasped at ever so small a kindness, even from one who appeared so depraved as our hero? For a few moments after the men had ceased speaking, Nelly waited in her secluded corner, half-frightened at her own thoughts, which urged her to protect this tipsy young man from these robbers. She crept through a hole in the fence, intending to cross the road and pass before the house, which was lighted brilliantly, for the purpose of seeing where the conspirators were. It was dark, the sky being covered with dark clouds, which portended a heavy downpour before morning, so she easily gained the opposite side of the road. Here she stood, almost too terrified to carry out her design; but a shadow on the window-blind of the room where she knew Paul Wright was either sitting or sleeping decided her, and she ran along quickly, till by stooping she could get a view under the blind—which did not quite reach to the bottom—of all that went on in the room. She saw Paul Wright's figure leaning back in his chair, his feet elevated to the table, his pipe in his mouth, his eyes closed in sleep,—apparently he was quite incapable, and in a drunken stupor. Beside him stood a bottle and a glass, the latter half full. She reached her coign of vantage just in time to see one of the men she had heard talking, in the very act of pouring some liquid from a small bottle into the tumbler beside the drunken man.

He stood close behind Paul's chair, his hand, in

which was the bottle, raised some six or eight inches above the glass. She could almost count the drops as they fell into it. Once the sleeping man stirred, and the pipe fell from his lips on to his lap. The conspirator merely closed his hand on the vial and turned round, pretending to examine the clock upon the mantel-shelf. But Paul slept on, and once more the hand was extended, and a few drops from the bottle again poured into the tumbler of spirits. At first Nelly's impulse had been to call out and surprise the man and waken the sleeper. But an instant's thought decided her to watch, and in some other way try and frustrate the designs of the two robbers, and bring them to justice. As she gazed upon the scene before her, and beheld what she supposed was poison being deliberately put for a helpless and unconscious man to take, she could hardly breathe for nervous excitement; several times she nearly betrayed her presence by an exclamation of horror, for though at the opposite side of the road to the house, she was quite near enough to be both heard and seen had she spoken or moved. But her spirit was roused now, and she resolved to save Paul Wright from the thieves he had fallen amongst. She saw the man raise the small bottle to the light to see how much there still remained in it. For a few seconds he appeared debating with himself as to whether to give more or not; then, with a glance at the sleeping man beneath him, he once more held the bottle above the glass, and poured all that was left into it. Then, to

her great relief, she saw him steal softly from the
room without awakening the sleeper, as she had at
first supposed he would.   She waited to see him join
his companion on the verandah, then very quickly
she retraced her steps, crept through the fence as
before, and regained the house just as Burgiss, half
tipsy, was staggering off to his bed, having just put all
the lights out.   She knew the two men were on the
verandah, evidently intending to wait a certain time
for the house to become quiet, and their victim under
the influence of the drug they had prepared for him.
Nelly trembled so terribly that she found herself
obliged to stand still every few steps or she would
have fallen ; she was in a pitable state of nervous
fright that Paul would waken and drink the stuff
prepared for him before she could reach him and
prevent it.   She had to wait till Burgiss had disappeared within his room before she could enter the
house, which, after the usual custom in the bush, was
left open all night ; then, very swiftly and silently, she
sped through the passage, and reached the door of
Paul Wright's sitting-room, which she opened very
softly, and, gliding in, closed as softly behind her.
The room was in total darkness, Burgiss having turned
out the lamp ; however, she knew where the glass was,
having seen it from across the road, and, reaching the
table, she now began to feel about for it.   Her heart
was beating like a sledge-hammer within her bosom,
and her hands trembled as if she had palsy.   A hidden
fear came upon her (as she failed to find the tumbler)

that Paul had drunk its contents while she had been coming to him, and in the excitement of her movements and gropings about the table the bottle was knocked over, and fell to the ground. It did not break; but the cork was knocked out, and the contents consequently flowed all over the floor, filling the room with the all-powerful odour of whisky. She stooped to pick up the bottle, and, as she rose with it in her hand, a match was hastily struck, almost in her face, and she met Paul Wright's eye fixed upon her in unfeigned half-tipsy astonishment.

'What do you want?' he asked angrily, just suppressing an oath, as he saw the intruder was a woman.

A burning blush suffused the fair face of the embarrassed girl, and she would have flown from the room, but she remembered that the fatal tumbler was not yet found. She did not know how to explain her errand; her courage had all deserted her, and she felt as if about to faint. After some little difficulty, Paul had managed to relight the lamp; but his hands shook so, that he was quite unable to place the globe on it, and after several futile efforts he desisted, letting the light flare and smoke upon the table between them. He was about to address his companion, when he stopped and glanced at the bottle, now very nearly empty. 'Not much there,' he said, 'you'll have to get me another bottle.' At that instant Nelly noticed the tumbler, and to her great relief it was still half full. Paul saw it at the same moment, and, with a nod and tipsy smile, lifted it to his lips. But the next instant tumbler and contents were both dashed out of his hand on to the floor, astonishing him past all power of speech. Though considerably muddled, he was not so tipsy as Nelly imagined ; his sleep had sobered him to a great extent, and her extraordinary onslaught brought him completely to his senses, though he could only look at her in surprise and wonder. When she met his astonished gaze, she whispered hurriedly,—

'Pray forgive my violence, sir ; but I came here purposely to prevent you drinking that glass of spirits. It was drugged. I saw that man who came by the down coach yesterday, dropping some liquid into it while you lay asleep in your chair there,' pointing to where he had been seated. 'For God's sake, Mr. Wright,' she continued, laying her hand upon his arm in her earnestness, 'don't drink any more in this house. If you *must* drink, let it be in your own home, where there is no danger of your being robbed or murdered, as there is in a disreputable house like this.'

She spoke so quickly and nervously, that the half-stupefied man could barely catch her words. He smiled at her eagerness, and asked thickly,—

'If it's so disreputable, why do you stop here, then?'

'Ah, why indeed?' was the answer; 'because I can't leave it,—because I've no money to take me away till my time is up. But you—you have nothing to prevent your leaving, save this wretched drink! Ah, Mr. Wright, do leave it and go home; you are just killing yourself, and wasting your manhood.'

For a moment or so he appeared to feel her words, and looked away as if ashamed to meet her eyes. But suddenly turning roughly upon her, he exclaimed,—

'What's it got to do with you, I'd like to know? Here, pass me that bottle, there's another nip in it.'

Nelly had her hand on the bottle all the while she was speaking. As he asked for it, and stretched out his hand to take it, she looked fixedly at him, and replied,—

'No, sir, I will not give it to you. Don't you believe what I have just been telling you, that at this moment *thieves* are only waiting till they think you sufficiently far gone to rob, perhaps murder you. Don't you understand me, or do you not believe my word?'

'Oh yes, I believe you right enough, and I'm much obliged to you for letting me know. But I must have another nip to steady me to face them,' he said, still unable directly to meet her glance.

'No, you shall not have any more drink,' she returned decidedly; 'if you do, you will not be able to grapple with those men if they do attack you. Go to your room, sir, and lock the door, that will be the best plan; and leave me to tell Mr. Burgiss to-morrow about what I saw and heard.'

'All right,' he said. 'Give me just one more nip and I'll go,—I must have it, see how I shake all over; and I am too far gone now to stop in a hurry,—just give me that drop you have in the bottle, and then I'll go off to bed quietly.' There was an anxious, wild look in his eyes, and he kept glancing over his shoulder, as if fearing an attack from some one behind him. Nelly stood considering for a while whether to give him what was still left in the bottle or not. She could hear the footsteps of the teamster and his mate, as now and then they passed the window, no doubt wondering what she was doing in their would-be victim's room. It was this sound that decided her, and very reluctantly she handed over the bottle, saying,—

'Well, here you are, sir, drink it, and then pray go to your room for the night.'

He seized the bottle and glass from the mantelpiece, and, pouring out what there was of the spirit, he drank it greedily without adding any water at all. Then, putting down the tumbler, he let her lead him towards his bedroom door. She saw him disappear within; then turning out the lamp, she closed and locked the outside door of the parlour, thus locking Paul in, and retired to her own room, having first convinced herself that the two men were still upon the verandah, waiting, no doubt, till the house was in darkness ere they visited their victim.

Next morning Nelly informed Burgiss of all she had seen and heard, and consequently the teamster and his ruffian mate were turned away from the house; nor were they seen again at 'The Bushman's Rest' for many a long day.

Signs of delirium now began to show themselves in Paul Wright, which was not very surprising, considering that for the last fortnight he had been drinking on an average between two and three bottles of spirits a day. Burgiss, who apparently was well skilled in the disease, took charge of him entirely, and Nelly, as she passed the room wherein the sick man lay, was horrified at his fearful ravings and cries of terror. One afternoon he escaped, and rushed away into the bush, under the impression that some one was pursuing to kill him. But they brought him back again, and from that day till he was considered nearly well, he was closely watched and guarded. For ten days he was very ill, and then came the long and weary convalescence, when the once strong, handsome young man emerged from his room a perfect wreck of what he had been only so short a time back. It was during these days he first began to notice that the pretty young girl, acting as servant and housekeeper in this wretched wayside public-house, was superior to any of her class whom he had come across.

And now sprang up a sincere friendship between the two. How it first began neither of them exactly remembered, but from the night Nelly had warned him of his danger from the teamster and his mate, and had actually saved him from them, Paul Wright began to feel an interest in the young girl, and when well enough to walk about he sought her society constantly, and bit by bit heard from her her sad story, and how she came to be in her present position.

There was no flirtation between them, it was

simply a case of pure friendship, and on Nelly's part pity for one who was cursed with so terrible a vice as intemperance. Her heart was very tender at all times, and more especially now that she was so lonely.

When once more the craving for drink possessed Paul, she tried to persuade him not to give way to it, using all her eloquence on behalf of his better nature. She made him the strongest beef-tea and soups, and coaxed him to take them, in the hope that they would supply the want. But in vain ; the madness was upon him, the terrible thirst for stimulant, and before it all her efforts were as grass before flame. And yet he did fight against it, tried with all his strength to resist the temptation. He would often put down the glass just as it touched his lips, and go away to his room for perhaps an hour at a time. He sent to town for all the advertised remedies against drunkenness,—so-called cures,—which he swallowed eagerly, and in the hope of casting out the devil that possessed him. Sometimes for a day or two he would fancy himself cured, then disturbing thoughts would come. Maud's fair face would rise before him, reminding him of her loss—thoughts of his dreary future without her, and without anything to live for. And in desperation to get rid of his wretched thoughts, and to forget how low he had fallen, he would rush to the bar, and before he could reason against it, would swallow glass after glass, till his brain was clouded and reason gone. At other times it would be the smell of the spirits as he passed the bar. In vain he would walk away out of the house, away into the paddock, in the fresh sweet air that should have been nectar to an unvitiated palate. Yet after a while he would find himself impelled by a force within him, and stronger than his better nature, to turn and retrace his steps, till he stood before the bar, and held the drink to his lips.

'Let it kill me,' he said, in reply to Nelly's warning that such would be his fate. 'Let it kill me, I do not care.'

'And are there not others to care, Mr. Wright? How will they feel when they hear of your terrible end?' she continued.

'There are no others to care,' he said gloomily. 'I haven't a relation in the world, or a friend either, who will care a brass farthing what becomes of me, or what death I die;' and with these words, and a sneer upon his still handsome face, he raised the glass of whisky to his lips.

But Nelly quickly placed her hand over it, and his moustache just brushed the back of her fingers. 'I care, Mr. Wright,' she said,—'I care very, very much. You are the only friend I have in all the country, the only one who has said a civil word to me since I landed in Australia.'

He laid the glass down with a strange look in his eyes, saying,—

'I daresay you wonder what makes me so reckless just now? I never used to be. They could tell you here that I never drank a glass of anything stronger than lemonade until five weeks ago. I gave it up for good and all, I thought, seven years back, when a girl at home promised to be my wife. She vowed she'd wait for me till I had a home for her. This year I meant to go and fetch her; but my cousin, a rich man, stepped in, and she has married him. She jilted me for him,—a little hop-o'-my-thumb, who wears stays, curls his hair, and is at heart the lowest little brute in creation. By Jove! if ever I do go home, I'll kick him first, and wring his wretched little neck after!'

Nelly laughed at his vehemence, as she said,—

'If he is all you say, surely he is not worth losing your temper over?'

'No, he is not, I admit,' he answered quickly. 'Nor is she either, I suppose; but it is she who has sent me to the devil this time, curse her!'

'Oh, hush, hush!' Nelly said, horrified. 'Remember, "curses, like chickens, come home to roost."'

Again he would have raised the glass of whisky to his lips, when she said gently,—

'Come, Mr. Wright, be a man, and don't give any woman the chance of boasting that you loved her so much that you couldn't live without her, or that you killed yourself for her sake. See, let me throw out that nasty stuff and bring you a glass of milk instead.'

'Indeed I won't,' he said sullenly, and drank off the spirits.

Grieved and disappointed, Nelly gathered up her

work and left the verandah, where they had been sitting together; nor did she appear again for some hours. When Paul did come across her again, her eyes were red as though she had been crying.

'You've been crying,' he said at once, in surprise. 'Has any one been bullying you?'

'No, oh no, Mr. Wright,' was the reply; 'I had a bad headache,' and she escaped from his questioning gaze.

But Paul Wright pondered it over, and wondered vaguely whether it could be on his account that those handsome eyes were swollen and red. The thought that perhaps it was the case gave him a strange quick thrill of pleasure, and in the very act of refilling his glass he paused, and the next moment flung the contents of both glass and bottle out over the verandah. Then going to find Nelly, he told her what he had done and why, and was rewarded by such a sweet smile and words of encouragement, that he began to think seriously of attempting to give up drink again for Nelly's sake. He was not at all in love with her; indeed, no thought of the kind had ever crossed his mind in relation to her. His thoughts were all about Maud, when he was sober enough to think at all; and his heart was so sore at her desertion and cruel treatment, that there was no room as yet for another.

At the same time, he was in that state when a clever woman could have caught his heart in the rebound by laying herself out to do so.

P

But Nelly Dunne was not that kind of girl; and, apart from the sorrow and regret she could not help feeling for Paul himself at times, she felt a loathing and horror of his besetting sin. Never once had it crossed her mind to engage even his attention, much less his love; and though they had drifted upon occasions into very confidential conversations, it had all been on the spur of the moment, and on her side at least had been regretted afterwards. Her only reason for allowing him to sit so much with her, and in her sitting-room, was because she hoped thus to keep him from drinking in the bar, and mixing with the rough company that frequented the place.

As may be supposed, the intimacy between the two was not allowed to go unnoticed or unremarked, and jests were made and bandied about from one to the other very freely on their account. At a house such as was 'The Bushman's Rest' they are not very particular, and often things are said—remarks passed and laughed over—which in reality are not meant, or even really believed by those who say them.

Thus remarks were made, Nelly's and Paul's actions and words watched, and meanings attached to them which neither of them ever intended or thought of. Nelly it was who heard most of this. The men 'chaffed' her, and talked at her, and in her hearing, till the poor girl was nearly mad with disgust, shame, and fear lest such things should come to Mr. Wright's ears, and shock his sense of refinement, or make him think her as vulgar and coarse-minded as those with whom she lived.

Thinking and brooding over all this, it was little wonder that she began to avoid Paul, and, when they did meet, became as stiff and cold in her manner as possible; the result being that, left to himself, thrown as it were back upon himself and his own miserable thoughts, he again gave way to drink.

When Nelly had first come to 'The Bushman's Rest,' Burgiss had taken a violent fancy to her; and, being an unprincipled, bad man, had endeavoured to make her aware of his feelings, greatly to her horror and disgust. Upon two occasions he had attempted rough familiarities with her in an apparently good-tempered manner, and each time had been pretty severely punished for his horseplay. The first time an ornament in her hair had scratched his face from eye to chin, making an ugly scar for some days. The next time a fork she held in her hand at the moment, and with which she defended herself, had pierced his arm, and made a rather bad wound. But his actual wounds were nothing to the soreness of his feelings, for the young girl hurled the bitterest terms of loathing and contempt at him. Over and over again he had returned to the charge, till Nelly was well-nigh desperate, and thought seriously of asking Bill the driver to give her a free passage down in the coach as far as the nearest town. But Mrs. Burgiss was expected home any mail day, and Nelly lived in the hope that when she returned she would either be

allowed to leave, or else her life be made more bear-
able.   Whatever Burgiss' feelings had been in the
beginning for Nelly, they had very soon turned to
bitterest hatred, though he covered it with a pleasant
face, while biding his time to pay her out for the
fancied slights she had put upon him.   For one
thing, he resented her interference with Paul's doings,
telling her plainly that it was her duty to encourage
him to drink rather than discourage him, on account
of his custom.   One day he said to her, 'What
business have you to keep telling him to go home?
you ought to make yourself pleasant enough instead,
to keep him dangling after you.   The more he drinks,
and the longer he's here, the better for me.   And I
pay you to do my business; and part of it is to draw
fellows to the house, not to send them away.   Now,
mind that, Miss Slyboots, or I may have to make
yer.'

Poor Nelly had felt humiliated enough before, but
when she was actually told that she was expected to
attract men to the house to drink and spend money,
her feelings were very much outraged, and, had she
been able to get away at all, or even had sufficient
money to take her to the next town, she would have
gone in spite of her agreement.   But, alas! she had
only a few shillings in the world, and Bill, who
might have helped her, was away taking another
driver's place for a month or so.   No, she was
helpless, and no one knew it better than Burgiss.

Two or three nights after the above incidents,

Nelly went to bed earlier than usual, with a bad headache. She lay awake thinking for some time, but finally dropped off to sleep, and was suddenly awakened by the *feeling*, more than the sound, of some one moving in her room. She sat up in the bed and asked, 'Is that you, Kitty?' thinking that possibly the half-caste girl had come in to see how she was, as she often did when Nelly was not well. But there was no reply; and, after she had twice put the question, she concluded that she was mistaken, or that possibly a cat in the stable below her room had caused the sound, and she lay down again. But she had hardly dozed off, when once more awakened, this time by what sounded suspiciously like a stealthy footstep on her floor, and she also fancied she could hear some one breathing close to her. Terrified now, and trembling in every limb, she stretched out her hand for the matches, which as usual she had left on the corner of the box-table within her reach. She secured them, and was just about to strike a light, when her hand was grasped and held as in a vice, while a voice hissed out the words, 'Screech, and I'll put a knife into you.'

Utterly regardless of the terrible threat, she gave two or three piercing shrieks for help, which very promptly brought Paul Wright to her assistance. It happened that Paul, who, as usual, had been drinking heavily all day, towards night had fallen into a sound sleep, from which he wakened sober, or nearly so; and, beginning to think about himself, and all Nelly had impressed upon him as to the probable result of his course of conduct, he suddenly asked himself if there was nothing he could live for? He was conscious that his feelings had undergone a change with regard to the young housekeeper within the last three days. Accidentally he had overheard part of a conversation between her and Burgiss, and her emphatic reply to the effect that she would never cease her efforts to prevent him drinking so long as she had breath to speak, had touched a chord in the drunkard's heart, and made him wonder how it was this girl took such an interest in him, and why he could not repay her better than he did.

Burgiss had said to her sneeringly, ' If yer think he's after yer to marry yer, yer can put the notion out o' yer head. He'd sooner cut his throat than marry a girl out o' *this* house, or any other o' the gents either,—so there!' And Nelly had replied bitterly, ' I never had such a thought, and you have no right to say I had. Do you think I don't know that no honest man, gentle or simple, would dream of offering marriage to a girl who has lived in *this* house? Do you think I don't feel the indignity of living beneath this roof, and that it will cling to me always? Yes, you may well say no man would ever marry a girl from here,—and Mr. Wright least of all. But as I am here, I'll try and do some good. I'll save him from your toils, see if I don't. Let me once see you trying to drug his drink again, as you did the other night, and I'll tell him there and then. I can't always save him from you, but I'll give him the means of saving himself by telling him.'

Paul had been lying half-asleep in one of the parlours when this conversation began, but he was very wide-awake before the end, and was just meditating discovering himself, when some one entered the room where the speakers were, and so put an end to it.

It had taken place in the afternoon, and all night Paul lay awake thinking over it, and also thinking a great deal about Nelly, and what she had said both to and of him. Did she care at all for him, or whether he lived or died? How would it be if he were to marry her? He knew her to be a good, honest girl, far superior to most of the girls he had met in the bush. He wanted an object in life; he firmly believed that if he had one he would reform. Nelly was miserable in this house; why should they not marry and be a mutual help to each other? Many men and women had come together from more ignoble causes. He took a sudden resolve to follow Nelly's advice, and leave 'The Bushman's Rest' at once, late as it was. Yes, he would 'sober up,' and then if Nelly would marry him he would be grateful and do all he could to make her happy.

He knew there was a horse in the small paddock adjoining the house, one his cousin had led over that morning, in the hope that Paul would be induced to come home with him on his return from a neighbouring station, where he was going on business. Fearing to let his good resolution cool, he started at once for the stable to procure a halter with which to catch the horse, and it was just as he reached the gate leading to the stables that Nelly's terrified scream for help fell upon his ears. He had to stand still and listen before he could be sure from where the sound came, or in which direction he should turn to render help. As soon as he realised that it was from the room over the stables, he was not long in making his way there. He stumbled up the narrow staircase or ladder, and, when his foot was on the last step, he was almost thrown back by a man rushing from the room past him. He tried to stop him, but in saving himself from being thrown to the bottom, the other wrenched himself out of his grasp and fled away in the dark.

When he reached the room and struck a match, he was horrified to find Nelly lying in the middle of the floor in a dead faint. For a second or two he gazed at her and around him in bewildered astonishment.

'What was the meaning of it all?' he asked himself. 'Was it a bad dream, or was he still under the influence of drink?' The squalid room, the mean bed, the young girl (whom he had really believed to be good and pure), and the strange man rushing away like a thief or worse. 'What did it mean? Was he wronging her in his thoughts? Was she all he had fancied her, and was this man who had rushed past him in the darkness a scoundrel, a destroyer?' Thus wondering, he stooped down and gently raised the senseless girl in his arms and laid her on the bed, lightly throwing over her its mean and scanty coverings. Then he found some water and bathed her head, dipping his handkerchief into the tumbler. The only evidence of ill-usage apparent was a dark bruise on the left temple. While thus occupied, he could not help noticing the extreme purity of the young girl's complexion, and the sad curves of the drooping mouth, which could be firm and stern enough in denunciation of evil. A strange tenderness and great pity came over the dissipated man for the lonely young girl, so defenceless in this bush public-house. He thought of her as he had seen her so often, treating with silent contempt the jests and jokes of the ribald men who frequented the house, and who seemed to look upon her as fair game for their low, coarse wit. Now that he was sober he loathed himself, and the hot blood came to his face as he remembered the state of disgusting intoxication in which Nelly had so often seen him; he felt utterly contemptible before this girl, whom he intuitively knew to be good and pure, and whose influence had constantly been used to save him from himself. All her words and advice came back to him with tenfold force, and there and then he registered a silent vow to try and deserve her good opinion in future. In the meantime the tired soul of poor Nelly came slowly back to its earthly tenement. With a soft little sigh she opened her bewildered eyes, to gaze in horror and amazement on the face of the man for whom she was conscious of feeling more than ordinary regard.

'Oh,' she exclaimed, with a great disappointment sweeping over her fair face, 'was it you? Oh, Mr. Wright, what made you come here? What have I done that you should think'—

'For God's sake, Nelly,' he interrupted, 'don't so mistake me; I'd as soon think of insulting my own sister as you. I heard you scream as I was coming to the stable for a halter to catch my horse, for I had made up my mind to follow your advice and to clear out of this cursed place, and I came to your assistance, to find you insensible on the floor, so I lifted you on to the bed; that's the true explanation of my presence here. And now, as you are all right again, tell me if you can what happened, and who the scoundrel was, do you think, whom I met rushing from the room? I'll go and settle with him.'

She covered her face with her hands and tried to think; her head felt sore and stupid; but after a few minutes she remembered what had taken place, and in a few hurried words told Paul. Then quite assured that she was better, and not likely to faint again, he was on the point of leaving the room, when the door was pushed back, and the angry, evil-looking face of Burgiss appeared.

'What the d—— is the meaning of this row?' he asked; but without waiting for any reply he turned to the girl with a diabolical sneer, saying, 'O ho! my lady; so after all ye're no better than the rest o' 'em, with all yer fine airs.'

Hardly were the words out of his mouth before

Paul Wright sprang upon him; and doubtless the brute would have fared badly, but suddenly the thought of the defenceless girl, in whose room they were, made him withhold the blow, and say to Burgiss, 'If you have an ounce of manhood in you, remember where we are, and come away out of this—we'll have it out below.' Then he turned to leave the room; but before he was half down the ladder Nelly was beside him, her hand firmly grasping his arm.

'Mr. Wright, oh, sir, don't fight him,' she begged. 'He is a bad, bad man, and will kill you,—I know he will,' and she burst into tears.

'Don't be foolish, Nelly,' he said to her. 'Go back to your bed, and try and get some sleep after this excitement. You'll have to leave here in the morning, for you can't possibly stay on after all this; so, like a good girl, go and rest, and leave it all to me. As I've got you into the row, I'll see you through it.'

'But you won't fight him, sir,—promise me you won't?' she begged again.

Paul stood thinking for a minute, then he said, 'Well, no, I won't fight him, if that will satisfy you; now, go back and get some rest before daylight.'

And then she went, though only half satisfied.

Burgiss was that pitiful thing, a bully; and when he saw that Paul Wright was determined to fight, he tried to laugh the whole matter off as a practical joke. But Paul was thoroughly angry—the excitement had done him good, and made a man of him again. When he saw that Burgiss was not willing to fight him, he strode away through the yard to his room, returning in a few minutes with the cutting whip he usually carried when not out on the run.

Burgiss was standing in the centre of a group of men, teamsters, bushmen, and loafers, who had been awakened by the noise, explaining to them the reason of it all, or rather he was giving his own version of the scene, which I may say was hardly within miles of the true one. As Paul Wright approached they did not see him, and he had time to hear one or two expressions uncomplimentary to Nelly fall from Burgiss' lips before he was observed. Directly he came among them the men fell back, and one or two of them slunk away into the stable shamed ; but Burgiss stood his ground till he noticed the whip in his opponent's hand, and then with one spring he made for the ladder to Nelly's room, doubtless intending to protect himself in her presence. But Paul was too quick for him, and caught him just as his foot was on the last step. He dragged him down and out into the yard, where he administered to him as sound a thrashing as only the arm of an angry man can ; then he flung him into a corner on to a heap of broken bottles, where the pitiful cur lay groaning and crying till some of his hired creatures carried him away to his bed.

Paul returned to his own room, and vainly racked his brains trying to think of a way to help poor Nelly out of her present difficulty. Suddenly he remembered a young couple who were living on a selection some

miles the other side of the station, and he began to
wonder whether they might not be persuaded to give
the helpless girl shelter until such time as she could
obtain another situation, for he knew there could be
no question of her stopping at ' The Bushman's Rest '
after what had taken place. He would go and see
these people, and ask them as a personal favour to
himself to take Nelly for a while. Having made up
his mind, he drew out his note-book and wrote upon
one page,—

' I go to try and find a new home for you with
friends ; will be back by dinner time, if possible.
Trust me, and believe me your friend,

' PAUL WRIGHT.'

He tore out the page, folded it in half, and then
once more started out to catch his horse. As he had
to go to the stable for his bridle, he went up the ladder
to Nelly's room and pushed his note underneath the
door ; then, satisfied that she would not think he had
deserted her in her trouble, he went down the paddock,
caught and saddled his horse, and was soon galloping
away through the sweet crisp morning air towards his
own home.

In the meantime poor Nelly was suffering all the
pangs of fear for Paul's safety, and reproaching herself
for being the cause of the trouble. It was quite
beyond her power to take rest, she did not even try,
so, huddling on her clothes, she wrapped a waterproof
round her and sat down by the open window (for it

had only a wooden shutter) to think.   She had hardly
taken this position when she heard Paul's voice, the
rush up to her door, and then the abject cries of the
pitiful coward as he received the beating he so richly
deserved.   As she listened to the merciless blows that
fell from Paul's strong arm, she found it in her heart
to pity the unfortunate creature though he so richly
deserved it.   It was nearly an hour after this that
she again heard steps upon the ladder leading to her
room, and just as she had begun to prepare herself for
some further development of her employer's spite, she
saw the slip of white paper pushed under the door,
and when the footsteps had once more died away she
secured it, and read the message Paul had sent to
reassure her in her loneliness.   And it had the effect
of comforting her.   She felt, after reading those few
words, that he was, and really meant to be, her friend ;
and with a sigh of relief she threw herself upon her
bed and sobbed herself to sleep.

The people whom Paul Wright purposed appealing
to on Nelly's behalf were a young couple named
Carrington, living on a small selection some four or
five miles from Morven Plains.   They were people
who had at one time been very well to do.   Mrs.
Carrington's father was a Presbyterian minister,
who periodically went round the different stations
holding services, performing christenings, marriages,
burials, etc.   He was almost entirely supported by
the squatters and selectors in the district, though, as
a matter of fact, he had a church and manse in one of

the neighbouring towns. Of late years, however, the old man had elected to live with his daughter and her husband almost entirely, giving up his manse to a younger man. He was not dependent upon his people ; on the contrary, he was in receipt of an income from property at home of £200 a year. His name was Garvie, and a very popular, good old man he was, while the Carringtons were no less popular. The Wrights had known Mr. Garvie ever since they had been in the district, and since the Carringtons had come to live so close to them a great intimacy had sprung up between the two families. Paul Wright was a special favourite with Mrs. Carrington, to whom he had confided all his love story ; and when she had heard from Herbert about his unaccountable outbreak, her woman's instinct had led her to the true solution of the mystery.

The Carringtons were just sitting down to their breakfast when Paul rode up to the house.

'You are just in time for breakfast, Mr. Wright,' was Mrs. Carrington's greeting as she shook hands with him in the passage between the house and the kitchen. 'Go to George's room and get a wash—I think you'll find him there too ;' and the kindly little lady bustled away to lay a plate and get a cup and saucer for the unexpected guest.

Paul did as desired, hoping for an opportunity at breakfast to introduce the subject of his early visit.

Mr. Carrington and Mr. Garvie were no less kind in their welcome than Mrs. Carrington,—all strove to

do himhonour, and to ignore his late outburst. Indeed,
he began to ponder whether they knew of it or not,
and wondered if he would have to give an account of
his own doings as a reason for knowing all about
Nelly. However, when breakfast was over, Mr.
Carrington was called away, and Mr. Garvie had
a letter to write which he wished Paul to post, so
finally Paul found himself alone with his hostess, and
free to tell his story. And this he did, at first with
many haltings and breaks; but when he came to the
events of the night before, his words flew glibly
enough, and he became quite excited.

'Then what is it you want me to do?' she asked,
when he had finished his strange story.

'Just what your own kind heart dictates,' was his
reply. 'It is quite certain the girl cannot stop where
she is after what has happened, and I, of course, would
do more harm than good by appearing at all in the
matter except through some woman.'

'Yes, I understand the position,' Mrs. Carrington
said thoughtfully. 'And you say she is, you think, a
lady by birth?'

'Yes, I am certain of it,' Paul Wright replied
impulsively.

'Well, I must see George; and if he says yes, I will
go back at once with you and see her, and offer her an
asylum here.'

'Oh, you *are* good, Mrs. Carrington!' Paul said,
grasping her hand warmly. 'I shall be so grateful,
for I feel as if it were almost my fault.'

'Oh, I don't see that exactly,' was Mrs. Carrington's reply; 'for, of course, you only did as any man worthy of the name would have done in going to her relief. However, here comes George—I will go and see what he says; and you can tell one of the boys to run up the buggy horses, for I know George will say *go.*'

But Mr. Carrington was not so willing to allow his wife to pay a visit to 'The Bushman's Rest,' or to accept any one from there as an inmate of their home even in the capacity of a servant. Like every other man in the district, he had heard of the place and its lawless character, and therefore was very doubtful about any one who had been, or was, an inmate of the house. However, the matter was decided by old Mr. Garvie, who said that he would go back with Paul and George, and if Nelly appeared all that he represented, they would offer her a home, and bring her back with them.

By eight o'clock that night Nelly was an inmate of Mrs. Carrington's little home, having favourably impressed the old minister as well as his son-in-law, George Carrington, who had gone to 'The Bushman's Rest' quite prepared to find her the very reverse of what she appeared.

And now began a very happy time for Nelly Dunne. Mrs. Carrington was her firm friend; the two women had been drawn towards each other by many similar tastes. Nelly sketched well, so did Mrs. Carrington, so they often took their materials and drove out together to different spots about the station for the purpose of

sketching. Then Nelly played and sang well and
brilliantly, accomplishments her hostess was not
perfect in ; so Nelly undertook to give her lessons
while she was there, for she had at once put an
advertisement into the Sydney papers for a situation
as governess. And all the time Paul Wright used to
visit the selection on an average four times a week, on
the pretence of helping Mr. Carrington with some
fencing he was doing. Several times the ladies had
been to Morven Plains to spend a day, or to sketch
some specially interesting piece of scenery.   Mrs.
Carrington saw plainly what his motive was in coming
so often ; but she was too wise to speak to Nelly about
it, though she most honestly hoped that a match would
result between the two.

One afternoon when the mail-bag arrived there was
a letter for Miss Dunne from a lady near Sydney, who
wanted a governess and companion to travel with her
and two little girls.   It appeared to be a most suitable
situation, the very thing to suit Nelly ; but though ad-
mitting all this, Mrs. Carrington was loath to let her
send a reply until Paul Wright had heard of it.   So,
having persuaded her to wait till next mail-day, Mrs.
Carrington wrote and told Paul Wright that Miss
Dunne had found a situation, and would be leaving
them very shortly, unless he could manage to prevent it.
And she wound up by advising him to come over on
the following day and take Nelly for a last ride,—a
hint he was quite willing to accept.

Accordingly next morning he rode over just at

lunch-time, and during the meal asked the ladies if they would go for a ride. Nelly never had ridden alone with Paul Wright, and Mrs. Carrington guessed she would not do so now, unless she contrived in such a way that she could not avoid it. So she at once said, 'Oh yes, they could go, she thought;' and Nelly expressed her willingness also. But when the horses were led up saddled and ready, and Nelly had even mounted, Mrs. Carrington came on to the verandah in her morning gown, looking the picture of (pretended) misery, and declaring that she had the most excruciating faceache, and could not possibly go for the ride.

'But you can go, Nelly; it need not make any difference to you, and particularly as this may be your last ride, dear.'

'Oh no, I'd rather not go,' Nelly began hurriedly, and preparing to dismount from her saddle, when Paul Wright came up to her and whispered, 'Why will you not go, Nelly? You may trust yourself to my escort, believe me,' in such an earnest tone, that she could not refuse him.

They rode along for three or four miles conversing on indifferent subjects,—Paul fearing, yet anxious to make the request that was trembling on his lips, and Nelly wondered why he was so unusually excited; for, though conscious that she loved him, she had never once allowed herself to dream of a future in which Paul Wright should have a part. They had both been silent for some moments, when suddenly Nelly said,—

'Did you hear, Mr. Wright, that I have at last the prospect of getting a situation?'

'Yes, Mrs. Carrington told me something about it, but I trust it is not true, Nelly. Surely you are not so tired of us all that you want to run away?'

'No, no; that is not the question at all. I must work and earn my living, Mr. Wright. I cannot afford to live on in idleness.'

For several moments Paul Wright made no reply, and they rode on in silence. He was debating in his own mind whether he had any right to ask this girl to share his life when he had so little confidence in himself. At last he said,—

'Nelly, you know the worst of me—you have seen me make a beast of myself, and you know my story. Yet, in spite of it all, will you marry me? Don't answer in a hurry, dear. I believe I could make you happy; and more than that, I feel quite confident that your influence could and would keep me straight. I am not such a bad fellow at heart. I am weak, I suppose, but for any one I loved I could do anything. And, Nelly dear, I do love you. I know what you will say—that it is not so long since I told you I loved some one else; that is true enough, but since I have known you that is altered. I could at this very moment find it in my heart to write and thank Maud for having thrown me over. You want a home, Nelly, and I want a wife; say you'll marry me, and continue the good work you have begun.'

'No, Mr. Wright,' Nelly replied. 'You have

made a mistake; it is only pity you feel for me, and by and by, when I am away, you will be glad that I did not take you at your word.'

He turned from her impatiently, a frown upon his face. ' Nelly, do you hate me ? ' he asked.

' Indeed, no,' she replied.

' Do you like me a little bit, then ? ' he continued.

' Yes, oh yes; better than any one in this '— She had spoken impulsively, and was going to say ' in the world,' but she suddenly stopped and blushed.

' Go on,' he said. ' What were you going to say—in the colony, was it ? Then there is some fellow in the old country, is there ? ' and he asked the question eagerly.

' I love no one in the old country.'

' Then were you going to say you liked me better than any one in the world ? ' He saw by her face that he had guessed aright, and he drew closer to her as he asked,—

' Nelly, can't you make liking become loving ? Couldn't you try to love me, Nelly ? '

Firmly believing that he only asked her to marry him under a mistaken idea that he had injured her, and so should thus make reparation, Nelly was on the point of answering in the negative; but a glance at his face, so near her own, and something in his eyes, prevented the untruth passing her lips; she kept silence.

' Nelly, I am waiting. I asked you if you could love me if you tried. Now give me an answer, Nelly ;

and be sure you don't tell me an untruth, or I shall
know it by your face. I am awfully vain, and I believe
at this moment that you love me. Now, for the third
time, Nelly, do you, or do you not?'

Still no reply came, and a spirit of mischief began
to twinkle in Paul Wright's brown eyes.

'Well, silence gives consent all the world over,
Nelly. Am I to draw my own conclusions from your
silence?'

'No, sir,' she said at last.

'What does "No, sir," mean—that you don't love
me? Oh, then I shall go back at once to 'The Bushman's Rest,' and drown my disappointment in another
month's spree. I'm a weak-minded fellow, and I can't
stand being disappointed,' and he turned his horse
round as if intending to carry out his threat. Nelly
put out her hand in sudden alarm, for she knew his
weakness, or thought she did.

'Oh, sir, you will not go? Please do not.'

'Well, will you love me, Nelly?' he asked, taking
her outstretched hand and looking into her troubled
face.

'I daren't, Mr. Wright,' she said, her voice trembling with agitation. 'What would your people say
if you married me?'

'Oh, that's beside the question altogether,' he
replied quickly. 'My people have nothing whatever
to do with it. I'm not in leading-strings, Nelly, though
I'll willingly be led by you if you will promise to
become my wife.'

She shook her head sadly, saying, 'It is all so sudden, sir ; and I know you are only making me an offer because you think my character has suffered through the affair at 'The Bushman's Rest.' No, Mr. Wright, I cannot marry you, but I am deeply grateful for your offer.'

'Oh, very well, then, there is no more to be said. You will be all right, Miss Dunne, if you follow this cattle track ; it will take you right up to the Carringtons' yards, and from there you will see the house.' With these words he made her an elaborate bow, and rode away back along the track they had come. For some minutes Nelly sat still on her horse, fully persuaded that Paul was playing with her, and would come back in a few minutes ; but when she turned her head he was out of sight, and she could hear the regular canter of his horse through the bush at some distance. Fully alive to her position, and terrified that he really meant to carry out his threat and leave her alone in the bush, she began to cry, and, slipping from her saddle, sat down on a tree-stump in a state of dejection not free from alarm. Her horse was restive, and kept neighing after his companion, and Nelly was a very timid horsewoman as yet.

She did love Paul Wright with all the strength of her young heart, but feared lest he were asking her to marry him from a mere sense of duty. Some weeks previously, before he had ever thought of her save as the barmaid of 'The Bushman's Rest,' Paul had said to her in fun,—

'You had better marry me, Nelly. Here we are, you homeless and alone in the world, and I just jilted : let's make a match of it, and astonish the natives !'

He had spoken the words in pure jest, just as many a man talks to a girl whom he looks on as outside the possibility of his marrying. At the same time, had Nelly taken him at his word there and then, he would most likely have carried out his offer, for he was madly reckless at that time, and ripe for any folly. Paul had forgotten the words ten minutes after he uttered them, but not so Nelly ; and now when he had said them again *un*influenced by drink, they had come back to her very vividly, and rankled in her mind. He had been unfortunate in alluding to her unprotected and friendless condition when making his offer, consequently she had jumped to the conclusion that he saw no other way of protecting her good name than by offering her his own. And she was too proud to suffer him to sacrifice himself on her account, though she knew quite well that the whole story of that night's incidents at 'The Bushman's Rest ' was known and talked about throughout the entire district.

So she sat on the log crying quietly, wishing that she had dared to be happy and accept Paul's love, if he really did love her, as he said he did. She glanced up to see if he was returning, for that he meant really to go away and leave her alone she could hardly believe. But there was no sign of him. Tearfully she sat watching her horse as he clipped

the tufts of long grass close by, till after a time the
stillness of the afternoon began to oppress her ; there
seemed to be nothing moving save the insect world
around her. She was utterly alone, and forthwith
began to get frightened, being indeed a most arrant
little coward in the bush, with no more knowledge
of tracks or roads than a baby. What would happen
to her if Paul never came back ? she wondered would
she be able to find the Carringtons' selection ; and if
she did, what story could she tell to them to account
for Paul leaving her ? Oh! it was terrible. She stood
up and looked round ; nothing was to be seen or heard
save the birds and bees as they flew here and there.
Was she really and truly alone ? Where were the
wild blacks she had heard so much about in the old
country ? were they indeed watching and spying upon
her from behind the huge gum trees which grew on
all sides ? Would they wait till night and then fall
upon her and kill her ? She was fast losing her
head and becoming hysterical, from pure nervousness
and fright, as her horse started and snorted suddenly,
frightened by the falling of a small branch, which
some bird had dislodged above him. It frightened
Nelly also—it was the last straw. She all at once
realised that she was left alone to die there in that
horrible bush, to be eaten by blacks and wild dogs,
and the poor half-crazy girl threw herself down upon
the grass in an agony of real terror and grief.

'Oh, Paul, Paul!' she cried, 'how could you be so
cruel, and I do love you so—oh, so dearly!'

'Why didn't you say so, then,' replied a voice at her side; and, starting up, she found herself clasped in Paul's arms, with no prospect of escape until she had admitted all, and replied to all his questions to his entire satisfaction.

He had ridden away out of sight, then turned, dismounted, and come back behind her.

'Then you do love me, Nelly?' he inquired for the twentieth time, holding her close to him. 'And you will marry me, dearest?'

'I did not say so,' she returned softly.

'But you will say so now—in fact you must, before I will let you go; and as we can't stand in this position all day, however amusing it may be for the jackasses, and as also we are some miles from home, I suggest that the sooner you say it the better. Come, let me hear you say, "Paul, I do love you, and I will marry you."'

But Nelly was still silent.

Paul waited several minutes for her answer, but when it did not come, he said,—

'Nelly, you think I want to marry you because of that night's work at the "Rest;" but, darling, you are wrong; though I tell you plainly, the thought did cross my mind that no one would dare to talk about you as my wife, and I even decided to offer myself to you without delay on that account. But, dearest, I did not do this, and I can honestly and truly say that I love you for your own sweet sake. I believe I loved you before that affair, for I really did value your good

opinion ; and I had it in my mind to clear away from
" The Bushman's Rest," get square, and then come and
see you again. I had, really, though doubtless you
find it hard to believe me. Nelly, I may not be a very
good fellow, but you will be able to keep me straight.
I am not altogether bad ; I have no real love for drink.
It is seven years and more since I had a turn like this,
and if you'll only marry me, I'll sign the pledge,
make any promise you like, and I'll not touch one
drop of liquor again as long as I live.'

He read her answer in her eyes, and in that instant
gathered her slight form to his breast ; and poor Nelly
was sobbing softly, very happy, yet half afraid of
what she had done. She did at last believe that Paul
loved her, and had she followed the dictates of her
heart she would have given in at once ; but she
could not reconcile it to her conscience to let him—
a man of good birth and good position—marry her,
as it seemed, all in a hurry, as if to save her
reputation.

'Then I am *not* to go to the dogs, Nelly ?' Paul
asked, smiling into the flushed face of the girl he loved.
'You will take me, faults and all, Nelly, knowing of
what has been my besetting sin ?'

The answer came at last, bravely spoken, 'Yes, if
you wish it so much, and really do love me.'

With a glad cry he bent his head and pressed his
first kiss upon her pure lips ; and it was no disgrace to
his manhood that there were tears in his eyes as he
did so.

'And you won't think the less of me for having been at that place?' she asked anxiously.

'The less of you, my own darling! I think the more of you for coming through the ordeal so grandly. I knew more of your trials than you ever told me, even though I was then so much under the influence of drink.'

'One kiss of your own free giving, Nelly?'

She raised her ripe red lips to meet his, and for several seconds there was a silence between them, more eloquent than any words that could have been spoken.

The sun had set when Nelly and Paul returned to the Carringtons'; and while the latter changed her habit, Paul told his story to the kindly little woman who had been such a good friend to the poor and lonely girl, and who now rejoiced at the good fortune that had befallen her.

At first Herbert Wright was very angry, and averse to the match; for, like many others, he looked upon Nelly as merely a barmaid, completely overlooking the fact of her being of gentle birth. However, after hearing the whole story, he was forced to admit that perhaps it was not such a very unwise step for Paul to take, now Maud had thrown him over. He felt convinced that unless some other powerful interest could be brought into his life, Paul would give way to drink, and eventually go to the bad completely. This was a state of affairs to be avoided for all their sakes, and greatly for his own (Herbert's), as it was Paul who managed the station, and through whose unflagging industry, perseverance, and determination they had, despite bad seasons, reached their present condition of prosperity. So Herbert was inclined favourably to consider any marriage of his cousin's under these circumstances. And, after all, he said to himself, 'She is very presentable, quite as much so as most of the girls one meets.'

Months afterwards, Herbert Wright admitted that his cousin had done well and wisely in marrying the girl he did, and eventually Nelly had no stauncher friend in the colonies than her husband's cousin.

It was just five weeks from the day she left 'The Bushman's Rest' when Nelly and Paul stood together before old Mr. Garvie, the minister, to be made man and wife. No sister could have been kinder than Mrs. Carrington proved to the friendless girl. It was she who stood beside her, and encouraged her with brave words and sympathy during the most solemn moment of her life, when she gave herself before God to a man of whom she knew little or nothing, save that he was cursed with the terrible vice of intemperance.

'And was it a happy marriage?' I can reply in all truth, 'Yes, it was; not a more united or more affectionate couple exist than Paul Wright and his wife.'

Many years have passed since these incidents took place. Paul Wright is a rich man now; and he has kept to his promise faithfully, never once has he touched spirits since he married.

There are still a few ill-natured and envious people

who point to pretty Mrs. Wright, and whisper, 'She was a barmaid, you know, when he married her, —and at a dreadfully low public-house, too. Such a pity, my dear!'

But these very people are none the less friendly when they meet Nelly, and never refuse an invitation to the Wrights' hospitable home. 'The Bushman's Rest' exists now under a new name, having become so notorious after Nelly's departure that the licence was taken away, and Burgiss had to leave that part of the country. It was granted again to a new proprietor, and is a respectable house under the present management.

THE STORY OF A PHOTOGRAPH.

THE STORY OF A PHOTOGRAPH.

THERE are not many more beautiful scenes in the world than that presented by Studley Park, near Richmond, in Victoria. I do not mean now, when it is probably fenced in and preserved as a public promenade or recreation ground, but twenty years ago, when it was untouched, fresh as it came from the hand of nature, without any of those so-called 'improvements' which, if they make it a better carriage-drive or smoother walk, yet take away that weirdness and wildness which are so characteristic of Australian scenery. In those days a man travelling in the bush might well fancy his own eyes were the first white man's to gaze on some romantic scene, or indulge the fancy, dear to the poetical spirit ever innate in the human breast, that he stood face to face with untouched nature ; now, even Australia is tolerably well known from coast to coast, and the ashes of the fires, or scorched hollow of the tree where the explorer boiled his billy and baked his damper, may be seen scattered far and wide.

Twenty years ago Studley Park was a wild romantic spot, whose glades the revelry of picnic and pleasure parties only invaded during the intense heat of Christmas. The tall white gums, with shattered untidy bark rattling in the fierce hot wind, presided like huge genii over the scene. On the hills and in the valleys the sweet-scented wattle threw its yellow tassels to the breeze, and beneath it blue star-shaped wild flowers—cyclamen, sundew, purple sarsaparilla, and the scarlet pea—peeped up from the short, crisp grass, where the children looked for the white, sweet manna in the season when it fell. In the distance, the Yarra Yarra wound its devious way around the bases of the hills, and stumbled and brawled fiercely over the stony falls by Dwight's Mills. A very un-English scene, indeed, yet one to remember and look back upon with affection if it at all belong to the country one calls 'home.'

Beneath these straggling, rattling gums (the leaves did not whisper together gently like English leaves, but hustled each other noisily), three young people were wandering about the time of which I write. One was a tall fair girl of apparently eighteen years of age, in whom it was easy to see the young man was deeply interested ; the other girl was one of those quick, energetic personages of whom it may be safely predicted that they will cut some pathway for themselves through the thorny thickets of the world ; short and strong, with dark curling hair, she formed a complete contrast to her friend who rose up languid and lily-like beside her. All three seemed wrapped in admiring the extreme beauty of the sunset which dyed the rippling waters beneath their feet in the colours of the dying dolphin, gilded the brown leaves of the gum trees with a tinge of red, stretched across the grass like a flood of fire, and crowned the sombre she-oaks with a blaze of glory. Awakening from his reverie, the youth was the first to speak, and he addressed her who resembled a lily.

'And now, Caroline, that we are *really* engaged, I suppose I may ask you for your photograph—that one of which the photographer has unhappily broken the negative ? At least I shall have your image with me, even if I cannot have you always just yet.'

'Yes, John,' was the reply, 'I will give it you when we get home. It is the only one I have ever had taken.'

'I shall value it more highly than anything else I possess, dearest,' he returned. 'And if Alma here ever becomes the great painter she hopes to be, after her voyage to England, and her studies in Rome, she shall paint me a still more beautiful portrait of you.'

'So I will,' said the girl addressed as Alma ; 'and as I have known Carrie so intimately all our lives, I think I should have the greatest chance of succeeding with her. And that puts me in mind to tell you that I am going to take my passage to England in the *Marco Polo,* which sails in a month from now. All difficulties are overcome, and I will go and try to make a name for myself, and be a credit to Victoria.'

'None will wish you greater success than we shall, Alma,' said the lovers, almost in one breath.

'I know it,' she said. 'Meanwhile I shall think of you both in your happy bush home, and sometimes, *sometimes* in the midst of all the art treasures of Rome, almost wish to be once more with you.'

These three never met again.

. . . .

A long white dusty road through the bush, bordered with the most uncompromising of three-railed fences ; in the distance, round you everywhere, an interminable plain, covered with short scorched grass ; overhead the clear Australian sky palpitating with heat, which seems so far off because there is no mist to give the effect of distance, beneath which nature appears to lie breathless, overcome. Fierce blasts of the fiery north wind speed across the plain, and when they come to the road arouse thick clouds of white dust, which either rush along in dense masses, or curl round and round in a kind of vortex, carrying dead leaves high in the air, as if they were enjoying a witches' dance. The intense, overpowering solitude is only broken by the harsh cries of the laughing jackass, who seems to have retired here from the world to chuckle over its mistakes and follies. But stay ! there is something else alive : in the dry grass beside the road a huge snake is curled, sometimes wriggling comfortably in its sleep, and so catching

gleams of light on its shining skin which betray its
whereabouts. A traveller on horseback, his clothes
white as a miller's from the eternal dust, now comes
slowly into view ; seeing the snake, which rises on end
at the noise of the horse's hoofs, with true bushman's
instinct, before it has time to escape, he hits it a heavy
blow with his loaded stock-whip—so heavy, that it
falls to the ground apparently to rise no more. Our
traveller (for it was no other than the John of the
former part of our story, now burnt brown by the sun,
and 'bearded like a pard') dismounted from his horse,
and, after examining the reptile, which was between
five and six feet in length, curiously for a while, took
it up, and saying to himself, ' I should like to have a
specimen of this species,' tied it in a double knot to
his stirrup-iron.

John Walton resumed his journey in the same slow
and melancholy fashion, but before long became
aware that the snake, far from being dead, had reared
itself up and was about to make a dart at his left
thigh ; to raise his whip and strike it again as hard as
he could, was but the work of an instant, and the
creature hung down as lifeless as before. Rather
unnerved at his narrow escape, he looked round for
some roadside shanty or inn where he might obtain
a little refreshment, and soon saw the blue smoke of
what proved to be a shepherd's log hut, curling up
among some gum trees. Here he was speedily made
welcome, and invited, with true Australian hospitality,
to share the mutton, damper, and tea just prepared

for the evening meal; while the snake, which he still intended preserving, was untied from the stirrup and thrown ignominiously on the dung-heap. John had scarcely seated himself on one of the benches which did duty as chairs, when he jumped up suddenly, exclaiming, 'My picture! my lost picture! Why, how did it come here? How glad I am to see it again!'

'That photograph?' inquired the shepherd.

'Yes, yes; it is the only likeness I ever had of my dead wife. She gave it me herself, and I coloured it with my own hand.'

'Well, now, that is extraordinary! My mate and I found it in an album which was in a small box lying by the roadside, about two years ago. Not far from this, either.'

'Indeed! Then I can only account for it this way. Two years ago, I was moving my furniture and things from one house to another, and the case containing the book must have fallen from the bullock dray without the driver's observing it. I missed it at once, and have advertised and inquired everywhere without success. But what made you stick it on the wall?'

'Oh, it is the likeness of such a pretty woman! Just for its beauty we put it there, because we liked to look at it. But, of course, it's yours, and you must have it again.'

'I will give anything for it. My wife gave it me when we were engaged; it is the only likeness I ever had of her, and she has been dead now more than two years.'

So the photograph returned to its original owner, who made the shepherd a handsome present, and spent the night at the hut dilating over their pipes and nobblers on the merits of the lost wife, a subject of which John Walton was never known to tire.

But the snake, which was the cause of the photograph's being found, was not idle meantime. In the morning six hens and two cocks were found lying in a bleeding heap on the dunghill, stung to death by the poisonous reptile, which, however, had safely decamped to the shelter of the neighbouring bush. John Walton, in order not to lose the valued picture again, took it with him to Melbourne, cut the tiny head out, and had it put in a gold locket, which he declared nothing on earth should ever induce him to part with.

Some years now elapsed, and the scene of our little story shifts far away—to no less a place than the imperial city of Rome itself. Here in the Forum, one bright spring day, a lady artist sat sketching. Around her were the gigantic ruins of the glorious past: broken column and statue lay at her feet; above her towered the noble pillars which have been for ages the models and admiration of the world. The Capitol was behind her; the stony road over which Cæsar passed in triumph encircled its base; the white and graceful arch which commemorates the victory of Titus over the Jews crowned the nearest height; to the left, the huge bulk of the

Colosseum filled an enormous space ; on the right rose the complicated arches of the Palatine, over-topped by cypress trees, through which the winds for ever moan the dead emperors who dwelt there ; while in the distance Monte Cavo and the Alban hills lay like clouds upon the horizon, alone unchanged and unchangeable as when Rome was the mighty mistress of the world, and the nations stooped in chains at her feet. Curiously enough, the church of Santa Francesca Romana, with its square tower, still occupies one end of the excavations of the Forum, blending the present with the past, representing mediæval, as the ruins do imperial Rome, and the new lines of white Parisian-like buildings the modern capital of the house of Savoy. Where elsewhere on earth is such a scene ? where such poetry, so much grandeur ? What memories crowd around the very name ! The history of the long centuries during which she has existed is all comprised within the one word—Rome ! and the poet and the artist will ever turn to her lovingly, as to the country which is by birthright his home, whatever land may claim him as her own.

The artist sat and sketched, oblivious, as artists generally are, of her surroundings, enjoying the sweet spring air, and absorbing, almost unconsciously, the melancholy spirit of the scene. For success—and success Alma had obtained—is ever mingled with sorrow : the loss of youth, the loss of friends, the loss of hope ;—perhaps failure and success are more nearly allied than we imagine. Amid these

sombre meditations she suddenly felt her elbow
touched, and, turning round, saw a lady and gentleman standing there, inquiring glances in their
eyes.

'I beg your pardon,' said the gentleman, 'but is it
—is it Miss Alma Lewis to whom I am speaking?'

'Mr. Walton! It is so long since I have seen you,
I did not recognise you.'

'So glad to see you again. May I introduce Mrs.
Walton?'

At first the name startled the artist; she did not
know her old friend had died many years ago,
and the new, unknown face, though so lovely and
genial, was a surprise.

After a few moments' conversation: 'Now I have
found you,' said John Walton, 'you must paint me a
portrait of my dear lost Caroline. Many artists have
tried and failed; but you, who were the friend of her
youth, and knew her so well, will be able to get the
likeness—to do her justice. I have only one photograph of her,—it is fading,—you can refresh your
memory from that. But take the greatest care of it;
it is the treasure I value most highly in the world.'

They then passed on to other subjects. Alma
related her struggles and successes, which were not a
few, though her fame had not yet reached the remote
part of the bush in which the Waltons resided. She
told of her life in the Schools of the Royal Academy,
London, of her labours for many years unrewarded,
of the medals she had gained, and the honour and

competence she had won. They in their turn gave her news of the childish friends, of whom, in the lapse of years, she had lost sight, and told her tales of that wonderful place by the sea which fifty years ago was a handful of huts and tents, and is now queen city of the South. John Walton also related how his wife had bequeathed her young children to the care of her friend, the lady whom he had since married. Finally, the young artist promised to go to London with them and paint the wished-for portrait from the precious photograph (which was entrusted to her for the purpose), and her own recollections of her early friend.

So Alma came to London and painted the portrait successfully—successfully even in the eyes of the still adoring husband. One day, when the picture was done, she looked for the photograph to return it. In vain! Knowing so well its value, she searched and searched for it, but always in vain—no trace could she discover. The tiny thing, taken out of the locket in which it was kept, had been pasted on a thin card, which was put in an undirected envelope, and this again carefully placed in a book. The servants were examined, every box and drawer turned out, with no success; and Alma, remembering Mr. Walton's repeated cautions, felt that she dared not tell him of the loss, for the bond which bound him to his first wife was of that kind which knows neither change nor diminution, here or in eternity, and he valued this little relic of her, her first gift and only portrait, more than all his flocks and stations.

'It is strange,' he remarked to Alma one day, 'what a fate there was about Caroline. Nothing belonging to her was ever lost.' Alma felt a throb like a knife go through her while he was speaking. 'She gave me this diamond pin, and one day I missed one of the stones. A few months after, I saw something sparkle in the hay in the bottom of a horse-trough; it was the diamond! You remember the story I told you about the photograph, which I found in a shepherd's hut more than two years after it was lost?'

'I do indeed,' replied Alma faintly.

'Well,' said he, 'I believe nothing that belonged to her ever was or will be lost. There is a charm about it.'

Poor Alma! that conversation cost her a *mauvais quart-d'heure.*

Long she pondered how to break the sorrowful news of her loss to him, and at length decided she could do it better by writing. But one day, while she still hesitated, she received a letter from a friend in Italy, with whom she had corresponded only since she had been in England, and in it was what gave her more delight than anything else could possibly have done—the much-loved photograph. How could it have come there? Alma had put the letter to her friend in the blank envelope, which had fallen from the book, without being aware of its presence there. Had the letter been sent to a less careful person, it might have been overlooked or destroyed, but her friend was a lady of minute observation, and returned the photograph to the sender. So the little picture was carefully restored to its place in the locket, where it still remains, unless, indeed, it has again commenced its wanderings, again to be found, as it bears a charm, and to form, perhaps, the subject of another story.

THE BUNYIP.

269

THE BUNYIP.[1]

——o——

EVERY one who has lived in Australia has
heard of the Bunyip. It is the one
respectable flesh-curdling horror of which
Australia can boast. The old world has her tales of
ghoul and vampire, of Lorelei, spook, and pixie, but

---

[1] While looking through files of the *Sydney Morning Herald* for
1848, I came across the following paragraph, under date August 1st
of that year. It was headed 'The Bunyip again.' 'A Mr. R.
Williams, of Port Fairy, a correspondent of the *Portland Gazette*,
reports the discovery of a real Bunyip in the Eumeralia. Mr. W. says:
'A stockman in the employ of Mr. Baxter was fishing in the Eumeralia,
when he was suddenly startled by what he at first imagined to be a
huge black fellow swimming in the river, but which I think must be
the Bunyip. I went with the stockman the next day, and was fortunate
enough to get a good view of him. He was of a brownish colour,
with a head something the shape of a kangaroo, an enormous mouth,
apparently furnished with a formidable set of teeth, long neck, covered
with a shaggy mane which reached halfway down his back; his hind
quarters were under water, so that we could not get a full view of him,
but if one may judge by what was seen, his weight must be fully equal
to that of a very large bullock. On trying to get a closer examination,
he took alarm and immediately disappeared; and although a strict
watch has since been kept, he has never again been seen, but it is
hoped that the exertions now being made by Mr. Baxter to catch him
will be crowned with success.'— ED.

Australia has nothing but her Bunyip. There never were any fauns in the eucalyptus forests, nor any naiads in the running creeks. No mythological hero left behind him stories of wonder and enchantment. No white man's hand has carved records of a poetic past on the grey volcanic-looking boulders that overshadow some lonely gullies which I know. There are no sepulchres hewn in the mountain rampart surrounding a certain dried-up lake—probably the crater of an extinct volcano—familiar to my childhood, and which in truth suggests possibilities of a forgotten city of Kör. Nature and civilisation have been very niggard here in all that makes romance.

No Australian traveller ever saw the Bunyip with his own eyes; and though there are many stockman's yarns and black's *patters* which have to do with this wonderful monster, they have all the hazy uncertainty which usually envelops information of the legendary kind. Some night, perhaps, when you are sitting over a camp fire brewing quart-pot tea and smoking store tobacco, with the spectral white gums rising like an army of ghosts around you, and the horses' hobbles clanking cheerfully in the distance, you will ask one of the overlanding hands to tell you what he knows about the Bunyip. The bushman will warm to his subject as readily as an Irishman to his banshee. He will indignantly repel your insinuation that the Bunyip may be after all as mythical as Alice's Jabberwock; and he will forthwith proceed to relate how a friend of his had a mate, who knew

another chap, who had once in his life had a narrow
escape from the Bunyip, and had actually beheld it—
and in a certain lagoon not a hundred miles from
where you are squatting. He himself has never set
eyes upon the Bunyip, nor has his mate, but there is
not the smallest doubt that the other chap has seen
it. When facts come to be boiled down, however,
'the other chap's' statements will seem curiously
vague and contradictory; and if the details are to be
accepted as they stand, a remarkable contribution to
natural history must be the result.

The Bunyip is the Australian sea-serpent, only it
differs from that much-disputed fact or fiction in that
it does not inhabit the ocean, but makes its home in
lagoons and still deep water-holes. For rivers and
running creeks it appears to have an aversion. No
black fellow will object to bathe in a river because
of the Bunyip, but he will shake his woolly head
mysteriously over many an innocent-looking water-
hole, and decline to dive for water-lily roots or some
such delicacy dear to the aboriginal stomach, on the
plea that 'Debil-debil sit down there.'

Debil-debil and Bunyip are synonymous terms
with the black fellow while he is on the bank of a
lagoon, though 'Debil-debil' in the abstract repre-
sents a much more indefinite source of danger, and
has a far wider scope of action than most mythological deities. 'Debil-debil' is a convenient way of
accounting, not only for plague, sickness, and disaster,
but also for peace, plenty, and good fortune. Accord-

ing to the religious code of the Australian aboriginal, Ormuzd and Ahriman do not work at opposite poles, but combine and concentrate themselves under one symbol. The supremacy of Debil-debil is uncontested, and he deals out promiscuously benefits and calamities from the same hand. A medicine-man professing to be in confidential communication with Debil-debil, may kill or cure a black fellow according to his pleasure. The natives have a superstition, in common with many primitive nations, that if an enemy possesses himself of a lock of hair from the head of one to whom he wishes ill, and buries it in the ground beneath a gum tree, the despoiled person will sicken and die as the hair rots away. In that case Debil-debil must be 'pialla-ed' (entreated) by the sick person to unbury the hair and cast it in the fire, when the charm will be dissolved. The medicine-man, therefore, has but to assure his patient that Debil-debil has refused or acceded to his request, and death or speedy recovery will be the consequence.

The blacks have an impish drollery and love of mischief, and they delight in imposing on the credulity of their white auditors. Thus the stories of their superstitions must not be accepted too literally. But it is certain that when they show a distinct reticence in regard to any reputed article of faith, it may safely be looked upon as genuine. The blacks never will volunteer information about the Bunyip; it has always to be dragged out of them. When a black fellow disappears, it is generally understood that the Bunyip has got hold of him, and the particular water-hole in which the monster is supposed to live becomes more than ever an object of terror, and a place to be avoided. The water-hole may have been hitherto uncondemned by tradition, and the blacks may choose to disport themselves in it ; but if one of them, seized with cramp or enmeshed in weeds, sinks to rise no more, the terrible cry of 'Bunyip' goes forth, and those waters are from henceforth shunned.

The Bunyip is said to be an amphibious animal, and is variously described : sometimes as a gigantic snake ; sometimes as a species of rhinoceros, with a smooth pulpy skin and a head like that of a calf ; sometimes as a huge pig, its body yellow, crossed with black stripes. But it is also said to be something more than animal, and among its supernatural attributes is the cold, awesome, uncanny feeling which creeps over a company at night when the Bunyip becomes the subject of conversation ; and a certain magnetic atmosphere supposed to envelop the creature, and to spread a deadly influence for some space around, rendering even its vicinity dangerous, is particularly dwelt upon. According to legend, it attracts its prey by means of this mysterious emanation, and when sufficiently near, will draw man or beast down to the water and suck the body under, and without sound or struggle the victim disappears, to be seen no more. It is silent and stealthy, and only very rarely, they say, and always at night, has been seen to rise partially from the black water which it loves, and utter a strange moaning cry like that of a child or a woman in pain. There is a theory that water is a powerful conductor for the kind of electricity it gives out, and that a pool with dry abrupt banks and no outlying morass is tolerably safe to drink from or to camp by; but a lagoon lying amid swamp has always an evil reputation, and in some districts it is very difficult to persuade a black fellow to venture into such a place.

One of the most famous haunts of the Bunyip, round which all sorts of stories gathered, though I never could really authenticate one of them, is a lagoon that we all knew well, and which used to furnish my brothers with many a brace of wild-fowl for our bush larder.

This lagoon is about four miles long, in some parts very deep, in others nothing but marsh, with swamp-oaks and ti-trees and ghostly white-barked she-oaks growing thickly in the shallow water. The wild-duck is so numerous in places that a gun fired makes the air black, and it is impossible to hear oneself speak, so deafening are the shrill cries of the birds which brood over the swamp.

We were none of us very much afraid of the Bunyip, though I confess to many an anxious shudder, and to having stopped and switched a stick behind me in order to make sure that all was right, when I found myself at dusk walking by the banks of the lagoon. A curious fascination, which was assuredly not the magnetic attraction of the Bunyip, used to draw me there ; the place was so wild and eerie and solitary, and appealed so strongly to my imagination. I liked nothing better than to go with my brother on moonlight nights when he went down there with his gun over his shoulder to get a shot at wild-duck; the creepy feeling which would come over us as we trod along by the black water with dark slimy logs slanting into it, and reeds and moist twigs and fat marsh plants giving way under our footsteps, was quite a luxurious terror. There were such strange noises, the faint shivering sound made by the spiky leaves of the swamp-oak, the flapping of the she-oaks' scaly bark, the queer gurgling 'grrur-urr-r' of an opossum up a gum tree, the swishing of the ducks' wings when they rose suddenly in the distance, the melancholy call of the curlews,—all these, breaking the silence and loneliness of the night, were indescribably uncanny and fascinating ; but I am bound to say that during these expeditions we never saw a sign of the Bunyip.

We were travelling once up country,—my brother Jo and I,—and had arranged to camp out one night, there being no station or house of accommodation on the stage at which we could put up. The dray, loaded with stores and furniture for the new home to which we were bound, had been started some days previously, and we had agreed to meet the drivers at a certain small lagoon, known as the One-eyed Waterhole, and camp there under the dray tarpaulin. We

were riding, my brother driving a pair of pack-horses
with our swags, and we were unable to carry any
convenience for spending a night in the bush.

It was the month of November, and the heat was
overpowering. The red gum oozed from the iron-
bark trees and fell in great drops like blood. The
deafening noise of the forest was in strange contrast
to the night silence and loneliness of the lagoon I
have described. All the sounds were harsh and
grating—the whirring of grasshoppers and locusts,
the chattering of parrots and laughing-jackasses, the
cawing of cockatoos and scuttling of iguanas through
the coarse dry blady grass. It was a relief to the
heat and monotony, when, as the sun set, we left the
timbered ridges and came down upon a plain, across
which a faint breeze blew, and where we could see, at
the foot of a distant ridge, the One-eyed Water-hole
and our dray beside it, loaded high, and covered with
a huge tarpaulin that hung all round it like a tent.

The men were busy making a fire and watering
the bullocks. They had got down their blankets and
the rations and tin billys and quart pots from the
dray, and Mick, who had been hut-keeper to a party
of shearers, was mixing Johnny-cakes on a piece of
newly-cut bark, ready for baking when the logs had
burnt down into ashes and embers. Some of the
others had cut tufts from the grass trees on the ridge,
and strewn them on the earth under the dray for us
to lie upon. Very soon we were all comfortably
camped, and as night closed in and the stars shone

out, the scene became more and more picturesque. Our fire had been lighted a few yards away from the lagoon, which, deep and black where the banks were high, widened out at the lower end into a swamp of she-oaks, their white lanky stems standing out against the darker background of ridge, densely covered with jungle-like scrub.

We had eaten our meal of beef and hot Johnny-cakes all together by the dray, and there was something striking about the appearance of the men, in their bright Crimean shirts and rough moleskin trousers and broad-brimmed cabbage-tree hats, as they lounged in easy attitudes, smoking their pipes and drinking quart-pot tea, while they waxed communicative under the influence of a nip of grog, which had been served out to them apiece.

They were telling shearing stories—how Paddy Mack and Long Charlie had had a bet as to which could shear a sheep the fastest; how Father Flaherty, the priest from the township, who had come over to see the shearing in full swing, timed them by his watch; how at the word 'off' the shears slashed down through the wool, and how the quickest man sheared his sheep in less than a minute, and the other a second and a half later. Then Mick had to tell of a man who used to shear his hundred and twenty sheep in the day, and on his way from the wool-shed to the hut jump over a four-foot-six post and rail fence, which after having been bent double all day was a feat he might be proud of.

Then somehow—perhaps it was the wildness and
loneliness of the place, or the wind across the plain,
or the sighing of the she-oaks, or the weird 'poomp'
of the bullock bells—the talk got on to eerie things,
and from the authentic story of Fisher's Ghost it was
an easy transition to the Bunyip and all its supernatural horrors. Most of the men had some Bunyip
tale to relate ; and as we talked a sort of chill seemed
to creep over us, and one could almost fancy that
the horrible monster was casting its magnetic spell
upon us from the dark swamp close by. After a bit,
when it was discovered that the billys were empty,
and that we wanted more water to make some fresh
tea, no one seemed inclined to go down to the lagoon
to fetch it, and Mick, taking a firestick to light his
pipe, said slowly,—

'Begorra, Charlie, we must look out here for the
Bunyip. You ask old Darby Magrath if he'd like
to camp down by the swamp of the One-eyed Water-
hole all night by himself. I remember Darby telling
me that when he was riding across this plain one
night after shearing, his horse stopped of a sudden and
trembled all over under him—just like a bullock in
the killing yard when you drop the spear into his
neck. Darby says he felt cold all through his bones ;
and then a queer sort of noise came up from the
water,—a kind of sound like a baby moaning,—and
he just clapped spurs into his old yarraman (horse),
and never pulled up out of a gallop till he had got
over the range and was at the "Coffin Lid" public,

five miles on. The horse was all dripping with
sweat, and poor old Darby as white as a corpse.'

'Well, I don't know much about the thing myself
—never had no Bunyip experiences myself; but
unless Gemmel Dick is *the* most almighty liar'—
began Long Charlie, taking out his pipe in prepara-
tion for a blood-curdling yarn and then stopping
suddenly, for at that moment there came a curious
sound from the lagoon, or the swamp, or the plains
to our left, we could not tell whence—a wild, thrill-
ing sound, which at first seemed scarcely human, but
which, when repeated after the interval of a moment
or two, struck my heart as if it were the cry of
some dying animal, or of a child in dire distress and
agony.

We all started and looked anxiously at each other,
waiting until it came again, and not quite liking to
confess our tremors, when one of the men exclaimed
nervously,—

'Say, what's that?'

'Wallabi bogged,' pronounced Long Charlie oracu-
larly, and was beginning once more,—

'Well, as I was telling you, if Gemmel Dick ain't
the most '—

But that strange, horrible cry from the lagoon—
yes, it must come from the swamp end of the lagoon
—broke the night silence again, and stopped Long
Charlie a second time. It was more prolonged, more
certain, than it had been before. Beginning low, a
sort of hoarse muffled groan, it swelled into a louder,

shriller note, which we at once imagined might be the strained broken coo-ée of a child in pain or terror.

Every one of us rose.

'By Jove! I'll tell you what I believe it is,' said my brother Jo excitedly. 'That's some free-selector's kid lost in the bush. Come along, you fellows. Don't be funky of the Bunyip.'

He darted down towards the swamp, which lay some little distance from our camp, the dark heads of the she-oaks rising above a thick veil of white mist, that shrouded completely the less lofty and more straggling branches of the ti-trees. The rest of us followed him closely. It must be said that we were not deterred at that moment by any thought of the Bunyip and its supernatural atmosphere. Long Charlie, the most practical of the party, waited to detach a rough lantern which hung from one of the staples of the dray, and caught us up as we reached the borders of the swamp. The sound had ceased now. Coo-éeing loudly, we peered through the cold clinging mist among the brown twisted branches of the ti-trees, which shook their scented bottle-brush blossoms in our faces. Under our feet, the ground, which had been trodden into deep odd-shaped ruts by the cattle coming down to drink, gave way at every step. We could hear the soft 'k—sssh' of the displaced water, and we shivered as the slimy ooze mounted over our insteps and trickled down through our boots, while the pulpy rushes sprang back as we forced ourselves through, and struck our hands with clammy touch.

It was a dreary, uncanny place, and even through our coo-ées the night that had seemed so silent on the plain was here full of ghostly noises, stifled hissings, and unexpected gurglings and rustlings, and husky croaks, and stealthy glidings and swishings.

'Look out for snakes,' said Long Charlie, flourishing his lantern. 'And don't all of us be coo-ćeing all the time, or when the little chap sings out we shan't be able to hear him.'

We stopped coo-ćeing, and presently the wail sounded again, fainter and more despairing, we fancied, and urging us to greater energy. Though we tried to move in the direction of the voice, it was impossible to determine whence it came, so misleading and fitful and will-o'-the-wisp-like was the sound. Now it seemed to come from our right, now from our left, now from the very depths of the lagoon, and now from the scrub on the ridge beyond.

I don't know how we got through the deeper part of the swamp without getting bogged; but we did at last, and reached the scrub that straggled down to the water's edge. Here was dense, and in places impenetrable foliage; rough boulders were lying pell-mell at the foot of the ridge, and creepers hung in withes from the trees, with great thorns that tore our hands and our clothes. We did not know which way to turn, for the cry had ceased, and the dead silence of the scrub was like that of the grave. We waited for a minute or two, but it did not come again.

'I believe it was the Bunyip after all,' said Mick, with a shudder. 'And look here, I shall head the lagoon, I ain't going to cross that swamp again. It's all nonsense about the little 'un, not a child nor a grown man or beast could have forced theirselves down here.'

Long Charlie flashed his lantern along the wall of green, and, stumbling over stones and logs, we walked as well as we could, skirting the scrub and making for the head of the lagoon. We paused every now and then, straining our ears for the voice that had led us hither, and once it sounded faint but thrillingly plaintive, and guided us on.

At last there came a break in the jungle, a narrow track piercing the heart of the scrub, and then a wider break, and a warning cry from Long Charlie in advance,—

'Hello! Look out! It's a gully—pretty deep. You might break a leg before you knew it. Keep along up the track.'

We kept along up the track, waiting to let Long Charlie go first with his lantern. Suddenly the moon, which had risen while we were in the swamp, sent a shaft of light down through the opening, and showed us, a little way ahead, where the track widened out and then stopped altogether, a tiny plateau, in the centre of which stood a great white bottle tree, its trunk perfectly bare, bulging out in the centre like a garment swelled by the wind, and looking in its fantastic shape like a sentinel spectre.

It gave one a strange creepy feeling to see this huge white thing rising up so solemnly in the midst of the gloom and the solitude. There was something else white on the grass—something almost the same shape as the bottle tree lying across at its foot. The moon was dim for a moment or two. Nobody spoke, we pressed up the ridge side, then a hoarse smothered ejaculation burst from Long Charlie's lips, and as he spoke the moon shone forth again, and he shifted his lantern so that its gleam fell athwart the white prostrate form and upon a snake, brown and shiny and scaly and horrible, which uncoiled itself, and with a swift, wavy motion disappeared into the depths of the scrub.

It seemed to us, we said afterwards, as though we could hear each other's hearts beating. The men were too horrified to utter a sound. At last Long Charlie said, in a deep, awe-stricken voice,—

'By God! that beats me.'

And then Mick, moving a little nearer, cried, with a sob in his brawny throat,—

'It's Nancy—little Nancy—Sam Duffy's girl from the "Coffin Lid," and it was only the other day she came out and served me with a nobbler.'

Paddy Mack was sobbing too, they all seemed to know and love the child.

'She wur so fond of looking for chuckie-chuckies in the scrub, and quantongs and things. And she might have knowed, poor little Nancy! that if she wanted quantongs, I'd have got 'em for her; and didn't I string her a necklace only last shearing! But she was always a child for roaming,—she wasn't afraid of snakes, nor blacks, nor nothing,—she said she liked to hear the bell-bird call, and that it seemed to be always calling *her.* I've heerd her say that— poor little Nancy!—always smiling when she carried a chap out a nobbler. And now the bell-bird has rung her home.'

Long Charlie only said again, 'That beats me.'

They couldn't account for it; the child had been dead some hours, they said. They couldn't believe it was that snake which had bitten her, and they declared that the cry we heard must have been the Bunyip, or little Nancy's ghost.

THE TRAGEDY IN A STUDIO.

THE TRAGEDY IN A STUDIO.

—o—

PART I.

THE DEAD MODEL.

I SUPPOSE it will ever be true, that one cannot be a prophet in one's own country. I had hoped it might have been otherwise in my case, and that mine might have been proud of me, the Australian-taught girl artist, who, after having gone 'home' for three years' study, had come back to Melbourne with the silver medal of the Royal Academy and two years' experience of one of the most reputed studios in Rome.

But no. The people who made a lounge of the studio on my 'days,' who gushed over this 'bit' or 'that study,' never so much as bought a sketch ; and had it not been for literary work in the magazines and newspapers, and a rare portrait, evil would have been those days in which I hoped and struggled and grew sick and weary of it all, and then hoped again and struggled on.

Other people who did not come to my studio said they really 'couldn't countenance a girl who lived alone, and was so peculiar-looking ;' my dress being of the plainest and simplest kind, the said 'peculiarity' could only be laid to the score of bright chestnut hair, and very black eyebrows and eyelashes, which perhaps did form a rather remarkable contrast to a face of ivory pallor. And as to my living alone, I had absolutely no relations, and could not afford to pay a companion. When my spirit was not stung by injustice of this kind, it was depressed by indifference, so at last I made up my mind to try if Fortune would not be kinder to me in the old country. I took my well-nigh worn-out courage into my wearied hands, and, having sold all I possessed—furniture, books, pictures—for whatever they would fetch, engaged a passage in a ship that was leaving a week from that time.

The last day but two had arrived ; but, short as was the time that lay before me, I hardly knew what to do with it, I was in such a feverish state of unrest and impatience to be gone.

The hotel was deserted that morning: everybody was on Flemington racecourse ; but, lounging idly on the verandah, I became suddenly aware of an arrival. A young man on horseback, leading a lady's saddle-horse by the bridle, had alighted, and was giving both horses in charge to one of the inevitable stable-boys, who, all the world over, seem to spring out of the ground at the first sound of a horse's hoof in the distance. A waiter was also to the fore; and I could almost fancy I heard my own name inquired for, and the response—'Yessir; cert'nly. Who shall I say?'

The doubt, however, became a certainty as the door of the room was flung open, and my unexpected visitor entered. I neither knew the name that was announced—Alston—nor the person to whom it belonged, a strong, sunburnt young fellow of about four-and-twenty, in high boots, and a light tweed suit dusty from riding, looking like any other twenty of his fellows after a long ride from some probably remote station. But I shall never forget the expression that met my gaze as his eyes looked into mine—the depth of sadness, the hurt, pitiful look of a wounded animal patiently bearing a pain it can neither realise nor understand. My woman's sympathy must have made itself outwardly visible, for his first words were,—

'You will come with me, will you not? I know you will come. Can you get ready at once? I have a lady's saddle-horse at the door. Please put on your habit, and bring your painting things with you —that is all.'

The abrupt strangeness of the request did not seem to strike me, and I answered in a natural manner, 'I am very sorry. I am afraid it is impossible; perhaps you are not aware that I am sailing the day after to-morrow for England?'

'And you don't even know who I am. But I quite forgot, Miss Challis—I have a letter with me that will explain.'

I took the twisted slip of paper he held out to me with an unsteady, tremulous hand, and motioned to a chair, into which he threw himself heavily with a long-drawn breath of fatigue or emotion. This is what I read :—

'You will probably have heard of me—Mordaunt of Telemon. My daughter, my only child, is lying dead. In the name of woman's charity I beseech you to come and paint her for her heart-broken father. The bearer, Dick Alston,—my son who might have been,—will bring you back with him and will take every care of you. I entreat you to come without delay.   P. MORDAUNT.'

I don't think I hesitated. I think I had made up my mind even before I had come to the signature. Every letter of the bold, manly writing, that should have been so firm and strong, was shaky, as if the palsied hand of age had held the pen. As I looked up I saw that Dick Alston had been watching me while I read, his hand nervously grasping the arm of the chair. Now he sprang up and followed me as I moved towards the door of the inner chamber.

'You are coming, I see. Thank God! You can't think how he has set his heart on having her picture, Miss Challis. He had seen the likeness you painted

last year of Judge Haughton's daughter. It suddenly
came across him that it would be a comfort. I don't
think he could have let her go, but for this.'

I paused with my hand on the door handle, and
the question forming itself on my lips—'When?'

'The day after to-morrow, I think. She died at
dawn, poor little darling! I started almost directly.'

The young fellow spoke with a strangled sob in his
throat, and I left him without another word to make
my slight preparations.

And thus it happened that I, Magdalen Challis, on
the very eve of my departure from my native land,
perhaps for ever, started on an expedition to an
unknown place with a perfect stranger, for the purpose
of painting the picture of a dead girl I had never seen,
for a man I had never heard of.

   .   .   .   .

After first starting off, we rode side by side for
about a couple of hours in almost unbroken silence.
A thirty miles' journey lay before us; and although
the horses had had a short rest, and were fully aware
of the fact that they were returning homewards, yet
we rode but slowly, with occasional stoppages. The
pretty little mare on which I was mounted fretted
and chafed at an unaccustomed touch; she was
evidently used to a lighter hand, and probably to a
far lighter weight than mine; and my companion's
animal began to show signs of distress.

'Poor brute!' said Dick Alston at last. 'I didn't
spare him riding in, this morning, and, but for you,

Miss Challis, I am afraid I should not be doing so now.'

I suggested that in any case we could not expect to arrive at our destination before nightfall, and I should not be able to set myself to my pitiful task until the morning. In this he acquiesced, but I saw that he was in a condition of feverish impatience to be back that was almost unendurable. My own feelings were the reverse of pleasant, as can well be imagined ; but while anxious not to intrude upon a great grief, or to appear inquisitive, I yet felt I had been thrust into a position in this sad drama in which a natural and legitimate interest in my fellow-actors could hardly be misconstrued into mere curiosity.

This thought must also have occurred to the young fellow himself, for he suddenly emerged from his gloomy musings to say,—

' It's real good of you, Miss Challis, to have come straight off like this on this miserable errand, and not to have asked any questions either. I think you ought to know something about us all, and poor little Lily.'

Thus it happened that by degrees I was able to piece together and connect the story that Dick Alston told me. It was nothing very new after all, and it seemed to me that in the telling of it the young fellow's love idealized and glorified the poor little heroine who was weak enough to let herself die, and selfish enough to break the hearts of two

men who loved her for an intangible and visionary
fancy based on no foundation.

He spoke of a motherless and only child, petted
and spoilt by a tender father, a doting old nurse, a
devoted young lover—taking all the affection that
was lavished on her as a right, something as natural
as the trees and flowers and the sunlight. And
then, tiring of her Paradise, and turning to the
stranger who entered its gates from another world of
which she knew nothing—a man who had *lived*—who
had the curious attraction that world-worn, travel-
stained wayfarers of his kind possess for such Eves
in their innocent ignorance. To this conclusion
jumped *my* travelled knowledge.

But, said honest Dick Alston, just even to a rival,
'I don't know that Gordon was what you would
have called a *bad* fellow, Miss Challis. He had
been extravagant, backed bills too, sold out of his
regiment, and displeased his father, who had shipped
him off to Australia—there was nothing worse
against him than that. But he made no friends on
the station, and always seemed as if he thought
himself rather superior to all of us other fellows.
And Lily was flattered by his notice of her, and
pleased to be taught little Italian songs, and to have
poetry read to her. Her father and I hadn't perhaps
treated her like a grown-up woman. I was waiting
till she was eighteen to ask her to marry me. Mind
you, I don't think he ever made actual love to her ;
and even if he knew he was turning her little head,

he didn't set about deliberately to break her heart.
But one day when he had ridden into town for the
mail letters, he sent back a hurried note to say im-
portant family affairs called him back to England at
once,—that a vessel was leaving the next morning, and
there would be just time for the messenger to ride
back with some things he specified, and the rest of
his belongings might be distributed among the
station hands. He thanked Mr. Mordaunt for much
courtesy and kindness, and sent his love to the
Australian lily. She was to keep his Browning, and
would perhaps sometimes read over the pieces they
had read together, so that he should not be quite
forgotten. That was six months ago, and from that
moment Lily drooped and pined like a broken
flower. We heard that Gordon had inherited a
property and changed his name, and a week since
news came out of his marriage. That was the
finishing stroke—the last nail that went home.'

The young fellow broke off with a shudder; his
own simile had conjured up a painful picture. I
knew that in imagination he heard the sound of the
nails being driven into his dead love's coffin.

'The day after to-morrow,' he went on, half to
himself, in broken sentences. ' Poor little girl ! Buried
on her birthday,—only eighteen,—and I was waiting
for that day !'

He said no more, but spurred on his tired horse,
and the rest of the ride was accomplished in
silence.

Darkness had fallen like a pall by the time we reached our destination. I felt unutterably weary, physically worn out, and almost fell prone on the threshold as I dismounted. Young Alston said something about looking after the horses, and handed me over to a grave, elderly serving-woman who had come forward, and ushered me into the house.

'You must not expect to see the master,' she said ; 'he will not leave the child to-night. But you must eat, young lady, and I daresay you will be glad afterwards of rest. You must be faint and very tired. I will bring you some refreshment here.'

She removed my hat, bathed my face and hands, and even took off my habit body, replacing it by a white dressing-jacket which she threw over my shoulders. I submitted without a word to her kind ministrations, and she waited upon me where I sat, drawing up a table by the side of the chair, on which she set a cold repast.

'You are very kind,' I said at last, when a little restored by the wine and bread and fruit of which I had partaken (I could eat nothing else), 'and I think I would like to go to bed directly.'

It was a bedroom into which she had brought me. She pointed to a little slip of a dressing-room partitioned off it. 'I am sleeping there, and shall be within call of you, Miss Challis. I am Lily's old nurse.'

Great tears welled up into her eyes and trickled

down her cheeks as she mentioned the girl's name ;
but she was bearing her grief quietly, and was
endeavouring, I could see, to restrain as far as
possible any outward demonstration of it.

'You will find all you may require,' she said, 'and
I shall not be long without looking in. Try to sleep,
Miss Challis;' and she wished me good-night and
left me.

I had been in a state of unrest for days past ; my
own preparations for departure and leave - takings,
though causing no heart - pangs, had somewhat
excited and fatigued me. Then came this unexpected and extraordinary summons. Perhaps the
exhausting ride of the day had been the best thing
that could have happened to quiet and calm me. At
any rate, I was too wearied to think either of myself
or others. Almost as soon as my head touched the
pillow I slept—a profound, dreamless, and unbroken
sleep.

When I awoke it was seven o'clock in the morning
of the next day. It was not until some moments
later that I realized where I was, and for what
purpose. After I was dressed and had partaken of
some breakfast, the nurse, who had again waited on
me, said simply, 'If you are ready, Miss Challis, I
will take you to Lily.'

.   .   .   .

It was a one-storied house, and the only room in
which I had hitherto been was on the ground-floor ;
but now the nurse preceded me up a flight of

shallow stairs, and quietly opened the door of a room, into which she entered reverentially, as into a church. I followed mechanically, almost in spite of myself, with downcast eyes which feared what they might see when their gaze should be raised and concentrated. Without looking, I became conscious of details—of matting on the floor, of cool-looking chintz coverings and draperies, of the heavy scent of flowers, of a white bed facing the door.

Slowly at last I looked up as I stood by the side of it. The bed was empty. But on a couch by the window, which was open to the verandah, lay a frail, white-robed form over which the nurse was bending. She beckoned me to her side, and I looked for the first time upon my dead model. A lily indeed! On earth, love's sweet virgin martyr, now one of Heaven's angels!

. . . .

I had never looked on Death before, orphan though I was. I had feared his unknown, nameless terrors and never dreamt of such calmly beautiful repose, such pure and passionless peace.

And peace fell upon me as I looked.

When I was at last able to turn away from my contemplation, I saw that the nurse was no longer there, and knew that the time had come when I must set myself to the task which had to be begun and completed that day.

I felt relieved that none of the ghastly paraphernalia of the grave surrounded the girl, who, clad in some soft white woollen garment, was lying on the couch, over which had been spread a large opossum rug ; a crimson shawl of China crape was thrown lightly across her knees and feet, and a mass of white flowers strewn over it.   On the edge of the couch a book was lying, which seemed to have just slipped from her grasp.   I did not need to look at it to know that it was the Browning, and one might have imagined she had fallen asleep while reading it.   Such was the picture that I saw and painted, at first calmly and steadfastly enough.

I must have been at work for several hours when the nurse came in, and, in the quiet but decided manner which she had adopted with me from the beginning, insisted on my leaving off for a time to take the food which she had prepared for me in the room downstairs.   I was probably away about half-an-hour ; as I returned, and had almost reached the top of the short staircase, some one passed from *that* room into another of which the door was quietly but quickly closed, and then the stillness was broken by the painful sound of a man's sobs.

.   .   .   .

I felt unnerved as I sat down again to my work. The sunlight that filtered through a trellis of leaves on the verandah seemed to cast strange shadows over Lily's face. . . . I could fancy that I saw her blue-veined eyelids quiver—that her long lashes trembled on her waxen cheek—surely a faint, wan smile was flickering over her mouth !

I threw down my brush, and buried my face in my hands. I think I must have remained long in that position, for it seemed to me when I once more raised my head that the room had grown almost dark. With a sudden desperation I seized my brushes again, and resumed my task. I painted quickly, feverishly, with hurried glances at the motionless form, whose face I hardly dared to look at. And then fell the sudden Australian twilight, and a breeze sprang up, and blew the muslin window drapery across my face. I could hear the soft pit-a-pat of falling raindrops, and my beating heart kept time to the sound. Then the wet leaves of a shrub on the verandah swung in at the window, and cast a shower of drops around. They fell chill and wet on my own warm hands, they fell on those other cold ones, and I bent forward trembling to wipe them off. Horror! what did I see? Tears on the dead face!

The ground seemed to give way beneath me. I felt myself sway and stagger. I fell across the couch. I remember no more.

.   .   .   .

The next day at an early hour I left Telemon with Mr. Mordaunt's cheque for £500 in my note-book, and with a haunting memory at my heart that will never depart from it. I saw Dick Alston for a few moments only, in which he acted as messenger for the host whom I was not to see at all.

An overseer 'who could be trusted' was to be my escort back to Melbourne, Dick Alston, of course, not being able to leave, as the funeral was to take place that afternoon. All through the long ride from the station—a solitary one to all intents and purposes of companionship, my escort either preceding or riding behind me in silence—I could think of nothing but Dick Alston's words: 'Buried on her birthday, poor little girl! Buried on her birthday!' For, by a curious coincidence, I remembered that it was my birthday too, and my heart sank with a vague foreboding of disaster that should result to me from the association.

'Who shall deliver me from the body of this death?' was the cry that rose unbidden to my lips, with an involuntary perversion of its meaning that I was powerless to prevent. Who should deliver me from an undying remembrance of death itself? Who shall break the link that must ever bind *me* living to the dead girl buried on my birthday? The thought pursued and remained with me even on board the ship that was to bear me away to new scenes and a new life. It took tangible shape and action, impelling me to perpetuate it by an outward and visible sign that should abide with me, and prevent me forgetting if I would. In the seclusion of my cabin it forced pencil and brushes into my unwilling fingers, till at first a faint sketch outlined itself on the canvas, and then the contours filled themselves in with all those accessories and details that seemed burnt in on my mental vision. A girl with closed eyes lying on a couch, her brown hair spread out upon the pillow,

a book fallen from a nerveless grasp, white flowers
on a crimson covering, wet leaves blown in at an
open casement, and always tears—tears on the wan,
white cheeks—tears escaping from the closed waxen
eyelids!

PART II.

THE VEILED PICTURE.

MY nervous system had received a shock which
resulted in an attack of utter prostration, accompanied by low fever. When the *Storm - King*
arrived in the docks, I was unable to stand, and
quite incapable of deciding for myself, or even
of giving directions as to my destination. I had
made no friends on the passage, and had rather
shrunk from well - intentioned proffers of assistance
and counsel. The question, however, had finally
resolved itself into what was to be done with me?
With me, Magdalen Challis, that strong and self-
reliant young woman, now lying there in her deck
chair, listening to the discussion as if it concerned
somebody else!

And the ship was actually in, and people coming
on board to look after their friends amongst all the
indescribable bustle and commotion of greetings and
collection of luggage, etc. Idly my gaze rested on a
lady who had come on board with a lovely petted

little daughter, to fetch and bring away her 'very own self' the king-parrot and yellow-crested cockatoo that some kind Australian friend had sent out to the little girl.

The interest which I had ceased to feel in myself and my own concerns, or those of any other human being, was suddenly roused and centred in the pretty English mother and child, who were standing close to my chair while waiting for their precious consignment.

I saw the little one clutch at her mother's dress to arrest her attention, and caught a look of wonderment in the big blue eyes that were fixed upon myself.

'What the matter with the pale lady, mamma?'

'Hush, Lucy! it is rude to make remarks about people. The lady will hear you.'

But the eyes of the speaker were turned upon me too, and I read a sweet soft pity in them, just as I had read the wondering indifference of childhood in those of her little girl. A sudden impulse moved me to speak.

'I have been very ill,' I said ; 'I am alone on board —I have money, but I don't know a soul in London, nor even where to go.'

I knew afterwards, when little Lucy's mother had become my one dear woman friend in the great world of London, that I had hardly finished speaking that day on board when I fell back fainting in my chair, and the parrot and cockatoo became a mere secondary consideration.

Mrs. Rivers held a hurried consultation with the doctor and the captain,—the latter, who knew who I was, being thus in a position to vouch for my respectability,—and carried me off then and there to lodgings that she knew of in a Surrey farmhouse, giving up the rest of the season, with all her engagements, to come there also, and herself to nurse me back to the health and vigour of which I had been so proud, and which, but for this sisterly hand stretched out in the hour of need, I might never otherwise have regained.

But though my splendid health and strength of body in time returned to me, I was never again quite the same woman I had been before the terrible ordeal which had so nearly overthrown my mental balance. I was for ever haunted by the remembrance of my dead model, and could not divest myself of the foreboding that some tragic result to myself was yet to follow the chance connection of my own birthday with hers on the day of her burial. Two anniversaries had come and gone with no special event to mark them ; the third was not far off.

.   .   .   .

Fortune meanwhile had been most kind, and had led me through pleasant paths to a pinnacle of success, where stood a flower - crowned temple of happiness of which she had given me the key.

From the day in which I had taken my studio in Chelsea, everything had prospered with me. In my wildest visions of success I had never aspired to

U

such a position as the one in which I found myself
on the eve of my twenty-fifth birthday, a woman of
ample means, admired and fêted, famous and envied,
beautiful and beloved.

   .   .   .   .

Yes—not only had Fame stooped to place her
chaplet on my brows, but Love had kissed me on the
mouth, and taken my hand in his. Between them
they had led me to the feast; and while the pungent
perfume of Fame's incense clung with subtle fragrance
to my garments and my hair, Love held out to me
the cup of rich red wine, of which I drank deep
draughts till the thrill of life ran through me to my
finger-tips. 'Twas in this supreme moment that a
formless shadow cast its gloom athwart the brilliant
sunlight, and a pale finger wrote upon the wall—
' Lily, Lily, Lily—buried on her birthday ! '

   .   .   .   .

That anniversary had now returned for the third
time, and I had nerved myself to meet and celebrate
it as usual. Shut up within my studio, admittance
denied to all, I offered up a propitiatory sacrifice ;
the sacrifice of one of those bright days of life that are
all too few and short—one whole day !

Taking from its resting-place the picture which I
kept jealously hidden all the year from my own eyes
as well as from those of others, I reverentially withdrew the crape that veiled it, and forced myself to
gaze upon the dead girl, who, I trust, unconsciously,
seemed to influence and mar the life which had never

so much as touched the fringe of hers, but which she had enchained and bound in those fetters from which death had released her.

The studio was transformed into a kind of *chapelle ardente;* the blinds drawn close, all light as far as possible excluded, wax candles burning on a table with a black velvet covering that stood in front of the easel, white flowers everywhere. Myself in white, girdled with a sash of deep violet, offering up my sacrifice to—whom or what—I knew not.

Thus did Una Rivers find me. She had been of late such a frequent visitor, that my orders to admit no one had probably not been considered to include herself. After a moment's pause of bewildered surprise, her laugh rang out like a silver bell.

'Why, Magdalen, what freak is this, and what new and startling picture does it portend? I did not know that artists " composed " in this way. I must own that it is all so very realistic, quite Tosca-ish, in fact, that I felt almost alarmed for a moment.'

For sole answer, I suddenly broke into a passion of hysteric weeping. Oh, the relief of those blessed, weak, womanish tears! Una wisely did not attempt to check them; she just held my hand in a firm, close clasp, and let the fit exhaust itself. A devil had been cast out of me, and after a time I was myself again, and able to tell her the story of the picture,— that story which for those three years had veritably held me bound and enchained under a kind of demoniac possession. I had never before spoken of

it to any human being : at the outset, I felt as if I
were committing sacrilege in doing so now ; but by
degrees, while I was speaking, all my morbid imaginings were dispelled, peace returned to my heart, and
the horrible, haunting, formless dread which I had so
long cherished, vanished like the troubled memory of
a dream.   I had passed through fire with a spectre
which was consumed while I was saved ; but from its
ashes had arisen an angel, with the sweet face of a
mortal woman, who held my hand in hers and smiled
upon me as she wiped away my tears.

'You are yourself again, Magdalen dearest.   This
terrible experience, I venture to say, will become to
you a sad memory, and nothing more.   By degrees,
too, even that will pass away, and for a beginning,
let us both set to work to alter all this gloomy *mise en
scène ;* come, help me to make your pleasant studio
bright again.'

We extinguished the tapers and let in the sunlight ;
the black velvet pall was replaced by a bright striped
Algerian cloth ; and even the blooms of my balcony
plants, the vivid scarlet geraniums and yellow
calceolarias, were ruthlessly plucked by Mrs. Rivers'
busy little fingers to mingle with the white waxen
scented blossoms.   The easel was moved into a
corner of the room, and its funereal drapery of crape
cast aside into a closet; but, with one of those
subtle delicacies of womanly feeling which none
but a woman can appreciate, as my friend took
off from my waist the mourning sash of violet that

encircled it, she threw it tenderly across the denuded
easel.

'All this explains much, Magdalen,' said she, 'that
has hitherto puzzled and even troubled me in your
conduct towards my brother Val. That you love
him, dear fellow, I know, and I believe you are proud
of the love he feels for you ; but that there was something on your mind which you had not told either of
us, has been patent to me since the first moment I
knew you. But I trusted you, dear, and believed
that in your own good time you would tell him
all.'

'I have had the feeling that there was a doom upon
me, Una, and I loved him too well to involve him
in it.'

'But that was a purely morbid fancy, darling.
You will not keep him waiting any longer now. You
will fix the day, will you not, to make him happy?
Sometimes I have thought,' she continued, 'that it
might seem to you too short a time had elapsed since
he lost his wife. Poor Gracie ! But it is nearly
eighteen months ago. She was our cousin, you know,
and we were both fond of her in a cousinly way ; but
Val never *loved* her, Magdalen. He has never loved
any other woman but yourself—never !'

'Tell me then—How was it ? Why did he marry
her ?'

'Don't you know, darling? But of course not—Val
would not tell. It was an act of pure generosity on
his part. Grace had offended Uncle Stephen by

marrying against his wishes,—a foolish, bad marriage it was; but she was an only child, and had always had her own way. Uncle Stephen, too, had set his heart on her husband, whoever he might be, taking her name, as she was quite an heiress. People thought he would eventually come round; but when he died, it was discovered that he had left all his money away from her to Val, who was to take his name and enter into undisputed possession at once. This was partly to punish Grace, and partly, I verily believe, to annoy our father, with whom he had quarrelled, by making Val independent of him. They were both men of stern, unforgiving spirit, and Val had also got into the black books at home, and had had to seek his fortune in Australia, whence he was hastily summoned by the news that this fortune had been left him. You know Val had been in Australia?'

I nodded my head in acquiescence. Yes, I knew; but as we had never met out there, nor had I even heard of a Mr. Lennox, I had not asked him any questions upon a subject on which he had not volunteered information. I had shaken the dust of my unappreciative country off my feet. I never meant to return there. I was trying to become thoroughly English in all my ways and mode of life. I wanted to forget Australia altogether.

'And so,' continued Mrs. Rivers, 'as Val had been summoned home by a mere bare telegram, he did not know any particulars. When he found that he was to be enriched at the expense of poor little Grace, who had become a widow only two days after her father's death by an accident that had befallen her drunken, good-for-nothing husband, he point-blank refused to take one penny of the money that had been left to him. Grace on her side was not to be outdone, and this kind of thing went on for months, and might have continued indefinitely — Val declaring he should go back to Australia, Grace saying she would go out as a governess, and a fortune lying idle between them— had not Gracie discovered one fine day that she had fallen desperately in love with Val, poor little thing! She told him, it appears, that it would kill her if he went out to Australia, and—well, I suppose it really amounted to asking him to marry her, if one could ever have got at the exact truth. However that may be, they were married after a decent interval of widowhood on her side, but she only lived six months to enjoy her happiness ; and if ever there were a happy wife it was Grace. She was quite utterly content and satisfied, and thought Val a perfect husband—as he was—to her. But it would require a very different kind of woman to make Val happy.

Una's soft brown eyes were fixed upon me with an expression that went to my heart. I could not resist their pleading inquiry.

'Do not fear, Una, I know I can do so, and, please God, I *will*.'

'Do you know, Magdalen, you look as I could fancy one of the vestal virgins, or a prophetess of old, taking a vow to devote herself to some lifelong duty and service. You are such a grand woman—the ideal wife for my noble Val.'

For all reply, I took her little curly brown head between both my hands and kissed her on her smooth forehead. What she had said was quite true. I felt as if I had solemnly dedicated myself to a lifelong duty and service which was at the same time the object of my fondest hopes, my deepest prayers, my highest aspirations, my most perfect and unselfish love.

For a time we sat there serious and silent—sisters in heart, as we hoped soon to become in reality. We were both recalled to a more everyday state of feeling by the striking of a clock on the mantelpiece.

'Five!' exclaimed Mrs. Rivers, springing from her seat. 'Why, I must have been here an hour at the very least, and I have not even told you what I came for. It went completely out of my mind when I came in and saw you.'

'Excuse me,' I interrupted, shrinking from a recurrence to the past, 'and sit down again, Una, for five minutes. I will ring for tea.'

'But indeed I ought to be at home now. I promised the child to have tea with her in the schoolroom, and we are dining at seven ourselves to-night. You have got to dine with us too, Magdalen, for Val has a box for *Lohengrin*. You said you wanted to hear your famous countrywoman, Madame Melba, in the part of "Elsa;" and everybody knows that a Wagner enthusiast like yourself would not want to miss one

note of the overture, so it was all settled I was to
come and let you know quite early, and about six
Val would fetch you himself, and bring you on to
Lowndes Square. I can't persuade my dear old stupid
Guy to come, so we shall have to share Val between us.
And I really must be off, darling. You can give Val
some tea when he comes instead of me.'

She was not to be persuaded to stay ; so, having
acquiesced in the arrangement, I kissed the little
woman and let her go.

. . . .

It was just striking half-past five when a tall, fair,
distinguished-looking man came leisurely down the
steps of the Reform Club and got into a hansom that
was in waiting. 'Cheyne Row' was the address given
to the driver, and thither we will follow him on his
way. But the drive, short as it was, was not to be an
uneventful one, for the vehicle nearly came into
collision with an omnibus that was coming down the
crowded King's Road thoroughfare, and as it drew
sharply to one side to avoid it, a little child, who had
just started to cross the street, was caught by the
wheel and thrown across the kerb upon the pavement.
She was not hurt in any way, a fact which the gentleman, who had sprung out of the cab to her assistance,
was careful to ascertain as he raised her up and
placed her in safety on the pavement. One of the
dirty little fat arms had been grazed just sufficiently
to draw blood. however, and the child was preparing
to set up a howl, which was promptly arrested at

sight of a bright new shilling laid in its palm, over which the fingers closed immediately. The gentleman got into the cab again and proceeded on his way, reaching his destination without further adventure. He did not dismiss it, but told the driver he should probably keep him about half-an-hour; and when the door was opened, entered the house without parley, as if he knew that the person he had come to see was in and would receive him. In the same way he closely followed the servant along a ground-floor passage, and was in the room as soon as, or even before, she had announced, 'Mr. Lennox, madam.'

There was only one person present, who rose up from a low seat to greet him; a woman not much shorter than himself, with the splendid proportions and noble carriage of a Greek goddess. But there was no mistaking the mere womanliness in the look she turned upon him, or in the tones of her low, full voice.

'Val, Val!' she cried, and threw herself upon his neck, and clung to him in a very passion of abandonment. The man himself turned pale with the surprise and joy of it, and the intensity of his own emotion. But as suddenly disengaging herself, she started back with a cry of horror—'Oh! what is it? What is it? Are you hurt? Blood on your wrist! For heaven's sake, Val, what has happened?'

She was now trembling like a leaf, and he gently guided her to the couch from which she had risen, and sat down by her side.

'It is nothing, my dearest, absolutely nothing. A little child fell in the street, and grazed its arm; in picking it up and holding it for a moment this must have been the result.'

But she persisted in asking for details of the affair, and he had to tell her the whole incident. She had turned a little pale, and he saw her shiver as he described the accident.

'Why, Magdalen, my queen, you are surely not quite your own brave self to-day? Come, let me look at you, silly Magdalen! And sweet Magdalen, and beautiful Magdalen—sweeter and more beautiful to-day than ever!'

He was looking at her, not only with the enraptured admiration of a lover, but with the critical appreciation of a man who knows how and what to admire, and can estimate at its proper value the beauty of a woman as of that of a picture or a statue.

Then suddenly his expression changed to one of proud and satisfied proprietorship, as he exclaimed,—

'Among all the handsome women in London, you will be the loveliest in the whole opera-house to-night, Magdalen.'

Well might he say so, for this was the picture that met his eyes. A noble figure robed in some soft white fabric embroidered in silver that draped her in classic folds. It was cut slightly low around the throat, which rose out of it like a polished column; but the beautiful contours of neck and bust were covered, only the massive rounded arms bared to their full length from the shoulder. In her sunny hair she wore a silver fillet, and a silver girdle encircled her waist. In each was thrust a cluster of blood-red blossoms of some rare tropical plant, which threw out the creamy tint of her draperies and the ivory pallor of her face,—a face from which the grey eyes looked steadily out beneath straight heavy black brows and lashes, which formed a curious contrast to hair of a bright chestnut that seemed to have caught and imprisoned the sunlight in its burnished masses. It was altogether a strange, wonderful face, with its curved, sensitive lips and dilated nostrils, its powerful chin and broad low forehead,—a face that flashed upon you its varying moods and its varied expressions, whose swift, sudden smile was like unexpected summer lightning.

On only two human beings did this smile ever linger and soften into tenderness, and these were Una Rivers and her brother. Such a look came across her now as she turned to the man who was gazing upon her with earnest intensity, while he attempted to speak with playfulness. She replied both to his look and words.

'Silly, am I, Val? and sweet, which is better; and beautiful, which is best of all? I am silly for myself, because it is my birthday to-day, and I don't want the least little miserable trifle to happen on such a day to spoil it. Silly Magdalen! And sweet for you, Val, because I love you; and beautiful for you, Val, so that you may love me.'

Happy Magdalen!

Val Lennox caught her to his heart.

'Your beauty is not what I care for, Magdalen, lovely as you are. It is not— Yes; it is, it is—my goddess, my idol. I love it, I worship it. Your beauty is driving me mad.'

He pressed her closer to him as he spoke, raining passionate kisses on her hair, eyes, throat, and arms, then threw himself at her feet, clasping her knees, and buried his face in her lap with a sob.

Magdalen bent down and laid her hand on it with a soft, caressing touch.

'Val, listen to me. It is my birthday, as I told you. You did not know it, and you brought me no gift, but I shall give you one instead. I promised Una to-day I would marry you whenever you chose to ask me. And I give myself to you now—this moment. I am yours when you like to claim me—do you hear, Val? Your very own, your wife.'

He slowly raised himself to a level with the woman who was bending over him, and, seating himself on the couch, threw his arm around her. Her eyes sank beneath the intensity of his gaze; she swayed towards him as it were involuntarily, but all at once sprang to her feet with a cry,—

'The blood, the blood on your wrist! Oh, let me wash it off, and then we will go, Val! We had better go—you *know* we had better go.'

She had taken hold of his now passive hand, and drawn him after her to a corner of the studio where a white marble nymph held up a vase from which water flowed into a shell beneath. Like one in a dream she turned on the little silver tap and took up a sponge from the basin. He was gazing almost mechanically before him, beyond the little fountain to the corner of the room where a small easel draped in violet stood with a picture upon it. All at once his glance was arrested, and a look of surprise came into his face.

'Lily Mordaunt!' he exclaimed, and made a step forward.

Whether in loosing Magdalen's hand, which was holding his, she lost her balance, dazed and bewildered as she was from the violent emotion through which she had just passed, or what happened to cause her to fall, was never known. She swayed and tottered for a moment, but he was not in time to catch her before she fell heavily backwards, overturning the easel. In her fall her temple struck on the sharp edge of the marble basin, and great drops of blood fell like a slow rain upon the picture. Horror-stricken he raised her in his arms, but the doom she dreaded had wrought its consummation—Magdalen Challis was dead.

THE END.

MORRISON AND GIBB, PRINTERS, EDINBURGH

1 M D—8 93.

A SELECT LIST OF BOOKS

IN

GENERAL LITERATURE AND FICTION

PUBLISHED BY

GRIFFITH FARRAN & CO.,

NEWBERY HOUSE, 39, CHARING CROSS ROAD, LONDON.

— ❖ —

The Standard Library of Fiction.

Crown 8vo.   Cloth extra, with Frontispiece.   Price 3s. 6d.

ASENATH OF THE FORD.   By " Rita."
BOND SLAVES.   By Mrs. G. Linnæus Banks.
HIS SISTER'S HAND.   By C. J. Wills.
THE WESTLAKES.   By Thomas Cobb.
HOW LIKE A WOMAN.   By Florence Marryat.
RISEN DEAD.   By Florence Marryat.
WHITHER?   By M. E. Francis.
A COVENANT WITH THE DEAD.   By Clara Lemore.
THE ISLAND OF FANTASY.   By Fergus Hume.
NO COMPROMISE.   By H. F. Hetherington and H. D. Burton.
THE "GOLDEN HOPE."   By W. Clarke Russell.
A DEFENDER OF THE FAITH.   By Tivoli.
EAGLE JOE.   By H. Herman.
AN EVIL REPUTATION   By Dora Russell.

THE DUCHESS. By Mrs. Hungerford.
A FATAL SILENCE. By Florence Marryat.
BROUGHT TOGETHER. Tales by "Rita."
HARVEST OF WEEDS. By Clare Lemore.
THE SMUGGLER'S SECRET. By Frank Barrett.
TUMBLEDOWN FARM. By Alan Muir.
THE BAFFLED CONSPIRATORS. By W. E. Norris.
THE PENNYCOMEQUICKS. By S. Baring-Gould.
THE PHILOSOPHER IN SLIPPERS : Zigzag Views of Life and
     Society. By the Author of "Three-Cornered Essays."
MISADVENTURE. By W. E. Norris.
LAZARUS IN LONDON. By F. W. Robinson.
LITTLE KATE KIRBY. By F. W. Robinson.
THE COURTING OF MARY SMITH. By. F. W. Robinson.
HARRY JOSCELYN. By Mrs. Oliphant.
A BORN COQUETTE. By Mrs. Hungerford.
NABOTH'S VINEYARD. By E. Œ. Somerville and Martin
     Ross.

Two Volume Novels, 21s.

A DAUGHTER OF MYSTERY. By Jessie Krikorian.
BRIARS. By A. M. Munro, Author of "Crane Court."
LOVE'S LOYALTY. By Cecil Clarke, Author of "Elsie Gray."

6s. Fiction.

MR. MEESON'S WILL. By H. Rider Haggard.
CASE OF DR. PLEMEN. By René de Pont Jest.
CRANE COURT. By A. M. Munro.
ICELAND FISHERMAN (*The Pêcheur d'Islande*). By Pierre
     Loti. Sole and Authorized Copyright Translation by
     Miss Cadiot. With original Portrait and Autograph.
PRINCE OF COMO, A. By E. M. Davy.
RHÈA : a Suggestion. By Pascal Germaine.
SECRET OF THE SANDS. By H. Collingwood.
SLAVE OF HIS WILL, THE. By Lady Fairlie Cuninghame.
STAR OF GEZER. By Sybil.
WRONG ON BOTH SIDES. By Vin Vincent.
BELLERUE. By W. M. L. Jay.

5s. Fiction.

CLEMENT BARNOLD'S INVENTION. By Lionel Hawke.

H. Rider Haggard's 3s. 6d. Novels.

Cloth. Fully Illustrated.

Allan's Wife. | Dawn.
Witch's Head.

Richard Pryce's Novels.

Uniform Edition. Crown 8vo, cloth, trimmed edges.
Price 3s. 6d.

An Evil Spirit. | Just Impediment.

3s. 6d. Fiction.

DOLLARS ARE TRUMPS. By A. Kevill-Davies.
GLENATHOLE. By Cyril Grey.
HARD HELD. A Sporting Novel. Being a Sequel to "Curb
and Snaffle." By Sir Randal H. Roberts, Bart.
HIGH-FLYER HALL. By Sir Randall H. Roberts, Bart.
J. S.; or, Trivialities. By. E. O. Pleydell Bouverie.
NEWTON DOGVANE: A Story of English Country Life. By
Francis Francis. With Illustrations on Steel by John
Leech.
RUHAINAH: An Afghan Romance. By Evan Stanton.
DEAD SOULS: A Russian Tale. By Nicholas Gogol. 2 vols.
WHO IS GUILTY? By Dr. Woolf.

2s. 6d. Fiction.

BABE IN BOHEMIA. By Frank Danby.
MISS LAVINIA'S TRUST. By Vin Vincent.
MYSTERY OF MRS. BLENCARROW. By Mrs. Oliphant.
THE SYREN. By Cecil Medlicott.
ROMANCE OF A MUMMY. By Theophile Gautier.
DUKE'S WINTON. By J. R. Henslowe.
IN A BLACK MANTLE. By Sybil Maxwell.

The Prison Series. 2s. 6d.

Crown 8vo. In a characteristic cloth cover. Price 2s. 6d.

THE MEMOIRS OF JANE CAMERON, FEMALE CONVICT.
By F. W. Robinson.
PRISON CHARACTERS. By F. W. Robinson.
FEMALE LIFE IN PRISON. By F. W. Robinson.

L. B. Walford's Novels.

2s. 6d. Cloth (with Etched Frontispiece), and 2s. Paper Boards.

1. Mr. Smith.
2. The Baby's Grandmother.
3. Cousins.
4. Troublesome Daughters.
5. Pauline.
6. Dick Netherby.
7. The History of a Week.
8. A Stiff-necked Generation.
9. Nan.
10. Two Stories ("A Mere Child," and "The Havoc of a Smile").

Dora Russell's Novels.

2s. 6d. Cloth and 2s. Paper Boards.

1. Footprints in the Snow.
2. The Vicar's Governess.
3. Beneath the Wave.
4. Annabel's Rival.
5. Lady Sefton's Pride.
6. Quite True.
7. The Broken Seal.
8. Crœsus's Widow.
9. Hidden in my Heart.
10. Jezebel's Friends.

James Daunton's Fate, 1s. and 1s. 6d.

Rita's Novels.

2s. 6d. Cloth and 2s. Paper Boards.

1. Dame Durden.
2. My Lady Coquette.
3. Vivienne.
4. Like Dian's Kiss.
5. Countess Daphne.
6. Fragoletta.
7. A Sinless Secret.
8. Faustine.
9. After Long Grief and Pain.
10. Two Bad Blue Eyes.
11. Darby and Joan.
12. My Lord Conceit.
13. Corinna.

Edelweiss, 1s. and 1s. 6d.

W. Stephen Hayward's Novels.

2s. 6d. Cloth and 2s. Paper Boards.

1. Love against the World.
2. Hunted to Death.
3. Perils of a Pretty Girl.
4. Ethel Grey.
5. Caroline.
6. Maude Luton.
7. The Three Red Men.
8. John Hazel's Vengeance.
9. Barbara Home.
10. The Secret Seven.
11. The Woman in Red.
12. The Stolen Will.
13. The Black Flag.
14. Diana's Defender.
15. Colonel's Daughter.
16. Left to the World.

Mary Cecil Hay's Novels.

2s. 6d. Cloth and 2s. Paper Boards.

1. Old Myddelton's Money.
2. Hidden Perils.
3. Victor and Vanquished.
4. The Arundel Motto.
5. The Squire's Legacy.
6. Nora's Love Test.
7. For Her Dear Sake.
8. Brenda Yorke.
9. Dorothy's Venture.
10. Missing.
11. Under the Will.
12. Bid Me Discourse.
13. Lester's Secret.
14. Among the Ruins.

A Wicked Girl, 1s.

Mrs. G. Linnæus Bank's Novels.

2s. 6d. Cloth.

1. A Manchester Man.
2. Stung to the Quick.
3. Caleb Booth's Clerk.
4. Wooers and Winners.
5. More than Coronets.
6. Through the Night.
7. Watchmaker's Daughter.
8. Forbidden to Wed.
9. Sybilla.
10. In His Own Hand.
11. Glory.

F. E. M. Notley's Novels.

2s. 6d. Cloth and 2s. Paper Boards.

1. Red Riding Hood.
2. Beneath the Wheels.
3. Love's Crosses.

Mrs. John Kent Spender's Novels.

2s. 6d. Cloth and 2s. Paper Boards.

1. Mr. Nobody.
2. Parted Lives.
3. Both in the Wrong.
4. Recollections of a Country Doctor.

E. Spender's Novels.

2s. 6d. Cloth and 2s. Paper Boards.

1. Restored.
2. A True Marriage.
3. Son and Heir.
4. Kingsford.
5. Until the Day Breaks.

Mrs. H. Lovett Cameron's Novels.

2s. 6d. Cloth and 2s. Paper Boards.

1. Vera Nevill.
2. Pure Gold.
3. Worth Winning.

Mrs. Power O'Donoghue's Novels.

2s. 6d. Cloth and 2s. Paper Boards.

1. Unfairly Won. | 2. A Beggar on Horseback.

E. S. Drewry's Novels.

2s. 6d. Cloth and 2s. Paper Boards.

1. Only an Actress. | 3. Baptised with a Curse.
2. On Dangerous Ground. | 4. A Death-Ring.

Percy B. St. John's Novels.

2s. Paper Boards.

1. Sailor Crusoe. | 4. My Beautiful Daughter.
2. Snow Ship. | 5. The Daughter of the
3. Young Buccaneer. | Sea.

Popular 2s. Novels.

Also in Cloth 2s. 6d.

EAGLE JOE. By Henry Herman. (*Cloth 3s. 6d.*)
MISOGYNY AND THE MAIDEN. By Paul Cushing.
WHO IS THE HEIR? By Mortimer Collins.
GUY DARRELL'S WIVES. By F. Iles.
PAUL NUGENT. By H. F. Hetherington and Rev. H. D.
     Burton.
CONFESSIONS OF A MEDIUM.
ADA TRISCOTT. By Capt. A. Haggard.
WAS HE JUSTIFIED? By C. J. Wills.
A SCARLET SIN. By Florence Marryat.
JAMES VRAILE. By J. Jeffery.
DENISE. By A. Dumas.
EXPIATION. By E. P. Oppenheim.
THE NICK OF TIME. By W. T. Hickman.
A HOUSE PARTY. By Ouida.
DOCTOR JACOB. By M. Betham-Edwards.
HARD HELD. By Sir R. H. Roberts, Bart. (*Cloth 3s 6d.*)
A WILY WIDOW. By Henry Creswell.
A MODERN DELILAH. By Vere Clavering.
A FAIR CRUSADER. By William Westall.
THE HAUNTED CHURCH. By James Murphy.
THE GAY WORLD. By Joseph Hatton.
DRIVEN BEFORE THE STORM. By Gertrude Forde.
A LOMBARD STREET MYSTERY. By Muirhead Robertson.
SCULLYDOM. By P. A. Egan. (*Cloth, 3s. 6d.*)
ANDRÉ CORNELIS. By Paul Bourget.
ALL OR NOTHING. By Mrs. Cashel Hoey.
GEHENNA. By Hon. Lewis Wingfield.

Popular 2s. Novels.—Continued.

THE BLUE RIBBON. By the Author of "St. Olave's."
ANNETTE. By the Author of "St. Olave's."
RECORDS OF A STORMY LIFE. By Mrs. Houstoun.
STORMY WATERS. By Robert Buchanan.
JACOBI'S WIFE. By Adeline Sergeant.
THE SON OF HIS FATHER. By Mrs. Oliphant.
MIGNON. By Mrs. Forrester.
A PRINCESS OF JUTEDOM. By Charles Gibbon.
CRADLED IN A STORM. By T. A Tharp.
JACK URQUHART'S DAUGHTER. By Miss M. Young.
THRO' LOVE AND WAR. By Violet Fane.
TWO LILIES. By Julia Kavanagh.
QUEEN MAB. By Julia Kavanagh.
FORESTALLED. By M. Betham-Edwards.
UNDER 14 FLAGS. By Capt. W. D. L'Estrange.

Popular 1s. Novels.

MONSIEUR JUDAS. By Fergus Hume.
ONLY A SHADOW. By D. Christie Murray and Henry
Herman.
PRESUMPTION OF LAW. By a Lawyer and a Lady.
JACK AND THREE JILLS. By F. C. Phillips, Author of
"As in a Looking Glass," &c.
A ROMANCE OF THE WIRE. By M. Betham-Edwards.
THE HAVOC OF A SMILE. By L. B. Walford.
EDELWEISS; a Romance. By "Rita."
NURSE REVEL'S MISTAKE. By Florence Warden.
ROLAND OLIVER. By Justin McCarthy, M.P.
MATED FROM THE MORGUE. By John A. O'Shea.
FORGING THE FETTERS. By Mrs. Alexander.
THE QUEEN'S SCARF. By D. Christie Murray.
THE HAUNTED FOUNTAIN. By Catherine Macquoid.
FAVOUR AND FORTUNE. By the Author of "Jack Urquhart's
Daughter."
99, DARK STREET. By F. W. Robinson.
A WICKED GIRL. By Mary Cecil Hay.
GABRIEL ALLEN, M.P. By G. A. Henty.
THE ARGONAUTS OF NORTH LIBERTY. By Bret Harte.
THE ABBEY MURDER. By Joseph Hatton
A MERE CHILD By L. B. Walford.
LOVE UNTIL DEATH. By R. Whelan Boyle.

Popular 1s. Novels.—Continued.

THE QUEEN'S TOKEN.   By Mrs. Cashel Hoey.

A RAINY JUNE.   By Ouida.

DON GESUALDO.   By Ouida.

JOHN NEEDHAM'S DOUBLE.   By Joseph Hatton.

JAMES DAUNTON'S FATE.   By Dora Russell.

BETTY'S VISIONS.   By Rhoda Broughton.

TOPSIDE AND TURVEY.   By Percy Fitzgerald.

BEFOREHAND.   By L. T. Meade.

LAYING DOWN THE CARDS.   By the Hon. Mrs. Featherston-
    haugh.

A FATAL AFFINITY.   By Stuart Cumberland.

DOUBT.   By James S. Little.

THE CRIME OF THE GOLDEN GULLY.   By Gilbert Rock

AGAINST THE GRAIN.   By C. T. C. James.

IN THE SHADOW OF DEATH.   By Sir Gilbert Campbell, Bart.

MAD LOVE; or, An Artist's Dream.   Translated from the
    Russian of Vsevolod Garshin.

GALLOPING DAYS AT THE DEANERY.   By Charles James.

AT WHAT COST.   By Hugh Conway, Author of "Called
    Back," &c.

THE WIFE'S SACRIFICE (Martyre!)   By Adolphe D'Ennery.
    Translated by H. Sutherland Edwards.

BAFFLED.   By Shirley B. Jevons.

SLOWBOROUGH; or, Rural Felicity.   By Frank E. Emson,
    Author of "Our Town."

INNOCENT OR GUILTY?   By Marion Greenhill.

THE SILENT SHORE.   By John Bloundelle-Burton.

THREE LUCKY SHOTS.   By Oscar Park.

THE CABMAN'S DAUGHTER.

SEIZED BY A SHADOW.   By Rose Mullion.

IMPRISONED IN THE HOUSE OF DETENTION FOR LIBEL.   By
    John Dawson.

CAUGHT IN THE TROPICS.   By a Lady Astronomer.

———————

STORIES FROM "NEWBERY HOUSE."   1st Series.   By Vin Vincent,
    Rev. Canon Benham Rev. George Huntingdon, Rev. J. Hudson,
    Helen Milman, Miss N. J. Blatchford, Marian Benham, H. G.
    Farrant, and Miss Amy Wilson.   Crown 8vo, paper cover, 1s.;
    cloth, 1s. 6d.

STORIES FROM "NEWBERY HOUSE."   2nd Series.   By J. Theobald
    Butler, Maggie Symington, Marian Benham, Austin Clare, S. H.
    Mitchell, and David Ker.   Crown 8vo, paper cover, 1s.; cloth,
    1s 6d.

Books for the Library.

£3 3s. Net.

A DESCRIPTIVE CATALOGUE OF THE COLLECTION OF PICTURES BELONGING TO THE EARL OF NORTHBROOK. Illustrated. On hand-made paper. Large 4to, parchment. Price £3 3s. net.

£1 1s.

LIFE OF BENJAMIN FRANKLIN, THE. Written by Himself. Now first Edited from original MSS., and from his printed Correspondence and other Writings, by John Bigelow. 3 Vols. Crown 8vo. Price £1 1s.

POLITICAL AND SOCIAL LETTERS OF A LADY OF THE EIGHTEENTH CENTURY. Being the Correspondence of the Hon. Mrs. Osborn, during the years 1721—1771. Edited by Emily F. D. Osborn. Demy 8vo, with four Photogravures, boards, uncut edges. £1 1s.

16s.

GENERAL CRAUFURD AND HIS LIGHT BRIGADE. By the Rev. Alexander H. Craufurd, M.A. Crown 8vo, cloth. Price 16s.

15s.

ETON OF OLD: or, Eighty Years Since. 1811—1822. By an Old Colleger. Crown 4to, cloth, Illustrated. Price 15s. Also an edition with illustrations on Japanese paper. Price 21s.

10s. 6d.

QUEEN'S BIRTHDAY BOOK, THE. With 13 Cabinet Portraits and Autographs of Royal Family. Edited by Mary F. P. Dunbar. 4to, cloth. Price 10s. 6d.

YOUNG PEOPLE AND OLD PICTURES. By Theodore Child. With numerous Engravings in the best style from Pictures by the Old Masters dealing with child life. Crown 4to, cloth. Price 10s. 6d.

HUNGARY AND ITS PEOPLE. By Louis Felbermann. Large Crown 8vo, cloth, fully Illustrated. Price 10s. 6d.

7s. 6d.

NEWTON DOGVANE: A Story of English Country Life. By Francis Francis, Author of "Sporting Sketches with Pen and Pencil," &c. With Illustrations on Steel by John Leech, coloured by hand. Imp. 8vo, cloth. Price 7s. 6d.

HIGH-FLYER HALL: A Sporting Story. By Sir Randal H. Roberts, Bart., Author of "Hard Held," etc., etc. Illustrated by G. Bowers. Imp. 8vo, cloth. Price 7s. 6d.

A COMPLETE GUIDE TO THE GAME OF CHESS. By H. L. F. Meyer. Pott 8vo, cloth. Price 7s. 6d.

THE LOOKING GLASS FOR THE MIND. A reprint of the Edition of 1792; with the original Illustrations by Bewick, and an Introduction by Charles Welsh. Crown 8vo. 7s. 6d.

6s.

TALES AND LEGENDS FROM THE LAND OF THE TZAR. Translated by Edith M. S. Hodgetts. Crown 8vo, cloth. Price 6s.

Books for the Library.

5s.

SOME NOTABLE GENERALS. Biographies compiled by Colonel J. Percy Groves, R.G.A. (late 27th Inniskillings). Illustrated by Lieut.-Colonel Marshman. Large 4to, cloth. Price 5s.

FORTUNES MADE IN BUSINESS. A Series of Original Sketches, Biographical and Anecdotic, from the Recent History of Industry and Commerce, by various Writers. Edited by James Hogg. First Series, with Six Portraits. Crown 8vo. Price 5s.

3s. 6d.

"1894 EDITION." READY REFERENCE: The Universal Cyclopædia, containing everything that everybody wants to know. By W. R. Balch. 800 pages, crown 8vo.

THERE IS NO DEATH. By Florence Marryat. Crown 8vo, cloth. Price 3s. 6d.

ROYAL WINCHESTER: Wanderings in and about the Ancient Capital of England. By Rev. A. G. L'Estrange, M.A. With numerous Illustrations by C. G. Harper. Crown 8vo, cloth. Price 3s. 6d.

LETTERS FROM DOROTHY OSBORNE TO SIR WILLIAM TEMPLE, 1652-54. Edited by E. A. Parry. With Portrait, &c. Crown 8vo, cloth. Price 3s. 6d.

AUSTRALIAN POETS, 1788—1888. Edited by Douglas Sladen. 662 pages. Crown 8vo, cloth. Price 3s. 6d.

YOUNGER AMERICAN POETS. Edited by Douglas Sladen. 686 pages. Crown 8vo. Price 3s. 6d.

2s.

EVERYDAY DICTIONARY OF THE ENGLISH LANGUAGE; containing 35,000 words. Edited by W. Balch. Crown 8vo.

MUSIC IN SONG. From Chaucer to Tennyson. By L. M. Carmela Kœlle. 32mo.

1s. USEFUL BOOKS.

AMBULANCE LECTURES; or, What to Do in Cases of Accident or Sudden Illness. By Lionel Weatherly. Illustrated. Fcap. 8vo.

DICTIONARY OF ABBREVIATIONS. Containing nearly 2500 Contractions, Signs, &c. Sq. 32mo.

HIGH SCHOOL NEEDLEWORK AND CUTTING-OUT MANUAL. By Harriet Baker. Fcap. 8vo.

ECONOMICAL COOK, THE. A Book of Recipes for every Season of the Year. By P. O. P. Fcap. 8vo.

HOW TO BE MARRIED: In all Ways and Everywhere throughout the British Empire and in Foreign States; with Appendix of all Legal Forms relating to Marriage, and a Summary of Marriage Statistics. By the Rev. Thomas Moore. Crown 8vo.

YOUNG WIFE'S OWN BOOK. By Lionel A. Weatherly. Fcap. 8vo.

CHILDREN: Their Home Training. How to Nurse them in Sickness and keep them in Health. By I. L. Richmond, with a Preface by Sarah Tytler. Fcap. 8vo.

The Newbery Classics.

A New Edition of the Poets. Crown 8vo. Attractive cloth gilt cover. About 600 pages in each volume, price 2s.

Also a choice edition, bound in ¼ cloth, gilt top, price 3s.

Longfellow.	Wordsworth.
Scott.	Shakespeare.
Browning (Mrs. E. B.)	Campbell.
Hood.	Byron.
Moore.	Burns.

THE NINETEENTH CENTURY CLASSICS.

Under this title we are issuing a series of illustrated volumes of world-famous books. In making the selection the idea has been to present some of those books, the names of which are familiar as household words, in a dress which shall be in every way worthy of their fame. The illustrations are specially drawn and engraved for each book, and in some cases, as in that of "The Lady of the Lake," artists have been sent to the scene of the story for the purpose. The type is clear and good, the paper of the best quality, and the binding is unique, striking in character—forming handsome volumes to read, to keep, or to give away. They are published at 6s. each.

Lalla Rookh. By Thomas Moore.

Faust. By Göethe.

The Lady of the Lake. By Sir W. Scott.

The Last Days of Pompeii. By Bulwer Lytton.

Longfellow's Poetical Works.

Whittier's Poetical Works.

The Scarlet Letter. By Nathaniel Hawthorne.

Tales from the Dramatists. By Chas. Morris. With an Introduction by Henry Irving, D.C.L. 3 vols. Fcap. 8vo. Cloth gilt, in box. Price, 10s. 6d. net.

The Bijou Byron. A New Edition, in 12 volumes, of the Complete Works of Lord Byron. Small oblong shape, convenient for the pocket, printed in good clear type, and issued in the following styles:—

The 12 volumes complete in box, bound in boards with parchment backs, 18s. 6d. net.

Also in an elegant cloth gilt box, bound in paper sides, cloth backs, all full gilt, 31s. 6d. net.

The volumes are also supplied separately :—Paper limp, 1s. net.; paper boards, parchment backs, 1s. 6d. net. ; cloth, richly gilt, and gilt edges, 2s. 6d. net.

The Entertainment Series.

Fcap. 8vo, Cloth, price 1s. each.

SHORT COMEDIES FOR AMATEUR PLAYERS. By Mrs. Burton Harrison.

DUOLOGUES. By Ina Leon Cassillis.

EVENINGS OUT ; or, the Amateur Entertainer. By Constance Milman, Author of "The Doll Dramas." Fcap. 8vo, cloth limp, price 1s.

"TWENTY MINUTES."—Drawing-Room Duologues, &c. By Harriet L. Childe Pemberton, Author of "Geese," "Prince," &c. Fcap. 8vo, cloth limp.

POSSIBLE PLAYS FOR PRIVATE PLAYERS. By Constance O'Brien. Fcap. 8vo, cloth.

POKER : How to Play it. A Sketch of the Great American Game, with its Laws and Rules. By one of its Victims. Fcap. 8vo.

EUCHRE, AND HOW TO PLAY IT. By Author of "Poker." Fcap. 8vo.

NORA, or the Doll's House. By H. Ibsen.
GHOSTS. By H. Ibsen.
Crown 8vo, cloth, 1s. each.

Birthday Books.

A Dainty Series. Well printed, and artistically bound in cloth. Price 1s. each.

Shakespeare.	Scott.
Mrs. Browning.	Shelley.
Moore.	Proverbial.
Longfellow.	Whittier.

The "Queen's," the "Favourite," and the "Anniversary."

GRIFFITH FARRAN & CO., LTD.
NEWBERY HOUSE, 39, CHARING CROSS ROAD, LONDON.
AUTUMN, 1893.

www.ingramcontent.com/pod-product-compliance
Lightning Source LLC
Chambersburg PA
CBHW021258050726
47498CB00003BB/895